I0685670

NIGHTMARES

IN

THE

NEIGHBORHOOD

**(Features "THE LAWYER'S SON,"
the basis for the suspense thriller)**

by

William Jaman Taylor

GB BOOK PUBLISHING

Books published by GB Book Publishing are available
at quantity discounts on bulk purchases for premium,
fund-raising, and special sales use. For details, please
call (404)-403-3570.

PUBLISHER'S NOTE

This book is a work of fiction. Places, events, and situations in this story are purely fictional. Any resemblance to actual persons, living or dead, is coincidental.

NIGHTMARES IN THE NEIGHBORHOOD

Copyright © 2002 & 2013 by William Jaman Taylor. All rights reserved. Except in THE United States of America, this book is sold subject to the condition that it shall not, by way of trade, be lent, resold, hired out, or circulated without the publisher's prior consent in any form.

The scanning, uploading and distribution of this book via the Internet or any other means without the permission of the publisher is illegal and punishable by law. Please purchase only authorized electronic editions, and do not participate in or encourage electronic piracy of copyrighted materials.

No part of this book may be reproduced, stored in a retrieval system, or transmitted by any means, electronic, mechanical, photocopying, recording, or otherwise, without written permission from the publisher/author. Your support of the author's rights is greatly appreciated.

Printed in the United States of America

ISBN: 061573223-2 (pbk.)
ISBN: 978–0-6157-3223–7 (pbk.)

The Library of Congress has catalogued this paperback as follows:

William Jaman Taylor,

The Lawyer's Son: Nightmares in the Neighborhood/William Jaman Taylor

Song lyrics to "Goodbye, My Love" and "Where Did I Go Wrong" written by William Jaman Taylor.

Ground Breaking Worldwide Entertainment (BMI) 2013

GB Book Publishing – rev. 9/07/2013

WEBSITE:WWW.GBWWENTERTAINMENT.COM
E-MAIL:GBWWENTERTAINMENT@HOTMAIL.COM
WWW.FACEBOOK.COM/GBBPUBL

DEDICATION

For my father, William Taylor, Sr.,

and my mother, Allie M. Taylor

ACKNOWLEDGEMENTS

Without hesitation, I must give the highest praise to God for my life, talents and career paths.

Love, peace and happiness to my sister Darlene, my two brothers, Sam and Calvin, my nephews, my nieces, my aunts, uncles, and to a host of relatives and friends.

Finally, I would like to thank everyone who has supported me from the very beginning.

William Jaman Taylor

Chapter 1

As Lisa Taylor walked toward the kitchen for her morning cup of tea, she maneuvered her robed frame down the canyons of stacked boxes that had seemed to claim dominion over most of the downstairs area. Lisa and her husband Mike had spent the last few weeks planning the move, and with the help of their seventeen-year-old son Jason, they had managed to get all of the packing done by moving day. Lisa was anxious to move into the new home. Getting ready to move out of the old one had become overwhelming and tiring.

More boxes filled the kitchen than the living room, making it a struggle to reach the sink, where the Chicago morning sun streamed through the small kitchen window. She yawned and lazily reached to pull the curtains closed, only to realize that the curtains had been packed snugly away. Lisa squinted as she fished a navy blue mug out of an open box that sat alone on top of the kitchen counter next to a packing tape dispenser. She had been mindful to leave that one box open, as she knew she would need her good morning dose of caffeine to get her through the day.

Jason had gone out with some of his friends the night before and that had allowed Lisa and Mike some time alone to do some serious celebrating. After all, they had quite a bit to celebrate. They were moving on up, thanks to a promotion and hefty pay raise Mike had recently received. He had been in structural engineering for almost fifteen years, and had been with his present employer for six of those years.

Mike was promoted to Regional District Manager of Corporate Operations for the Northwest region of Drake and Nash Commercial Construction and Management Company.

When the realtor showed them the house, in the affluent Arlington Heights neighborhood, on Chicago's West Side, they were sold. The house itself was remarkable, and Lisa had fallen in love with its contemporary stucco frame almost immediately as soon as they pulled into the driveway.

The inside was very spacious, with a finished basement that could have assumed many different uses. The neighborhood was lovely and quiet, neurotically neat with beautifully manicured lawns and brick-encased mailboxes standing guard at the end of each driveway. Three weeks after parting with the realtor, they closed on the purchase.

The microwave beeped. Lisa had removed the hot mug and begun dipping an Earl Grey teabag. With a smile, she sniffed at the welcoming aroma of the tea. After Lisa took a sip, she started to go over the day's schedule in her mind, but lost her train of thought when she heard her husband coming down the stairs. Lisa knew it had to be him, because their son, Jason, had made it his summer routine to sleep in as late as possible.

Michael Taylor entered the kitchen, dressed in a navy blue business suit and striped tie that had been a Father's Day gift just two months ago. He had declared it his lucky suit after he'd worn it during the interview that landed him the promotion. Lisa held her tea tightly in front of her breasts as she surveyed her husband's handsome appearance. She joked that there was something about a man in a tailored suit or crisply ironed uniform that would make her weak in the knees. In all honesty, it was only Mike who has ever had that effect on her. He leaned his six-feet-two body over and gave her a good morning kiss, and allowed her to breathe in the scent of Chanel Egoist, probably the only bottle of cologne to evade the packing box.

"Good morning," Mike said and nibbled his wife on the earlobe.

"It is now," Lisa said with a smile and placed the navy blue mug on the countertop.

"I'll assume that's because of me and not because of the tea," Mike said and hugged Lisa from behind as she spooned more sugar into her steaming mug.

"Don't you start anything time won't allow you to finish," Lisa teased as she wiggled free of his hold, and retied the belt on her robe.

"With a grin he said, "I'll always have time for a morning or afternoon delight," as he glanced at his watch.

"You're so naughty," Lisa chuckled. What time is Reggie supposed to be here?" she asked, with a lingering chuckle.

"One o'clock," Mike said, referring to his cousin, a professional mover, who agreed to move them into their new home.

"Well, I'm just thankful he offered to help us out. Lord knows I don't want to see another brown cardboard box after all of this is over with," Lisa confessed and shook her head at the overwhelming thought of it.

"Hey, I'm with you on that one. I wish I didn't have to go to this meeting this morning, but I should be back here by noon," Mike said as he pushed some of the boxes aside to allow for more space. "When I get back, we'll pack up the rest of the things, and bid a farewell to Evergreen Avenue."

"On your way back home, stop by Potbelly's and pick up some sandwiches. I want to at least have some lunch for Reggie and his crew when they get here. They're going to have their work cut out for them," Lisa said as she looked around the kitchen at the sea of cardboard boxes.

"They do this for a living, babe. This is probably nothing compared to what they usually move, but I'll call you before I leave the office," Mike said.

"Hopefully, our little Rip Van Winkle will grace us with his presence before we're completely moved out of here," Lisa joked.

"I'm sure he's up now. I showered to the beat of house music reverberating from his room," Mike said.

"I thought I told him to pack up all his DJ equipment," Lisa said and sighed.

Mike chuckled and leaned over again to give her a goodbye kiss. "Take it easy this morning. Don't get all stressed out. We definitely have a busy weekend ahead of us," he said and exited the kitchen.

"Don't remind me," Lisa said as she followed her husband through the maze and to the front door to see him off.

After a final kiss goodbye, she weaved her way back through the scattered boxes again. Lisa went back upstairs to call her mother. She sat down on the edge of the bed, lifted the cordless phone from off the nightstand and punched in the number.

Jon and Madeline LaRue were now both retired, but Lisa could still count on them to be up at the crack of dawn. Both Lisa's parents were from New Orleans. Both were of Creole heritage. Lisa had always found it to be interesting how their ethnicity was evident in very different ways. Jon LaRue had all the physical features generally attributed to a Creole Southerner, from his hair texture, skin tone and sharp facial features. Madeline LaRue's heritage was more of a cultural and spiritual aspect. She was a very wise woman who had many gifts passed down through her family bloodline, including the uncanny ability to see further into or through things than most people. In the past, Jon had joked with her about having "old voodoo traces" in her blood, but Madeline would simply refer to it as a gut feeling that was usually stronger and more reliable than a typical hunch or inclination.

Madeline, affectionately called Maddie, was as comfortable with French as she was with English. But having mastered Creole as a young child, and having learned proper French as a student, she rarely spoke the language.

Lisa's parents migrated to Chicago, Illinois, where she was born and reared. Even though they'd left the South, it was evident that the South had not left them.

Later in life, Lisa had learned that her parents moved to Chicago, like so many other black Southerner, during the great migration, for its rich history and culture, housing, education, achievements, business and job opportunities. Maddie was especially intrigued when she learned Chicago's first black settler, Jean Baptiste Point Du Sable, had migrated to Illinois in the mid to late 1770s. Because of this well-known documented fact, she swore on her life that the city of Chicago would produce the country's first African-American president.

Lisa, an only child, had spent countless years of alternating Thanksgiving holidays between Chicago and her mother's now deceased sister, Bessie Mae Davis' home, in New Orleans. Regardless of location, the meals were almost identical with helpings of well-seasoned collard greens, baked macaroni and cheese, cornbread dressing, corn pudding, spicy gumbo, chitterlings, fried turkey, honey-baked ham, and an assortment of homemade cakes and pies. In fact, Lisa had no idea that Thanksgiving dinner was prepared any other way until she was twelve-years-old and invited to Thanksgiving dinner at the home of her childhood best friend Brenda Nelson. Lisa's chin almost hit the floor when she realized that Brenda's mother was not going to be returning to the kitchen to retrieve any dishes filled with chitterlings or gumbo. After enduring the Cornish hen, green bean casserole, corn-on-the-cob and boxed stuffing dinner at the Nelson's home, she rushed home and indulged herself in extra helpings of her mother's traditional Southern holiday feast.

Lisa was still deep in thought after the third or fourth ring when her father had finally answered the phone.

"Hello?" a deep and familiar voice answered.

A smile had instantly tugged at the corners of Lisa's mouth. "Hey, Daddy," she said.

"Hey, baby girl, how are you?" Jon asked, his voice hinting at his Southern roots.

"I'm doing fine considering all the packing, but other than that, everything appears to be right on schedule. I was just checking up on you and Mom," Lisa said as she traced the stitched pattern on the down comforter with a neatly manicured index finger.

"Everything's just fine. I just walked in from getting the newspaper, and your mother is in the kitchen making a mess and just a fussing over this pineapple upside-down cake she's about to bake," Jon reported.

"This early in the morning?" Lisa asked.

"You know your mother," Jon reminded. "That woman's determined to make the most of her day."

"Who are you telling?" Lisa chuckled as she thought about her mother's delicious pineapple upside-down cake.

Once Maddie had sensed that she was the topic of the phone conversation, Lisa heard her mother in the background as she entered into her parents' living room.

"Is that my favorite daughter?" Maddie asked as Lisa heard her voice got closer to the telephone her father was holding.

"No, Maddie, it's our only daughter," Jon said.

"Hush now, husband, and give me that phone," Maddie said and snatched the cordless phone from Jon before he returned to the kitchen. "Lisa?" she called in a cheerful tone.

"Hey, Mom, how are you?" Lisa asked.

"Child, I'm doing just fine. I'm trying to get this here cake made for Sarah from across the street. She tasted a slice last week before we went to bingo, and child don't you know that woman has been bothering me ever since about baking her a cake. I told her I would do it just this once as long as she would stop worrying me," Maddie explained.

Lisa smiled to herself, knowing the fact that no matter how much her mother seemed to have complained, Madeline LaRue loved to be complimented on her cooking.

"So, today's the big day, huh?" Maddie asked and quickly abandoned her discussion in regards to baking a cake for Sarah from across the street.

10

"*Yes!* Finally, we'll be out of here by this evening. Did Mike give you the new phone number?" Lisa asked.

"Yeah, he did. I wrote it down on the calendar. I've been calling y'all at the same phone number for sixteen years, so you know I'm not going to memorize this new one anytime soon," Maddie said as Lisa recognized the sound of her mother opening the oven. "How's Mike's new job coming along?" she asked.

"Great. Mike said as soon as he got the promotion, they had him to just jump right in and start the new position immediately. His division had put in a bid on that O'Hare International Airport deal I was telling you about, so he has been hard at work putting together a proposal. As a matter of fact, he's on his way to a meeting with the Airport's Operations and Planning Board right now," Lisa informed.

"Well, congratulate him for me when he gets the contract," Maddie said as she turned on the kitchen sink faucet, and rinsed the mixing utensils. "How's my favorite grandbaby?"

"Jason is a seventeen-year-old member of the 'it's all about me' generation. Need I say more?" Lisa said with a sigh.

"Hush now, child," Maddie fired back. "You can't expect him to accept the idea of moving away from his friends and school over night. Don't you realize that those four walls you're in right now make up the only home that he's ever known? So I don't blame him for jumping for joy."

"But Mom, he didn't even want to go house hunting with us," Lisa explained.

"Just give him some time. He'll come around. You'll see. Especially when he starts thinking about turning that finished basement into his own music studio that you told me about," Maddie assured.

Lisa smiled to herself at how well her mother knew Jason.

"Well, he'll have to discuss that with his father. Mike has thought about turning the basement into a media room," Lisa said. "Once we get moved in and settled, you and Daddy must visit soon and see the new house."

"I can't wait. I feel as if I've already seen it. You've practically provided me with every detail about the house," Maddie said. "Did you see any of your new neighbors when the realtor had shown you the house?" she asked.

"No," Lisa said slowly and sensed where their conversation was headed.

"Well, I hope they take kindly to the new family in the neighborhood. Y'all might be the only people of color," Maddie said.

"I haven't decided whether or not that would be such a bad thing," Lisa teased, knowing full well that her apathy about such details would surely irritate her mother. "Don't worry, Mom, I hardly think we would ever have to extinguish a burning cross on the front lawn. And besides, the realtor that we'd dealt with assured us that it was a diverse neighborhood."

"Well, I still have my reservations. I just want to make sure that you all are safe," Maddie huffed, somewhat relieved by Lisa's words of reassurance.

"Mom, we'll be just fine. You know, I could use your help this weekend if you feel up to the forty-five minute drive," Lisa suggested hopefully.

"No, child, an old woman like me will only get in the way," Maddie said.

"If that's your final answer, I guess I'll have to accept it," Lisa said and sighed. "Well, I'm about to get back to work. There are still quite a few things that we haven't packed up. Mike will be back in a few hours. Reggie and a couple of his co-workers will be here with the moving truck around one."

"Okay. You all take care. Call me Sunday evening. Love you," Maddie said.

"I will. Love you too, Mom. Kiss Daddy for me," Lisa said.

"Okay, baby. Kiss my grandbaby and Mike for me," Maddie said.

"I promise. I'll talk to you on Sunday. Bye, Mom" Lisa said.

"Bye, daughter," Maddie said.

Lisa returned the phone to the nightstand, before she stood up and stretched. She'd run her hand over her short-cropped hair and walked into the closet. Even that small area contained its share of boxes, but Lisa had managed to get to a charcoal gray jogging suit, which she took into the bathroom. She planned on taking her morning jog, showering, and then getting Jason to help her pack up the rest of their things. Lisa thought that it would then be a good idea to move all of the packed boxes that remained upstairs down to the living room and hallway area, so that the movers would only have to go up and down the stairs to move the heavy furniture.

Lisa thought about the new house and the inviting fireplace in the master bedroom on-suite. She thought about the autumn and winter nights that she and Mike would share snuggled cozily in their bed in front of a warm crackling fire. She could hardly wait.

Chapter 2

Approximately eleven o'clock found Mike still in his morning meeting with the Chicago O'Hare International Airport Operations and Planning Board. They had already gone over extensive plans and projections for the upcoming project, for which Mike's firm was pitching a bid. The airport was planning on renovating one of its major annexes and two of its boarding terminals. In addition, complete makeovers of the food court and Central Pavilion were being considered. This was actually the second meeting Mike was having with O'Hare's IAOPB. During the first, the chairman, seemingly impressed with the projected plans and overall expense estimates, requested that they schedule another meeting to go over budget details. Mike took that as a good sign, but it was ten fifty-five, and they had been discussing the budget details for almost two hours. The bad part was that the chairman had not shown any of the same signs of interest that he'd initially expressed. However, Mike continued his pitch, highlighting the positive aspects of the proposed budget and explained thoroughly the more costly projections.

O'Hare's IAOPB, made up of six members, sat directly across a black marble conference table in an executive conference suite. The room was dimly lit, due to Mike's use of the slide projector. The litany of questions had finally ceased, and Mike sat patiently directly across from Mr. Karl Anderson, Chairman, who was giving the printed budget one final review before making his determination.

Robert McAllister, Mike's assistant, a young man with freckles and copper red hair, appeared to be physically spent from the meeting. He sat to Mike's immediate right and operated the projector that had just displayed its last slide. Robert was noticeably uncomfortable with the new element of silence that had taken over the conference room. He recently completed a grad program at the University of Chicago and had come highly recommended by a couple of very influential professors there. He was a quick learner, and he and Mike both put in a great deal of work on the O'Hare bid, so Mike was sure Robert had his fingers mentally crossed. Mike smiled at the thought of how he was a nervous wreck, when he'd handled his first bid proposal. Over time, the pitching and waiting game would become routine and less unnerving.

Robert switched the humming projector off, which reactivated the lighting alongside the walls of the conference room. Mike stroked his goatee slowly and patiently. He studied Chairman Anderson, who was attentively studying the bid proposal that Mike had provided. The other board members were jotting down notes and shuffling through some of their own paperwork. The chairman, a short middle-aged man with balding brown hair and a moustache that was frosted with traces of gray, cleared his throat and closed the manila portfolio.

"Mr. Taylor, I must say that we were very impressed with your presentation," Mr. Anderson said, instantly causing the board members to look up from what they had been doing.

Mike calmly took a sip from his glass of water before responding. "Well, Mr. Anderson, our firm is very interested in assisting you with this particular project," he assured.

"Fortunately, your team managed to make that very obvious. Your projections had actually met our approval unanimously after the initial meeting," Mr. Anderson said. "The purpose of this meeting was simply to look more closely at your cost and budget analysis. I think I can speak for everyone else in saying that we are still equally impressed," he added as the other board members nodded their heads in assent.

"Thank you, sir. That's very good to hear," Mike said as he removed his reading glasses, and carefully placed them inside their hinged case.

"As far as I'm concerned, Drake and Nash has the deal," Mr. Anderson said as he removed his own pair of glasses, and placed them on top of the manila portfolio beside an authentic Montblanc Meisterstuck Solitaire Doue Gold and Black Fountain Pen.

Robert breathed a sigh of relief, and consequently allowed his posture to relax a bit.

"Well, I can assure you that Drake and Nash will not disappoint you," Mike said with an appreciative smile. "In addition, the company will be very pleased to hear the good news."

"We're very pleased as well, Mr. Taylor. We'll have all the necessary paperwork drawn up and have the package delivered to your office via courier later this afternoon. If the contract you left with us in the first meeting still stands, we'll have that signed, notarized and delivered as well," Mr. Anderson said.

"Sounds great," Mike said as he stood and shook Mr. Anderson's hand. "We'll definitely be in touch."

Robert, who was obviously excited about the deal, questioned Mike as they rode back to the office about how he managed to be so calm, cool and collected.

"Believe me, I'm just as excited as you are, but that was the easy part. Now, we have our work cut out for us. From start to finish, we have to make good on the deal," Mike said.

Mike was back at Drake and Nash by noon, briefing Mr. Drake on the meeting with O'Hare's IAOPB. After briefing Mr. Drake, inside his office, he called Lisa to find out exactly what kind of sandwiches she wanted him to pick up from Potbelly's Deli. He didn't relay the outcome of the meeting just then, because he wanted to tell her in person. Having already planned to work only half of the day, Mike left the office immediately after hanging up the phone, reminding Robert of the important courier delivery on his way out.

At approximately twelve forty-five, Mike pulled his smoke gray Lexus GS 300 into their driveway for what he knew would be for the very last time. He had received an alpha-page from Reggie confirming that he and his crew would be there by one, so everything was fortunately going as planned. Mike entered the house to the sound of thumping house music, a clear indication that Jason still hadn't dismantled the audio equipment. He was shocked to have seen that all the boxes cluttering the living room and hallway had more than doubled.

Lisa trotted quickly down the stairs, looking tempting even in what she called her "bum sweats." She was surprised to see Mike standing in the living room, since the loud music had not allowed her to hear the security system chime upon his entry. Lisa's face lit up with a smile as she walked over and planted a hello kiss on his lips.

"I see you two have been working hard this morning," Mike said as he looked around the congested living room.

"Yes, we have. Jason's on his way downstairs now with the very last of the boxes," Lisa said.

Mike headed toward the kitchen with the deli bags in tow. Lisa, having forgotten whatever it was she'd rushed downstairs to do, followed him.

"How did the meeting go?" Lisa asked anxiously.

Mike turned to her with a wide grin, both arms extended.

"You got the deal?" Lisa shrieked, jumped into his arms, and planted a kiss on his cheek, to congratulate him.

"Who's the man?" Mike bragged and laughed at Lisa's enthusiastic response.

"You're the man," Lisa said in between planting a couple more kisses on his cheek. "*Congratulations.*"

"Thanks. But just as I'd stated to Robert, that was the easy part. Now, the division has to make good on all its promises and get the job done."

"You know my mother pretty much said you would get this deal," Lisa said, released her embrace, and tried to smooth out the wrinkles she caused in his sweats.

"How's Maddie?" Mike asked.

"She's her usual self. I spoke to her this morning. I tried to get her to come over the weekend to help us out. She wouldn't hear of it. She said an old woman like herself would only get in the way," Lisa said.

"Did you ask Madam Madeline LaRue for the six winning lottery numbers so we can pay off the new home, and get you your new dream car?" Mike joked.

"Now you know my mother won't have anything to do with lottery gambling," Lisa said flatly.

"One thing I can say about your mother is that I've never known her to take part in any form of gambling except for bingo. She swore up and down it isn't gambling. Instead, bingo is elder entertainment, with the possibility to supplement their income. That's if the player won of course," Mike said.

"Remember the time shortly before our one year anniversary when she bet me fifty bucks that I was pregnant with Jason. And boy she was right," Lisa said matter-of-factly.

"Did you ever pay her?" Mike asked.

"No," Lisa said and shook her head.

"Speak of our future music mogul," Mike said and acknowledged his son's entrance.

"Hey, Pops," Jason said as he opened the refrigerator only to find it bare.

"We just talked you up. We were just talking about the time your grandmother knew I was pregnant before I did," Lisa said with a chuckle.

"Are Grandma and Grandpa coming over?" Jason asked hopefully.

"No, your grandparents are not coming over this weekend to spoil you. I'm pretty sure they'll come and visit next weekend once we're moved and settled into the new house," Lisa said. "We have some sandwiches from Potbelly's Deli."

"Thanks. I sort of felt like a sandwich anyway," Jason said in a subdued voice as he picked up the sandwich wrapped in white deli paper and headed out of the kitchen.

"Jason, where are you going?" Mike asked.

"I'm going upstairs to my room," Jason said dryly. "I guess I should say what used to be my room," he corrected, with a hint of sarcasm. "That's about the only place I can find a seat that's not already taken by a box."

"Could you just try to maintain your excitement about the move?" Lisa asked, with a hint of sarcasm of her own.

"Hey, son," Mike intervened. "I know this move has happened kinda fast. I know you'll miss your friends and your high school of three years, but it won't be so bad. Give it a chance. Just wait until you see the size of your new room."

Jason stood quietly, a woebegone look on his face, dropped his head, and begun fidgeting with the sandwich in his right hand.

"Somehow, I've managed to get my hands on two tickets for the Cubs home game this Sunday afternoon," Mike revealed and extracted the tickets from his shirt pocket, looked and winked at Lisa. Instantly, he got Jason's undivided attention. "I'm not quite sure what to do with them," he added as Jason's eyes widened, fixated on the two tickets. "I mean, I'm going to be very busy with unpacking, and getting things in order with the new renovation project at work."

Jason's eyes were still fixated on the tickets. Baseball was his favorite sport. The Cubs were his favorite baseball team, of course.

"I wonder if a couple of young teen-aged baseball enthusiast would want to check out the game," Mike said as he stroked his goatee inquisitively, referring to Jason and his friend Jerome, a.k.a. Romeo.

Mike gave Lisa another wink. She stood with one hand covering her mouth, quite amused by Mike's overly dramatic theatrics.

"Dad, Romeo and I will go and check out the game for you," Jason offered eagerly.

Mike paused for a moment, turned to Lisa, and gave her a questioning look. Jason's gaze followed Mike's over to Lisa who removed her hand from her mouth and nodded.

"I guess it would be okay," Lisa said finally.

"*Yes!* I'm going to a home game, baby!" Jason exclaimed as he eagerly reached for the tickets. "Thanks, Pops," he said and hugged him. "Thanks, Mom," he said and kissed her on the cheek.

"I'm sure you want to run on down to Jerome's and tell him the news," Lisa said.

"You know it," Jason said and beamed from ear to ear. "I'll be back by the time Reggie gets here.

"You better, or else we'll just have to save you a good share of hauling and loading boxes on the truck when you get back," Mike warned as Jason walked briskly out of the kitchen.

"I hope you're this enthusiastic about the new high school on Monday!" Lisa yelled behind him as he rushed out the front door, and closed it behind him with a thud.

"Now that we're alone, won't you come upstairs and help me get undressed and into my birthday suit that you seem to love so much?" Mike whispered in a seductive voice.

Lisa smiled at her husband's sly and seductive innuendo as she considered her answer.

"I don't think we have time for what you want to do," Lisa whispered in her own seductive voice.

"Babe, we have about ten minutes," Mike said as he looked at his watch.

"Ten minutes? I'm just getting started. *Hmm*! It's very tempting," Lisa whispered into his ear, and rubbed her breasts

20

against his hard muscular chest. "I'll follow you to the bedroom."

"That's what I'm talking about . . . an afternoon delight. Let's do this," Mike said and unbuttoned his shirt as he walked steadfastly out of the kitchen toward the stairs with Lisa close behind.

It was exactly ten minutes later when they emerged from their bedroom, having spent their last moments of a 'quickie'. Reggie and his buddies were downstairs ringing the doorbell. Jason still had not made it back from Jerome's. Mike galloped down the stairs, into the foyer and opened the door.

"Whassup, cuz? Y'all cooking fish up in here? Reggie asked, with his eyes averted as he sniffed the air, and then looked to Mike with a sly grin. "Gotta go out with a bang, huh?"

"Ha ha, very funny, cuz," Mike said and looked at Reggie as he walked passed him. "Hey, Craig, Aaron . . . you two ready for this?"

"We're ready to get y'all moved out of here, and into your new place," Aaron said.

"I've picked up some deli sandwiches from Potbelly's for you guys. They're in the kitchen."

"Hi, guys," Lisa said as she walked down the stairs.

"Hello, Lisa. The perfume you're wearing smells good on you," Reggie said in a snarky tone and looked over at Mike.

"Thanks," Lisa said.

"Lisa, this is Craig and Aaron," Mike introduced after he cleared his throat, and allowed Lisa and the guys to exchange greetings.

"Come on in the kitchen and get something to eat. You didn't think we'd put you all to work without feeding you first," Lisa said cheerfully as she motioned for the men to follow her into the kitchen.

Approximately three hours later, the 26 foot moving truck was all packed up, with the house now completely empty, except for the Taylors who stood in the foyer, looked around one last time, bidding adieu to the home of sixteen years.

"Well, this is it," Mike said, staring blankly into the living room.

"Yeah," Jason said dryly.

"I don't know about y'all, but I'm just dying to get moved into the new house," Lisa said anxiously.

"Well, let's be on our way," Mike said.

Jason flipped the light switch off, and they all walked outside, where Reggie, Craig and Aaron were waiting in the moving truck. Mike led the convoy to the new house on Chicago's West Side of town. The moving truck followed him, with Lisa and Jason following the truck.

On the ride across town, Lisa reminisced about how excited she and Mike were sixteen years ago when they first moved into the home that they had just moved out of. It had been her dream to return from their honeymoon, and move into their own home, and Mike made that dream come true for them. They returned from their honeymoon to a week of unpacking, but she enjoyed every minute of it. She shook her head at the idea of how fast time had gone by, and she chuckled to herself about how one's attitude toward packing could change so drastically over the course of sixteen years. She was pleased with the fact that they've "finally got a piece of that pie" that George and Weezy from the hit sitcom, *The Jeffersons,* had bragged so wholeheartedly about for years. That was their dream, and it was a good feeling to see the dream of theirs had materialized.

It was actually Mike's goals in life that had initially attracted Lisa to him. Of course, they had the physical attraction going on, but Lisa was more impressed when she learned that there was more to Michael Taylor than his good looks and charm. He had dreams that were even bigger than hers, and he was not ashamed to share them. One of Lisa's dreams was finding someone like

22

Mike, and he had remained her own personal dream come true.

Approximately forty-five minutes later, the Taylor family had reached their new neighborhood. As Mike, Reggie, and Lisa pulled into the subdivision, they were unaware of their new next-door neighbor, Rachel Martin, a woman in her mid-to-late forties. She's an attractive and sweet-looking woman, wearing a V-necked, red, thin cotton dress from Nordstrom's, stood in the living-room window watching them. Rachel had peeped through one of the slats of the mini-blinds as her husband, Thomas Ray Martin or Tom, as he's called by family, friends and co-workers, slept on the sofa. He's pushing fifty, with light silver streaks beginning to permeate his corporate haircut that made him look like the high-powered attorney that he is, with a patch of white hair on the left side of his head.

Tom dreamed of a black man, a stranger passing through town, doing odd jobs for food or very low wages as he headed north. In the stifling heat, he chopped the last piece of wood and neatly stacked them into a nearby woodpile for the Martin family. He wore a filthy long-sleeve white shirt, frayed blue jean overalls, worn-out work boots and a dark-colored cap.

Two rusted-out Chevy pickups approach in the distance. A rebel flag license plate adorned both of the trucks' grills. There were a total of thirteen white men, drinking bottles of Carling's Black Label Beer, hooting and hollering and pounding on the roof of the trucks. The black man stopped dead in his tracks, removed his cap, wiped away the sweat from his forehead, just as the first truck passed; two passengers are in the front, four in the back of the truck. He stared at the truck hypnotically, as if under a spell. The second truck approached; two passengers are in the front, five in the back of the truck. Someone spat a disgustingly lump of phlegm in the stranger's face, as if to break the spell.

"Mind your business, boy!" a passenger yelled from the bed of the truck. The men laughed as they disappeared into a thick cloud of dust. The black man wiped away the disgustingly lump of phlegm from his face, flung it to the ground.

The Martins' son, Tommy Ray, quickly scurried toward the worn-out screen door, caught a glimpse of the distant trucks. He looked over a shoulder at his mother who'd just set a wooden table for supper, where his father was seated reading *The Fayetteville Observer*.

"Can I go fishing?" Tommy Ray asked.

"After you eat your supper," Mrs. Martin said.

The black man walked up the rickety wooden steps, took off his cap, held it in both hands as he peered through the screen door.

"I done finished choppin' the wood, sir, ma'am," the black man said politely.

"Well, now, that's perfect timing. C'mon in. Supper's ready," Mrs. Martin said.

* * *

Approximately an hour later, everyone had finished eating supper and the black man had just finished entertaining the Martin family. He played the harmonica, sang a blues song.

The family, especially Tommy Ray, beamed and applauded the black man's performance. He graciously nodded, put on his cap, picked up a sack, and hoisted it over his left shoulder. Mr. Martin pointed him in the right direction heading north.

Tommy Ray and his mother looked on as the black man walked off. After he'd walked a yard or so, the black man turned, extended his right hand and offered Tommy Ray his harmonica.

"A gift for you," the black man said.

Tommy Ray dashed toward the black man and accepted the gift.

"*Gee!* Thanks, mister," an elated Tommy Ray said and raced

24

back toward his parents, flanked between them, and showed them his gift.

The black man smiled, turned and quickly disappeared into the rural, wooded area on the outskirts of Fayetteville, North Carolina.

Tommy Ray looked up toward his mother, "Can I go fishing now? he asked.

"Sure, honey," Mrs. Martin said as Tommy Ray raced toward the house, grabbing his fishing rod and pail before skipping off. "Make sure you're home before sunset."

* * *

Later that evening, the black man had traipsed deeper into the woods. He spotted the white men whom had driven by him earlier. He removed the sack from his left shoulder, propped it up against a nearby towering oak tree, crouched down behind it, and observed their activity. Eleven men were being initiated into a college fraternity group. The black man hid behind a few trees, as he inched closer toward the men. He crouched down behind each tree, as he looked on. Suddenly, the black man heard the sound of something shuffling through leaves. He slowly turned his head and peered over his left shoulder.

CRASH!

A beer bottle was smashed over the black man's head. His head and face are bloodied, and he's out cold. The white man, who smashed the beer bottle over the black man's head, grabbed him by his feet, and dragged him toward the forefront of the group.

"Well, well, well, look what we have here?" Andy, one of the two pledge masters said. "*Get up!*" he commanded and kicked black man in his right shin. The black man, somewhat dazed and confused, had managed to stumbled to his feet.

"Boy, didn't I tell you to mind your business?!" Stan, the other pledge master said and grabbed the black man, with both hands, by his shirt, and slammed his back against a tree.

"I sorry, sir," the frightened black man said.

"I guess we're gonna have to teach this boy a lesson," Stan said to the group.

The black man shuddered with fear, and shook his head. One of the eleven frat members punched the black man in the face. Another frat member lowered his head, and charged him like a battering ram. The black man doubled over. Still another frat member produced a powerful kick to the black man's bloodied face, and sent him crashing to the ground. The men had formed a phalanx around him and begun to kick and pummel him.

After what seemed like an eternity, the black man laid on the ground, in a supine position, pummeled and dazed. The vicious attack had left his left eye dislodged from its socket, hanging on his face.

Andy jumped into the driver's seat of the truck and started the engine. The black man slowly sputtered back to life.

The truck sped off, kicking up gravel and dust. The black man was chained, by both his ankles, to the back of the truck. For several miles, he was dragged along a dusty and bumpy country-logging road. The men were hooting and hollering, as they celebrate their cruel and inhumane act.

The black man cried out in agonizing and excruciating pain. His shoulders, back, arms and buttocks are skinned, ground to the bone.

Within minutes, the black man's right arm had become completely severed. One of the frat members riding in the back of the first truck noticed. His eyes had widen, mouth agape.

"*His arm!*" a frat member said hysterically.

The second pickup driver swerved to avoid running over the severed limb, and screeched to a complete halt.

Stan sat in the front seat on the passenger's side, with a Granny

26

Smith apple in his left hand, and a 15-inch overall jungle master hunting knife in his right. As he looked over his left shoulder a moment, he turned to Andy. "Turn the goddamn truck around. We'll hang him," he said as cut a piece of the apple, and stuck it in his mouth.

Andy slammed on the brakes and swerved left. The truck's tires spun rapidly, slid off-road on dirt and gravel, and screeched to a halt.

Abruptly, Tom was awakened from his engaging dream by a truck's screeching wheels. Simultaneously, a moving truck was backed into the Taylor's new driveway; its rear end facing a garage as it comes to an abrupt halt. Tom's eyes snapped open. He released a deep breath as if he'd just emerged from deep waters, and starred up at the ceiling. A moment, he sighed and closed his eyes. Tom heard a shrilled whisper, "Help me, please!"

Again, Tom's eyes snapped open. The black man's ghostly figure hovered over him. The face was horrific, beaten to a pulp with the left eye dislodged from its socket, hanging on his face. A knife was stuck in his right shoulder. A noose hung around the neck.

Tom, with a blanched face, bolted upright on the sofa and was panting profusely.

"Our new neighbors have just arrived. Oh, I'm sorry, sweetheart. Did the moving truck wake you up?" Rachel asked as she looked over her left shoulder at Tom, and closed a slat of the mini-blinds.

"Yeah, yeah, it did," Tom said as he sat straight up on the sofa, still panting.

"You look as if you've just seen a ghost," Rachel said as she continued to look over her left shoulder at him. "I wonder what they're like," she pondered the thought as she turned around, inserted a finger into one of the slats of the mini-blinds, and peeped out of the window at the new neighbors.

"So do I," Tom muttered and released a deep sigh.

Chapter 3

Saturday morning, the Taylors awoke in their new home with an entire weekend of unpacking ahead of them. The night before, Reggie and his moving buddies seemed to have moved them in quicker than they had moved them out. Just as Mike and Lisa had expected, Jason was obviously impressed with the new house, especially his bedroom, even though he tried his best to withhold his approval.

At the very moment when they had first arrived, it seemed that the sun was setting right outside the kitchen windows as a welcome to them all. The orange and purple color variations, projected through the kitchen's tall traditional-style windows, and the overhead skylights turned the bare walls into a canvas of color. Lisa thought it was absolutely breathtaking. She looked out the window at the backyard. Sunlight filtered on the hard surface of the patio outside. Shadows of leaves, sharp edges danced over the cracks in the stone pavers.

That night, they'd managed to set up all the bedrooms, so everyone could get a good night's rest. Of course, the first things Jason had set up in his new bedroom were his turntables and stereo equipment. Maddie had always called her grandson a gifted child of music, the spiritual product of melody and rhythm. All Lisa and Mike knew was that high-energy electronic dance or house music, usually yielding at least one hundred and twenty beats per minute, was their son's passion. It was his most time-consuming hobby, with baseball running a close second. Jason had expressed that he wanted to become a Disc Jockey for a dance music radio station, so his parents had encouraged him to pursue a college degree in mass communication. However, with graduation nine months away, he had yet to decide on a particular college.

That coming Monday, Jason was going to be attending his first day of school at Arlington High. He was not exactly enthused, but it helped that he had the entire summer to spend hanging out with his friend, Romeo, who just happened to be a respected and well-known local deejay, and his other buddies from the old neighborhood. Although they had all been within five minutes of walking distance of each other, the move had separated them by a forty-five minute drive, so they would definitely be seeing less of each other. Jason, a former member of the baseball team at his old high school, had played against Arlington High on several occasions. From Jason's point of view, Arlington's bad track record in baseball didn't exactly make his upcoming transfer any more appealing. After all, baseball was his second passion, but Jason rationalized to himself that nine months was not a very long sentence.

After putting the finishing touches on his room, with his baseball cap collection and posters in full display, Jason made his way downstairs, his right hand on the smooth polished oak as he descended the staircase. A light in the foyer was on, he turned it off. At the bottom of the stairs, he went left, opened a door that led to the garage, and grabbed an armload of broken down moving boxes. The garage door was open. Jason walked down the driveway toward the curb. He thought the neighborhood was decent enough. The difference between Arlington Heights and their old neighborhood across town was obvious. It was evident by the luxury cars parked curbside or in the homeowner's driveways. Jason was taking it all in.

In the driveway next-door to theirs, Jason spotted his new neighbor, about his height and possibly his age, clean-cut, but with dark haunting eyes. He was washing a black car with the license plate that read: "BTM 1013." What was even more interesting was that his suburban neighbor was sporting an Arlington High red and white baseball T-shirt.

Jason stood admiring the car a moment, a black 1980-something

Monte Carlo, which appeared to be in very good condition, and then walked off. His new neighbor looked up from swilling a sponge in a bucket of hot soapy water, and shook his head as his eyes followed Jason. He stood up and dropped the
sponge into the bucket, walked into the garage as he wiped his hands dry with a towel wrapped around his neck.

Moments later, Jason's neighbor emerged from the garage. He looked menacing as he walked briskly across the separate lawns, brandishing some sort of weapon. The sunlight beamed off of it.

Jason furiously stuffed the last box in the rolling outdoor plastic trash container. As he turned, he's face-to-face with his new neighbor who thrust forward his right hand. Jason froze with wide eyes. A moment, he slowly peered down toward his stomach.

"I thought maybe you could use this," the new neighbor said and offered Jason a box cutter. Jason relaxed his stance. "I'm Brad, by the way," he said and offered his hand.

"Thanks. I think I've stuffed them all in there. I'm Jason," he said and offered Brad a hip-hop handshake. Surprisingly, Brad did not miss a beat with the hip-hop handshake.

"You guys just moved in, huh?" Brad said as he secured the blade and put the box cutter in his back pants pocket.

"Yeah. We've just moved in yesterday," Jason said.

"Will you be attending Arlington High on Monday?" Brad asked.

"I don't have much of a choice," Jason said with a wry chuckle.

"Transferring to a new high school must really suck," Brad said. "What's your classification?" he asked.

"I'm a senior. What about you?" Jason asked, feeling a little relieved that Brad didn't seem as square as he previously thought when he'd initially seen him.

"Class of 2-G," Brad said, thrown up one hand and made a symbol with only his thumb and pinky fingers extended.

"That's whassup," Jason said and turned slightly to get a full

31

panoramic view of the neighborhood.

"This is a good neighborhood. It's very quiet," Brad said, noticing Jason surveying the neighborhood. "I spend a lot of time inside playing PlayStation, and then there's baseball camp in the summer," he said and pointed toward the front of his T-shirt.

"You play ball, huh?" Jason said with a grin.

"I play third base. I'm also a fill-in southpaw," Brad said.

"Huh?" Jason said.

"A left-handed pitcher," Brad said.

"Oh, all right," Jason said as he nodded and surveyed the expensive homes and cars in the up-scale suburban neighborhood.

"What about you? Do you play ball?" Brad asked.

"A little," Jason said dryly as he debated whether or not he'd considered playing on Arlington High's baseball team, due to their horrible track record.

"Well, maybe you should try out for the team," Brad suggested.

Just then, Jason recognized his mother as she rounded the corner and jogged into the cul-de-sac, with her white Discman bouncing on her left hip. She wore a blue and white warm-up suit, with a white sweatband, across her brow.

"I like the car," Jason complimented and turned his attention back to Brad. "Is it yours?" he asked.

"Yeah. My parents purchased it for me last year soon after I'd gotten my license. It didn't look this good at first, but me and my dad put a lot of work into it."

"Well, it's definitely paid off. It's nice," Jason said.

"Thanks," Brad said.

Lisa had just approached the driveway and jogged toward Jason and Brad with a friendly smile, already engaged in her cool down breathing exercise, and blew short continuance puffs of breath through her pursed lips.

"Morning, Mom," Jason greeted.

"Good morning, ma'am," Brad said politely.

32

"Well, good morning," Lisa said as she jogged in place. "I see you've already made a new friend."

"This is Brad; he lives next-door," Jason said.

"Nice to meet you," Lisa said with a nod. "I'm Jason's mother."

"Nice to meet you too," Brad said.

"Brad had just giving me the lowdown on 'The Heights'," Jason said.

"I'm sure they were all good things you had to say about the neighborhood," Lisa said to Brad as she patted Jason's on his right shoulder. "We nearly had to drag him here kicking and screaming like a big old baby."

"They were all good things," Brad said and chuckled. "I told him that it's a good neighborhood."

"Thank you, Brad, for the positive reinforcement," Lisa said, looked at Jason, and folded her arms across her chest.

Just then, the front door of Brad's home was opened, and a female voice from inside called out, *"Braaaaaad!"*

"Sounds like you two will get to meet my mom," Brad said and turned to respond to his mother's beck and call. "I'm over here!"

A blonde-haired woman, who looked quite demure, wore khaki pants and a pink polo shirt, stepped out of the house with her left hand positioned over her eyebrows to block the morning sun. Once she spotted Lisa and Jason, her face was flushed with embarrassment. She smiled politely as she walked across the separating lawn toward the Taylors' driveway.

"Hi, I'm Rachel Martin," she introduced and shook both Lisa and Jason's hands. "Usually I'm not this loud, screaming out the front door and all, but a certain teenager truly believes that 'mother' is synonymous with 'maid'."

Lisa chuckled as Brad scrunched his face, his eyes averted as he turned away from his mother. "Tell me about it," she said. "Hi, I'm Lisa Taylor, and this is my son Jason, who's mistaken me as his live-in maid."

Jason scrunched his face and rolled his eyes sarcastically. "Well, welcome to the neighborhood," Rachel said cheerfully.

Lisa noticed a slight Southern accent, and tried to figure out where Rachel could have been from. "Thank you," she said.

"I'm going to assume the tall, dark and handsome man I saw picking up the newspaper this morning was your husband," Rachel said.

"That was my husband, Mike. At times, he's like my eldest teenager," Lisa said.

"I can relate," Rachel said as they both shared a quaint chuckle.

Brad and Jason had apparently become bored with the turn of both their mothers' conversation. They stood by quietly until Brad had suggested, by motioning, that Jason walked with him over to his car while he finished washing it. The two had casually strolled off, barely being noticed.

"Is it just the three of you?" Rachel asked, squinting in the sunlight.

"Yeah. It's me and my two guys," Lisa said. "What about you?"

"We're a family of three as well. My husband Tom would've probably been out mowing the lawn this morning, if he didn't have to go into the office today," Rachel informed.

Lisa smiled and seemed genuinely surprised at how openly social her new neighbor was. She thought about her mother, Maddie, and how she could not wait to introduce her to Rachel as extra reassurance that they didn't move into the middle of Klan County.

"Hey, I have an idea!" Rachel exclaimed enthusiastically that it startled Lisa. "How about I cook dinner tonight?" she suggested.

"I don't know," Lisa said reluctantly. "I wouldn't want you to go through the trouble. And besides, we still have quite of bit of unpacking to do."

34

"It's no trouble at all. As for your unpacking and putting things away, that's all the more reason for you to want to get away from everything for a while, and enjoy a nice home-cooked meal," Rachel said.

"I guess we could use a nice home-cooked meal after eating fast-food and sandwiches the past few days," Lisa said as she reconsidered the idea. "It's very kind and thoughtful of you to offer."

Rachel waved the thought away with a flick of her wrist. "It's no problem. By the way, just so you know, I'm a Southern gal. I can throw down in the kitchen," she reassured with a little added Southern twang to her voice.

The women shared another quaint chuckle.

"How does seven o'clock sound?" Rachel asked.

"Seven o'clock sounds great," Lisa said as she looked past Rachel and focused on Jason and Brad talking across the lawn.

"*Great*," Rachel said. "They seemed to have hit it off pretty well," she said as she looked over her left shoulder. "How old is Jason?" she asked and turned back to Lisa.

"Jason's seventeen. He'll be starting his senior year of high school on Monday," Lisa said.

"Well, it seems as if we'll both be attending the same graduation ceremony," Rachel said proudly and released a sigh. "Well, Lisa, it has been absolutely a pleasure meeting you, and I do look forward to having you all over for dinner tonight. I'll let you get back to your unpacking, and I have to get back inside and play Mrs. Cleaver. I'll see you all at seven," she reminded.

Lisa chuckled and thanked Rachel again, before they both parted and walked in the direction of their respective homes. She couldn't wait to reveal the dinner plans to Mike, who was inside hanging artwork.

Lisa entered the house to the sound of a nail being hammered into the wall. She followed the sound into the living room, where she found her husband who stood shirtless on a short step ladder as he prepared to hang a painting of two little black girls running through a field of violet and pink wildflowers in the South. Two years prior, Lisa had purchased the painting while attending the Dogwood Festival during a visit to Atlanta, Georgia. When she first saw it, she instantly thought of her favorite movie, *The Color Purple*. Lisa had to have the artwork, despite the costly price displayed on the dangling tag. She was a freelance artist herself, and she had produced a good bit of the artwork in their home, but that didn't keep her from appreciating the talent of other artists.

As Lisa watched her husband extend his arms upward to position the second nail, she noticed his back and shoulder muscles flexing and catching the light and shadow at all the right angles. She only wished she was able to paint him just like that at the very moment. Unfortunately, her art supplies were still packed away in one of the remaining few boxes.

Lisa cleared her throat forcefully, to get Mike's attention.

"Hey, babe," Mike said, identifying her without turning away from his task. "Would you hand me the box of nails from off the mantle?"

"Sure," Lisa said and walked a few steps across the living room toward the fireplace.

As she handed Mike the box of nails, he kneeled over from his position on the stepladder, and gently kissed her on the forehead.

"Thanks, babe," Mike said.

"We've been invited to dinner," Lisa said nonchalantly.

Mike stepped down off of the ladder with a curious expression. "Who invited us to dinner?" he asked.

"Our new next-door neighbor, Rachel Martin," Lisa said with a smile.

"Did you just meet her?" Mike asked, still curious.

"Well, I met Rachel when I got back from my morning jog. Jason was standing in the driveway talking to her son, Brad, and she came outside and introduced herself shortly afterwards. She seemed to be very nice. I mean, she practically insisted that we come over for dinner tonight," Lisa informed.

"I hope she can cook," Mike said.

"Well, she told me not to worry. She's a 'Southern gal' who can throw down in the kitchen," Lisa said as she tried to imitate Rachel's Southern twang.

"Yeah, right," Mike said sarcastically.

Lisa laughed and slapped Mike playfully on his bare chest.

"She said she saw you this morning, when you went out to get the newspaper. She inquired about 'that handsome man'," Lisa teased and crossed her arms.

"That would be me," Mike said proudly and stroke his goatee. "I'm sure you don't need this Rachel Martin person to tell you that your man is fine as wine," he said as he grabbed Lisa, uncrossed her arms, pulled her in tightly to his hard muscular chest and planted a passionate kiss on her lips. "What time is dinner?"

"Seven o'clock," Lisa replied.

"Well I guess we don't have to worry about being late," Mike said.

"It would be a shame if we were. They live right next-door," Lisa said as she walked over to a box containing a pair of drapes that she wanted to have hung.

They spent the rest of the day hard at work, and by five o'clock, they had already set up the living room, dining room, the master bedroom on-suite, Mike's office, and all three full bathrooms. On Sunday, they'd planned on completing the kitchen, the den, a guest bedroom, hanging more artwork on the walls, and putting the finishing touches on the halls and foyer.

Approximately five minutes to seven, they were just about ready to go. Lisa was dressed in a comfortable, yet classy, light blue pantsuit, and she had styled her hair that had initially been made famous by Halle Berry herself. The color that she was wearing looked great against her light mocha complexion. Mike had on a pair of khaki slacks with a blue oxford shirt, and Jason wore a pair of black jeans with a blue, black and white short-sleeved knit shirt that was neatly tucked.

"How do I look?" Lisa asked with a confident smile as she checked her lipstick in the hall mirror.

"Stunning," Mike said.

"Don't you two look handsome," Lisa complimented, turned from the mirror, and walked down the hall toward her two escorts who were waiting patiently in the foyer.

Mike extended his right arm to Lisa. "Shall we?" he said.

Lisa smiled as she and her husband walked arm-in-arm, with Jason close behind them, as they made their way across the lawn that separated the Taylor's home from their new neighbors.

Chapter 4

Lisa pressed the doorbell button.
DING, DONG!
DING, DONG!
DING, DONG!

"Coming," Rachel said in a cheerful tone as she opened the door and ushered the Taylor family inside. "Hi, come on in. Dinner is almost ready, and I'm expecting my husband any minute now. That's a lovely outfit, Lisa. It looks so comfortable," she said.

"Thank you. It's very comfortable," Lisa beamed. "Rachel, this is my husband, Mike. Mike, this is Rachel," she introduced.

"Hello, Rachel," Mike spoke cordially and extended his right hand.

"Hello, Mike. I'm pleased to meet you. Hi, Jason," Rachel beamed as she spoke and shook Mike's hand. "He's better-looking up close," she said to Lisa. Mike blushed with embarrassment.

"Don't even get him started," Lisa muttered with a wry grin tugged at her mouth. She had begun admiring the Martins' lavish and beautifully decorated home as Rachel led them into the living room. "You have a beautiful home," she complimented.

"Thank you. I must confess that I visited your home when the realtor first held an open house a couple of months ago. I wanted to see the upgrades done by the previous owners. Overall, I think the layout of the floor plan and the finishes were absolutely exquisite," Rachel said.

"Well, we'll have to invite you all over once we get everything situated," Mike said.

"I'd love that," Rachel said as she swept a stray lock of hair back behind her ear. Jason, Brad is upstairs playing video games. You're welcome to join him, if you like. It's the second door on the left, once you reach the top of the stairs."

"All right, thanks," Jason said and ascended the stairs, happy

39

to get away from the seemingly uninteresting adult interaction and conversation.

"Have a seat. Make yourselves comfortable. Can I get either of you something to drink?" Rachel asked and looked from Mike to Lisa.

"A glass of water would be fine," Lisa said.

Rachel turned to Mike. "How about you?" she asked.

"No thanks. I'll wait until dinner," Mike said politely.

"All right. I'll be back in a flash," Rachel said and headed toward the kitchen.

Lisa was admiring a bevy of African artifacts that were displayed in a large cherry oak curio case. She nudged Mike and nodded in the direction of the elaborate display. They were both more or less surprised that the Martins had chosen to adorn their living room with colorful masks and trinkets from the motherland. Lisa got up from her seat on the plush sofa, so that she could take a closer look. Mike, obviously impressed as well, followed her over to the curio case.

"I bet these are from South Africa," Lisa surmised, and cocked her head to the side, to get a better look at the detail of one particular ceremonial mask.

"I never expected to see an exhibit like this tonight," Mike said, massaging Lisa's shoulders as they both peered through the spotless glass.

"Nor did I. I wonder if she went out and set this all up to make us feel comfortable," Lisa joked, knowing full well that certainly wasn't the case. From looking at the contents of the intriguing collection, she could tell that someone had a good eye for authentic African art.

"Don't be silly," Mike whispered as Rachel returned to the living room.

"Here you go," Rachel said and handed Lisa the glass of ice water along with a bamboo coaster.

40

"Thank you, Rachel. We were just admiring your art collection," Lisa said as she and Mike returned to their seat on the sofa. "Did you actually go to South Africa?"

"As a matter of fact, we'd just vacationed there last month, and that's when I got the large tribal mask with the red, green, and orange detailing," Rachel revealed with a flustered look, sat on the armchair, and stared blankly toward the mask she was referring to. "The rest of the pieces were collected from an African Novelty Shop. I think they're absolutely wonderful pieces, all from South Africa."

"I thought so," Lisa said. "Artists in that particular region have a unique creative sense that makes their artwork easily identifiable."

"I'm impressed," Rachel said with a raised eyebrow. "Do you collect?"

"Everything she manages to get her hands on," Mike interjected with a chuckle.

Lisa smirked, rolled her eyes and dismissed his comment with a flick of her wrist. "Don't pay him any mind. Men don't know how to appreciate the finer things in life such as fine artwork," she said.

"*Oooh!* I am not even going to go there," Rachel laughed.

Just before Mike could respond, a key turned in the door, and a briefcase entered the foyer, followed undoubtedly by Tom Martin.

"Lucy, I'm home!" he shouted from the foyer in a pretty good Desi Arnez impersonation. Tom hadn't noticed that the dinner guests, who Rachel had informed him about earlier, were already seated in the living room.

"Tom, we're in here!" Rachel shouted toward the foyer.
Tom entered the living room, loosening his tie with a pleasant smile, walked up behind his wife, bent over, and kissed the back of her neck. Rachel stood up and greeted him.

"Tom, these are our new neighbors I told you about," Rachel

reminded. "This is Mike and his lovely wife Lisa," she introduced. Their son, Jason, is upstairs playing video games with Brad."

"Nice to meet you both," Tom said with a smile as he leaned in to shake both of their hands.

Mike stood up. "Likewise," he said, and then sat back down.

"We were just discussing your recent trip to South Africa," Lisa said, causing Tom's face to light up with recollection as he looked to a flustered Rachel who sat in the armchair.

"I must say, South Africa was absolutely breathtaking. It's almost tropical even. We just loved it. In fact, we've been meaning to plan another trip there next year," Tom said, taking a seat on the arm of the loveseat.

"Now you're talking," Mike said. "I had the privilege of visiting Durban, South Africa during my senior year in college. The beaches were so beautiful that I could have sworn I was in the Caribbean. I only wished that my baby could've been there with me," he said and kissed Lisa on the cheek.

Rachel and Tom both exchanged tremulous smiles before Rachel rose to her feet, and clasped her hands together.

"Okay. I, for one, can sit here all evening and talk about vacation paradises, but I refuse to let you all miss out on this wonderful dinner I've prepared," Rachel said as her voice had begun to falter.   Tom, Mike and Lisa collectively chuckled. "Tom, would you go upstairs and get the boys away from the video games so we can all have dinner?" she asked.

"Sure, honey," Tom said as he ascended the stairs. "Hey, Brad," he yelled.

Rachel ushered Lisa and Mike into the inviting dining room, where the eight-seat dining room table was set for six, complete with place cards. Lisa was further impressed and found Rachel Martin to be more and more interesting by the minute. She was very fond of elegant dining and loved dinner parties. Lisa had managed to drag Mike to quite a few informal dinner parties, celebrating various events in the Chicago art world, but he had always remained bored and uncomfortable. In contrast, she tried to explain to him that it was very similar to the formal executive dinner parties, in which she had accompanied him. Mike preferred that the line not be blurred between formal, and informal and was more open to participate in either extreme. But the dinner parties that were thrown by his wife's circle of friends in the art world were too informal, in his opinion. Lisa thought that was exactly what added to their appeal.

"Rachel, do you need any help?" Lisa asked as she took her seat in front of the fancy gold and white plate that supported a place card with her name written in gold calligraphic letters.

"No, Lisa, you're a guest. Perhaps next time, I'll take you up on your offer," Rachel said with a smile, obviously excited about the meal she was about to present. "I'll be right out."

Rachel left the dining room and turned on some mellow jazz that was projected from the small Bose speakers in the kitchen at just the right volume. Tom entered the dining room with Brad and Jason following close behind. After introducing Brad to Mike, they all took their seats in front of their respective place cards.

"I'm famished. I didn't have time for lunch today?" Tom said and removed his napkin from inside the wine glass and placing it on his lap. "Rachel doesn't get to host dinner parties that often. But when she does, she goes all out," he explained to Lisa and Mike.

"I must say, Rachel is quite the host," Lisa complimented as she picked up her place card from her plate, and looked intently at the formation of the letters. Despite her artistic talent, Lisa had yet to master the art of calligraphy. Instead, she created her own font style that was of course inspired by calligraphy with a twist of her own creative interpretation.

"Indeed, she is," Tom agreed and redirected his attention back to Jason. "So, Jason, do you play any sports?" he asked.

43

Brad glanced at his father, and answered, "He plays a little baseball."

"A little . . ." Mike said, with a raised eyebrow.

"I play a little ball," Jason affirmed, fidgeting with his place card.

"Son, I'd hardly say that you play a little baseball," Mike said as he braced his elbows on the table, looked to Tom. "Tom, this kid has been a stand-out player on the high school's varsity baseball team since his freshman year at Fitzgerald. He's even won the MVP award two years in a row," he boasted.

Brad's mouth fell open with surprise when he'd finally recognized Jason. "Oh snap! I remember you," he said.

Rachel entered the dining room with a couple of covered ceramic dishes matching the china, placed them on the dining table, and returned to the kitchen for the rest of the food.

"You got mad skills," Brad said.

Jason, undaunted by the attention, continued fidgeting with his place card and mumbled, "Thanks. That was at Fitzgerald. I might not play this year."

"I'm sorry you feel that way, which is too bad. Arlington High could definitely use your talent," Tom said.

"That's true. We could really use you on the team," Brad agreed. "Doug Kirkpatrick is going to be the new head coach. Rumor has it that the coach will be thinning the herd this season. He's only accepting the best talent. A lot of us veteran players are biting our nails."

Jason looked up and wondered if he'd heard Brad correctly. Doug Kirkpatrick was the winningest baseball coach for Wheeling High School, in Illinois state history, for the past eleven years. In fact, Wheeling High had claimed solid victories over Fitzgerald over the past ten seasons. Jason was definitely interested in the new details.

"Coach Kirkpatrick . . . from Wheeling High?" Jason asked

enthusiastically.

"The one and only," Brad said.

Just then, Rachel reentered the dining room, carrying the last and biggest dish.

"I hope everyone has brought a hearty appetite to the dinner table," Rachel said as she placed the last dish in the center of the table.

"Everything looks and smells great," Lisa said. "I wish you would allow me to help you serve."

Rachel contemplated Lisa's offer to help a second time, before smiled and said, "On second thought, I could use your help. I'll bring out the serving utensils, and we can serve everyone."

"My pleasure," Lisa said as she slid her chair back from the table and stood up.

Rachel returned to the dining room with the serving utensils. She and Lisa distributed portions of roast beef, corn-on-the-cob, roasted garlic mashed potatoes and green bean casserole. Afterwards, Rachel picked up a bottle of Dolcetto D'Alba, a medium-bodied red wine, uncorked and poured wine into the glasses of the adults. Lisa twisted off the cap of a 2-liter bottle of soda, and poured a glass full for Brad and Jason.

After Brad said the grace, he and Jason continued their conversation where they'd left off about Arlington High's baseball team, as the adults listened intently.

"You probably don't want to be part of a losing team," Brad said and surprised Jason by hitting the nail on the head. "I think Coach Kirkpatrick is definitely going to turn the team around this season."

"Jason, you should really give it some thought," Tom said.

"I agree," Mike said, leaving Jason to consider the idea.

"Mike, if you don't mind my asking, what line of work are you in?" Tom asked.

"Well, I've earned my degree in Structural Engineering. I'm

currently employed with Drake and Nash Commercial Construction and Management Company as a Contractor. We specialize in commercial and residential renovations," Mike said.

"I'm very familiar with Drake and Nash. You guys do remarkable work," Tom said.

"Thanks. We pride ourselves in the craftsmanship and unmatched quality of our work," Mike said.

"Well, I work for a firm," Tom said. "A legal firm, that is."

"You're an attorney, huh?" Mike said.

"*Guilty!*" Tom said with a chuckle. I've just made partner. Actually, effective September fourteenth, it will be Mossberger, Weinstein, Stewart and Martin," Tom confirmed.

"Congratulations," Mike said.

"Well, isn't that something," Lisa said. "Mike was promoted to a Regional District Manager of his division, just a couple months ago."

"A toast . . . to Tom and Mike," Rachel said and raised her glass.

"*Cheers!*" Everyone chorused and made a toast.

CLINK!

CLINK!

CLINK!

CLINK!

CLINK!

CLINK!

After a sip, Tom removed his table napkin from his lap, dabbed the corners of his mouth, and then turned to Mike.

"You know, now that I think about it, I need to get one of your business cards. One of my clients is looking to renovate a church and restaurant," Tom said.

"I have one right here," Mike said and reached into his back pants pocket, removed his wallet, extracted one of his business cards and handed it to Tom.

"Our firm is planning on renovating and expanding into an adjacent building, and will be publishing an RFT in the Chicago Tribune pretty soon," Tom added.

"Would part of the expansion project include your new office? Lisa asked.

"*Guilty again!*" Tom said and chuckled.

"Honey, what's an RFP?" Rachel asked inquisitively and took a sip of wine.

"Request for Proposal. It's a document that a company posts to elicit bids from potential clients," Tom explained. "I'm sure Mike can better explain the process."

"You've pretty much summed it up," Mike said. "How soon are you guys looking to expand?" he asked, definitely interested in learning more about the law firm's future renovation and expansion plans.

"Very soon," Tom said. "I'm set on a nice corner office.

"Well, we'll definitely have to talk more about this," Mike said. "If your office is located outside of my region, I'm certain that division would be just as equally interested in the RFP."

"What region does your division handle?" Tom asked.

"The Northwest region, and the surrounding business districts.

"Well, then, I think this project might actually be applicable to your division. We're actually located in Green Oaks," Tom said.

"Green Oaks is within my region. I don't imagine your building is extremely large, to be in that neighborhood, so I'd expect it wouldn't be a very drawn out project. We get some of our smaller renovations done in as little as four to six weeks," Mike said.

"Then we definitely need to get together soon. I strongly encourage you to submit a bid on this one," Tom said.

"Rachel, how do you spend your days, when you're not playing Mrs. Cleaver," Lisa joked and caused Rachel to laugh out loud. She's clearly buzzed from the wine.

"Well, when I'm not playing the role of June Cleaver, I do volunteer work. I put in a few hours a week at the Women's Center, conveniently located off Goebbert Road. I help out with project coordinating, fundraising, light office duties . . . things like that. It keeps me busy," Rachel said.

"It sounds very interesting and rewarding," Lisa said.

"Oh, it is. The majority of our memberships are mother-daughter, and I just love to see that type of interaction. Some of our programs are really good for mothers who have careers and volunteer their time encouraging and mentoring their own daughters as well as other girls. We have such a diverse group of members, and it's just a joy to work with these impressionable girls," Rachel boasted.

"Well, I'm not exactly a career woman myself, unless you consider being a wife, a mother and homemaker a full-time job," Lisa said.

"You might as well. It's just as demanding. When I'm not at the Women's Center, I'm home cooking and cleaning. I do all the laundry, and attend all the PTA meetings. Hell, I should have a lock of white hair in my head instead of Tom," Rachel said, quaffed the wine, and then looked at both men a look as if to dare them to challenge her analysis. Neither Tom nor Mike said a word. Lisa chuckled quietly to herself.

"I agree one hundred percent. As a matter of fact, I used to do volunteer work for a local charter school. There, I taught an arts and crafts class, and conducted a weekly fitness and wellness program. I did that for almost three years before I'd fully submerged myself in my artwork," Lisa said.

"You're an artist, huh? I knew there was something artsy about you," Rachel said, pointing her fork at Lisa.

"Well, I'm a self-taught artist. My mother noticed my talent early on and encouraged me to pursue it. She said my artistic talent would someday come in handy. I'd planned on opening my own art gallery, but Mike feared for my safety," Lisa said.

"Would we have seen any of your work?" Tom asked curiously.

"Not unless you've frequently attended local art festivals, but judging from your art collection you have in your living room, I wouldn't be a bit surprised," Lisa said.

"Actually, Lisa, we have quite a few paintings stored in the basement simply because we haven't taken the time to have them hung. I'm going to have to check to see if 'Lisa Taylor' is signed at the bottom of any of them," Rachel said and smile.

"Rachel, dinner was delicious," Mike said and removed his napkin from his lap, and placing it neatly on top of his plate.

Jason and Brad had already finished their dinner and they were engaged in their own conversation.

"Mom, dinner was great," Brad said. "May Jason and I be excused?"

"Yes, you may. There's some ice cream in the freezer if you two want dessert," Rachel said.

"All right," Brad said, slid his chair back from the table and dropped his napkin on top of his plate.

"Jason, I see you enjoyed dinner as well," Lisa said as she noticed Jason had nearly cleared his plate except for a few green beans, and a very small portion of mashed potatoes that he probably left out of politeness.

"Dinner was very good, Mrs. Martin," Jason complimented as he slid his chair back from the table, placed his napkin on top of his plate, stood and followed Brad toward the kitchen.

"All these compliments . . . I'm beside myself," Rachel said and added, again, an extra helping of her Southern twang. "I couldn't pay for a compliment on any other day."

"Rachel, I love your Southern accent. I've been desperately trying to figure out where you're originally from," Lisa said, nearly finished with her own meal.

"Fayetteville, North Carolina. I've been gone from there for over twenty years, and I haven't been able to lose the accent. Are you originally from Chicago?" Rachel asked.

"No. I was born in New Orleans. My parents moved to Chicago approximately thirty years ago, but I've had my share of visits to the Deep South," Lisa said.

"I see," Rachel said and turned her attention to the finished plates that sat in front of her. "If everyone's finished with their dinner, we can all go back into the living room.

"Why don't you two go into the living room? Mike and I will take care of the dishes, if that's all right with you?" Tom said, with a wink and nod to Mike. "No more June Cleaver stuff," he whispered.

"*Gotcha!*" Mike agreed. "This will give us a chance to further discuss business."

Without saying a word, Rachel and Lisa looked at each other as they got up from the table, left the dining room, and   returned to the living room.

"I've learned not to question a man when he's offered to do the dishes or any other work around the house," Rachel said matter-of-factly.

"Who are you telling?" Lisa said and chuckled. "I have really enjoyed myself this evening. Dinner was fabulous. We must do this again soon. Next time, I'll prepare dinner."

"We've enjoyed having you. Perhaps, one day when you're free, after you've finished unpacking and all settled in, I'd love for you to join me in paying a visit to the Women's Center."

"I'd love to," Lisa beamed.

"Sounds like a plan," Rachel said cheerfully. "Hey, ten bucks that they're both fast asleep with their heads face down in their plates."

The women shared another laugh at their husbands' expense.

50

"There are two things that would do that to them," Lisa said. "The first is good food. The other is great sex."

Lisa and Rachel continued joking, shared laughs and friendly conversation. This was the beginning of a friendship that would last a lifetime. Like Jason's buddies, Lisa's friends lived all the way across town. One of Lisa's friends in particular, Dameeka, known for being prone to say just about anything that popped into her comical mind, had already warned, "I don't care how grand the villa is, I'm not about to leave the comfort of my abode, to trek all the way across town to sip tea, with a raised pinky finger, and eating crumpets with your uppity ass. Ms. Thing, you'd better reach out and dial somebody." Lisa remembered and laughed at Dameeka's animated candor, who always appeared to be so serious, despite how comical her words were.

Tom and Mike had finished the dishes and joined their wives in the living room. They all talked some more about a little bit of everything from politics to their sons' college futures. After that, Tom ascended the stairs once again to summon Jason and Brad in order that everyone could say their goodbyes.

"Mom, Dad, can Jason stay over a little longer? We're really into the video games," Brad asked as they all stood around in the living room.

"Well, if it's all right with Mike and Lisa, it's fine with us," Tom said and looked to Rachel.

"It's fine with us," Mike said and looked to Lisa who nodded in agreement.

"If he starts to get on your nerves, send him home," Lisa said.

The adults said good night, as Brad and Jason bolted upstairs boasting how one was going to outwit the other.

Moments later, Mike and Lisa were in their new master bedroom on-suite. Lisa was feeling romantic. She hugged Mike and whispered softly in his ear, "How about you and me take a nice hot bath and continue tonight's celebration," she said and kissed him on the lips, causing his eager smile to grow even more.

"Let's do this," Mike said without hesitation.

Lisa smiled, and then said, "I'll go run the bath water."

"You do that," Mike said and playfully tapped Lisa on her backside.

Lisa smiled devilishly at his naughty innuendo and stepped inside the bathroom. Instantly, Mike had stripped down to his underwear, dropped to the floor, and started doing push-ups as if he was cramming a last minute warm-up, to increase his stamina, for what the night had in store. After doing one set of twenty-five push-ups, he flipped over onto his backside, and started doing one set of twenty-five sit-ups.

A few moments later, Lisa called out seductively from the bathroom, "Mike, I'm waiting."

Mike jumped to his feet with a slight grunt and yelled, "You ain't said nothing but a word."

He stepped out of his underwear and headed toward the bathroom.

"Hurry up, baby," Lisa said and tried not to stare so hard at her husband's body in the buff, even though he stared intently at hers.

Lisa bit her bottom lip to keep her mouth from dropping open. It was amazing how his naked body still had the same affect on her after so many years of marriage. She thought that was a real good thing. His erection had already grown to half-mast as he walked through the candle-lit bathroom. Lisa noticed that the flames from the candles seemed to bend and curl, also checking out her man, as he walked toward the antique cast iron slipper claw foot bathtub. She smiled to herself at the idea that her man was so fine even the candle flames were breaking their necks to check him out. She leaned forward, giving Mike enough space to step into the tub and sat behind her. She was so eager to lay her head on his chest and enjoy a relaxing bath with her husband. The steaming water had

52

just the right amount of bath oil so they wouldn't shrivel up too badly; regardless of how long they indulged themselves.

"I hope there's enough room for you, me, and Moby," Lisa smirked and chuckled amusedly, her gaze at the length and girth of Mike's penis.

Mike grinned slyly. "Yeah I hope so too. Otherwise, we'd have to take this party to the bedroom."

Mike put one foot in the tub and quickly snatched it out with a surprised look on his face. *"Ahh!* This water is hot! Why do you women like to bathe in scorching hot water?"

Lisa laughed, and then said, "I know my big daddy isn't afraid of a little hot water."

"Are you referring to me or him?" Mike asked with a coy smile and pointed to his fully erect penis.

"Both of y'all need to get your big heads in this tub," Lisa said playfully.

Bravely, Mike stepped into the tub, slowly giving his body enough time to adjust to the temperature of the hot bath water. He assumed his position behind his wife, who always seemed to fit perfectly between his muscular thighs. She leaned her back against his chest as he massaged her shoulders, nibbled on her earlobe, and kissed his way down her neck. His hands worked their way down to her arms, and then in toward the cocoa colored circles around her nipples, hardened like bullet points. He gently traced circles around them with his fingers, kissed and sucked even more passionately on her neck. Lisa let out moans of pleasure as she allowed her head to roll back onto Mike's shoulder. She was really getting turned on, and she could feel Mike's full erection pressing forcefully against the small of her back. With one hand, he massaged one of her nipples with his thumb and forefinger, while his other hand searched the water for the beige porous bath sponge. Mike had found the sponge and squeezed the hot bath Water onto Lisa's chest while his other hand made its way down past her belly button to massage the nicely trimmed area where her firm and toned legs met. Lisa continued to moan with pleasure, as she held on tight to Mike's thighs, which were serving as perfect armrests. She started to grind her back against his throbbing erection, and this made the muscles in his legs flex as he exhaled a long warm breath onto her neck. Things were heating up immensely for the both of them, and even though they were both enjoying the attention that their bodies were receiving, neither one of them wanted the bathtub to be the main course of their erotic evening.

"How about we take this party to the bedroom? I think we've succeeded in scalding off all the impurities," Mike whispered into his wife's ear, his penis still pulsating behind her.

Lisa giggled breathlessly and nodded her agreement as Mike continued to tongue her neck passionately. She pressed down on his muscular hairy legs to try to raise herself out of the bathtub, but she found that her legs were weak from the aquatic interlude. Lisa noticed that Mike had begun to raise his body behind her to help her out of the bathtub. While doing so, his penis slid up along her backside, and was positioned once again against the small of her back. Holding onto her from behind in somewhat of a bear hug, they stepped out of the tub together and stood dripping wet on the plush floor mat.

"I have a surprise for you," Mike whispered, with his head nuzzled into Lisa's neck and shoulder.

"*Hmm!* I bet you do," Lisa said slyly.

"Go pull the covers back and lay out a couple of towels on the bed, and I'll get the surprise," Mike said as he loosed his embrace, and leaned over to reach into the tub to let the still steaming water out.

Lisa gave him a curious look. She kissed him on the lips, stuck her tongue into his mouth, gently stroked his firm manhood, and commanded that they both hurry back. Lisa released her gentle grip with a playful tug, and then walked into the bedroom to prepare the bed. This time, Mike was the one left biting his bottom lip as his eyes followed his wife's perfect butt into the bedroom.

"All right, we'll be right back," Mike said as he peeped out of the door, one hand doing a terrible job of concealing his manhood, before his naked body darted downstairs and into the kitchen.

Lisa was waiting patiently on the bed, stretched out on her back in the middle of two very thick towels that were absorbing all the warm water rolling off of her body. Mike quickly returned. He stuck his head inside the bedroom, winked at her, and then stepped inside, with one hand positioned behind his back hiding something, as the other closed the door gently behind him.

"What are you up to?" Lisa asked and slightly lifted her head up.

"*Ssh*," Mike silenced her question with the brush of his index fingertip against his lips, giving her another sly wink.

Mike stepped over to the bed, stood over Lisa, and revealed a bottle of wine and one glass flute. He poured wine into the glass flute, and then put it up to Lisa's lips. She took a long sip. While Mike stood over her, he slowly poured the remaining glass flute of wine onto his wife's bare chest and stomach, allowed the chilled liquid to overflow, run down her sides, and made her release a surprised gasp. He was well aware that her threshold for cold sensations was just as high as her threshold for hot, so he smiled devilishly at his opportunity to treat her to a tongue bath. Mike sat the bottle of wine and glass flute on the nightstand, moved onto the bed and licked and lapped up the excess wine off of her body. Lisa's body writhed with pleasure as her husband's tongue teased her nipples. Mike moved down to her belly button, worked all the way down toward her clit, and tongued her feverishly, intent on satisfying her.

Lisa wriggled delightedly as she opened her leg as wide as she could, and bent her knees upward to offer herself fully to him. Even though Mike had recently eaten dinner at the Martin's, he'd begun to devour her, like some sort of wild animal. Lisa had always told him how good he was at cunnilingus. But Mike didn't need her to tell him. By the way she'd offered herself to him, he knew from experience that his tongue action always immediately heightened her pleasure. As Mike greedily licked her clitoris, he started to feel her stomach muscles contract, a sure indication of the very early stages of orgasm. He moved even lower toward the perineum, the area between her vagina and her anus. The overwhelming sensation sent Lisa into a sexual frenzy. She opened her mouth wide; the small of her back arched up off the bed, moaned softly with pleasure and started moving her hips with added vigor. With Mike fully erect, he slid his penis inside her, she moaned loudly. For several minutes, he slowly thrust in and out of her, passionately kissing her on the lips and neck. From time-to-time, he licked, sucked, and nibbled at her tits.

"Oh, Mike, baby!" Lisa exclaimed. Mike knew she was about to climax.

He could now concentrate on his own pleasure, knowing Lisa had been completely satisfied. Mike had begun to thrust in and out of her, quickening his rhythm. Lisa gripped him, her arm around his neck. Suddenly, her hands moved, fingernails raking his back. She sent a jolt tingling down his spine.

"Oh, God, I'm coming!" Mike exclaimed. After unloading insurmountably into her, he collapsed on her, staying inside her, gasping hard. Lisa released a stifled scream, a rigid shudder passed through her body as she wiggled beneath him.

After their night of torrid lovemaking, they both cuddled in the afterglow, satisfied and thankful that they could still enjoy such passion over sixteen years into their marriage.

Chapter 5

The first day of school had crept up on Jason Taylor much sooner than he would've liked. He and Brad rode to Arlington High School together, and on the way, Jason filled him in on every detail of Sunday's Cubs game. Jason and Romeo had watched the game from section 221, row 16 of the Wrigley Field, which allowed for a fantastic view of the game. What made the experience even better was the Chicago Cubs' victory over the opposing Houston Astros. Jason was still excited about the game, until Brad turned onto Tucker Drive, which presented Arlington High School in full view. There was a crowd of high school kids arriving. Many arrived by school buses. Some drove up in expensive cars. Others were on foot.

Although Jason's mother had already taken care of his transfer and registration a few months prior, he had yet to actually review his class schedule. Upon doing so, he and Brad had learned that they were scheduled for the same advanced college prep courses of *English*, *Chemistry*, and *American Government*, which insured a conveniently accessible study partner.

Brad and Jason entered the school building and parted ways to find their respective lockers and classes. On the first floor of the building, Brad located his locker, opened it to view the inside. It met his approval. He closed the locker, and secured it with a combination lock. Brad turned to locate his first class when he was confronted by Chad Parker, Zack Foster, Melissa Warwick and Josh Zuckermann, a group of skinheads he was almost once part of.

"Well, well, well, if it ain't Brad Martin. You've grown all of your hair back. I liked it better bald," Chad said.

"Who's the reggin' we saw you with? You brought him back from South Africa?" Zack said.

The skinheads collectively laughed.

"I guess the trip to South Africa has deprogrammed you, huh, Brad?" Melissa said.

"The idea of wanting to become a skinhead, makes you a skinhead. That's what Ted believes. You do remember him? Chad said.

"People can change," Brad said.

Chad had become furious. He walked up close to Brad, face-to-face. They locked eyes. "You think a few therapy sessions and a trip to South Africa has really changed you? Fuck you, Martin," he barked and spat in Brad's face, and then shoved him up against his locker. Brad retaliated, leveled him with a solid punch to the jaw. Zack and Josh quickly stepped in-between them.

The school's resource officer appeared, holding a hand-held metal detector. "Is there a problem here?" he asked. There was no answer. The first of the two warning class bell sounded.   "Let's break this up . . . get to class."

Aggressively, Chad shoved a pamphlet into Brad's face. "Keep it real pure, bro," he said with a scowl and rubbed the right side of his jaw as he, Zack, Melissa and Josh headed off to class.

Jason spent most of the first half of the day going from class to class, strategically following the color-coded guide that was included in his transfer packet. Approximately 11:00 o'clock, he had met up with Brad for lunch, who seemed a little reserved. Jason concluded that the school year probably wouldn't be as bad as he'd originally thought. Arlington High was actually rather typical, and although it lacked the friends that he had made throughout his childhood, the student body contained quite a few seemingly interesting characters, one of which being a young lady by the name of Shauna Davis.

Jason noticed Shauna when she first walked into his third period *Conversational Spanish* class, flashing a pleasant smile, as she took the seat directly in front of him. He spent the whole period staring at her hair, which cascaded down her back and happened to be the blackest and straightest hair he'd ever seen on a female of his ethnic persuasion. He knew exactly whom he'd want to partner up with, should the class ever provide the opportunity. After the class had ended, and the students begun shuffling out of the room, Jason sparked up a conversation.

"Excuse me. I'm looking for room 211, *Calc II*. Can you direct me?" Jason asked.

"You must be new," Shauna said in a tone as pleasant as her smile.

"How did you know?" Jason asked and flashed a charming smile.

"The school's guide you have rolled up in your hand clued me in," Shauna said and pointed at the guide that Jason held in his right hand.

"All right, you got me," Jason confessed. "That was the best I could come up with. But you gotta cut me some slack. I just wanted to meet you."

"Well, I'm flattered you made the effort," Shauna said. "Even though it wasn't well planned or thought out. So where did you transfer from?"

"Fitzgerald High," Jason answered, glad that she was still engaging in the conversation. "Actually, my family just moved to Arlington Heights this past weekend."

"Think you'll survive?" Shauna said.

"I think I'll manage," Jason said and nodded. "You've been the highlight of my day."

"Glad I could be of help," Shauna said and stopped in front of *Drama and Theater* classroom. "Well, this is my next class."

"Are you telling me that so I can meet you here afterwards and escort you to your next class?" Jason asked as they moved closer toward the classroom wall to escape the bustling hall traffic.

"No, I think I pretty much have the layout of the building down, so I'll be fine. Thanks anyway," Shauna said and removed her maroon canvas book hag from over her shoulders.

"You're kinda quick. I like a challenge," Jason said. "By the way, I'm Jason."

"Shauna," she said and extended her soft delicate right hand.

Jason kissed the back of her hand. "See you around," he said and flashed his charming smile.

"Maybe," Shauna said simply, turned and stepped into her class.

Jason watched as his new acquaintance walked into the classroom. Maybe the school year won't be so bad after all, he thought as he unrolled his school guide so that he could find his *Calc II* class.

* * *

Lisa had just finished breaking down the very last cardboard box in the entire house and adding it to the pile in the garage. She entered the living room, sat on the sofa, picked up a remote and turned on the TV.

On the TV, a news reporter was wrapping up an updated segment. Over her, footage rolled of a 16-year-old teen girl, who simply walked up to an unsuspecting woman, doused sulfuric acid in her face and stole her purse. After police released part of surveillance tapes from a nearby business, it showed several individuals leaving the scene after the July 28th attack. The investigation led to California where police officers there saw the tape and called Chicago police. The juvenile was brought back to Chicago where she had given a statement implicating herself, another juvenile female and three adults who were all charged with armed robbery and heinous battery.

"In other news today, an entire community is still on edge. For the fifth time, the Arlington Heights serial rapist has struck again. The rash of recent rape cases in the area has added a sense of urgency to capture the perpetrator. The police chief would not comment at this time due to the pending investigation nor would he tell us their latest victim's name. A source has told us that the victim is the wife of a prominent local businessman. We will keep you updated on this on-going story as we get more details. Reporting live, I'm Angela Adams, TV 2 news.

The doorbell rang.

DING, DONG!

DING, DONG!

DING, DONG!

"*Coming!*" Lisa yelled as she walked into the foyer, and opened the door.

"It's me, Rachel! I just stopped by to say hi," she smiled and waved.

"Hi, Rachel. What a pleasant surprise," Lisa said and chuckled. "Come in."

"Well, I really didn't want to come over unannounced. I'm sure you probably want to get everything situated before you have guests," Rachel said as she stood on the other side of the door. "I realized that we hadn't exchange telephone numbers."

"Girl, get in here," Lisa chuckled as she gestured for Rachel to come inside. "We actually finished getting everything unpacked last night, and I've just finished taking the last empty box out to the garage."

"Good deal," Rachel said and stepped into the foyer. "What do you have planned for the rest of the day?"

"No plans. I thought I'd be unpacking today and tomorrow, but Mike and Jason really pitched in yesterday and now, it's all done," Lisa said.

"Well, I'm happy to hear that you're done. I was wondering if you wanted to get out of the house for a couple hours," Rachel said.

"What do you have in mind?" Lisa asked.

"I thought maybe we could stop by the center. Afterwards, we could go get manicures and pedicures," Rachel said.

"If we can add grocery shopping to the list, I'm all for it," Lisa said.

"I think that's doable. I have to pick up a few things from the store myself," Rachel said, glad that Lisa would be able to join her.

"Well, just give me a moment to change," Lisa said as she stood up and looked down at her jeans and T-shirt.

"Sure. Just come over to the house when you're ready," Rachel said. "By the way, the decor looks amazing in here. It actually goes so well with the house."

"Thanks. I'm just glad the move is over," Lisa said, releasing a deep sigh.

"I do understand. I've been there," Rachel said and chuckled. "I'll see you shortly."

After seeing Rachel out, Lisa walked upstairs to the master bedroom's walk-in closet, which was neatly arranged with all of her clothes and shoes on the left wall and those belonging to Mike's on the right. Of course Lisa contained her overflow of clothes and shoes in a closet in the guest bedroom. She picked out a pair of black Capri pants and a white shirt with pearl-toned buttons. Using Rachel's casual attire as a guide, she was sure that she'd dressed appropriately enough as she gave herself a final look in the mirror, right after giving her hairdo some much needed attention. Lisa gave Mike a call, got his voicemail and left him a message, letting him know that she would be out and about with Rachel, and that he could reach her on her cellular phone.

After double-checking to make sure she had unplugged the iron and cut off any potentially dangerous appliances, Lisa walked next-door. Rachel answered the door with her purse over her shoulder and a pair of sunglasses in her hand. She had pulled her light blonde hair into a neat ponytail since she'd left the Taylor's home about thirty minutes earlier. She quickly placed the shades on top of her head and took her keys off of the key rack that hung just beside the door.

"I'll drive," Rachel volunteered and shook her keys in front of her.

"Okay," Lisa said.

"It's such a beautiful day that I had to get out and do something," Rachel explained, disarming the security alarm on her white 2-Door Mercedes-Benz SL 320 Convertible, parked in the driveway.

"I agree," Lisa said.

The Chicago sky was pleasantly clear and the temperature comfortably moderate. They drove with the sunroof open and the windows down, listening to the music of a local oldies station. They had arrived at their first destination shortly after departing their Arlington Heights subdivision. Rachel's excitement about visiting the Women's Center made Lisa very anxious to actually experience the place for herself. She had briefed Lisa on many details about the programs the Women's Center offered, its day-to-day operations and goals for 1999. Rachel had rambled on and on, barely stopped to take a breath, made Lisa wonder if Rachel was taking her to some occult organization. She dismissed the idea, when she realized that in a neighborhood like Arlington Heights, for homemakers, volunteer work or participating in any social organization offered a degree of benevolence in their lives as opposed to eating hot cross buns, and watching soap operas all day.

"I won't be long," Rachel said as she parked in the lot facing a two-story building, which appeared to be no more than a decade. "I just want to introduce you to a few acquaintances, one being Joan. She's the director and such a sweetheart. You'll just love her."

"It's a well-maintained building," Lisa said as she exited the car, and pulled her pocketbook strap over her left shoulder.

"You know, that's one of the things I really like about this place. The facility is clean and well-maintained," Rachel said. She and Lisa started walking toward the front of the building, where about fifteen steps, all the width of the building itself, stood between the sidewalk and the entrance. "First, let's go check to see if Joan is in her office."

"Sure," Lisa said, trying to study the artwork along the main hall and keeping up with Rachel's hurried pace. "Slow down a bit. I've already had my morning jog.

"I'm sorry, but I think Joan takes a one o'clock lunch, and I want to catch her before she leaves," Rachel said.

They both turned off of the main hall and walked into a small waiting room, where administrative assistant, Amy Byers, with a pencil wedged between her teeth, was seated behind a solid cherry oak desk. She's multitasking—answering the phone, stuffing envelopes, sorting an accessory pile.

Amy removed the pencil wedged between her teeth. "Hey, Rachel, how are you?" she said, with a welcoming smile.

"I'm doing just fine," Rachel said. "How are you two doing today?"

Amy leaned back in her chair, exposing her baby bump. "Actually, we're both fine. I'll be even better if he stops kicking," she said and rubbed her belly. Amy had strawberry-blonde hair that fell in wavy curls all around her face.

"Oh, where are my manners? I'm sorry, Amy, this is Lisa Taylor, my new neighbor. Lisa, meet Amy Byers.

"Hello, Lisa. Nice meeting you," Amy said, smiled and extended her right hand across the neatly organized desk.

"Nice meeting you too," Lisa replied.

"Is Joan in?" Rachel asked as she pointed at the closed door behind Amy's desk.

"Actually, Joan just walked in. I'll buzz her and let her know you're here," Amy said as she picked up the black telephone, and dialed Joan's extension.

"You're right, this place is well-maintained," Lisa whispered to Rachel as she surveyed the office and all its contemporary furnishings. Rachel simply smiled.

"Joan will see you now," Amy said and returned the phone to its base.

"Thanks, Amy," Rachel said, motioning for Lisa to follow her.

The door led to a larger office, decorated in a similar contemporary style. Lisa could tell by the warm colors throughout the office that Joan possessed a creative spirit of her own. Joan Grutner was a woman who appeared to be no more than fifty years of age, but Rachel had already revealed during the ride over that Joan was nearly sixty. Joan wore her mid-fifty something years as if she created age. She had obviously taken good care of herself, and her graying black hair even appeared to have more tones of silver than the usual dull gray. Joan sat behind a desk that was a larger version of Amy's. She stood with a smile as soon as they entered the office.

"Come on in, ladies," Joan invited and stepped from behind her desk and beckoning Rachel and Lisa to the more informal sofa and armchair setting against the office's right wall. "Have a seat. Who do we have here?" Joan questioned, shaking Lisa's hand.

"This is Lisa Taylor," Rachel said and sat on the sofa.

"Well, hello, Lisa. I'm Joan Grutner," she said and shook Lisa's hand.

"Hello, Joan. It's a pleasure meeting you," Lisa said cordially.

"Have a seat," Joan said and motioned for Lisa to be seated.

"Thank you. Rachel has told me so many good things about you and the Women's Center," Lisa said and sat next to Rachel on the sofa.

"Rachel has told me some good things about you as well. I hear you're an artist and aerobics instructor," Joan mentioned.

Lisa glanced over at Rachel. "Yes, I am. I was just admiring some of the artwork in the main hall," she said.

"Those pieces were from an old estate sale. I purchased them during a visit to Virginia. They caught my eye, and I knew they would be perfect for the center," Joan said.

"You have a good eye," Lisa complimented.

"Why, thank you, Lisa." Joan said and looked to Rachel. "I like her already," she whispered and crossed her legs. She looked very professional and poised in a taupe skirt and white blouse.

"Actually, just yesterday, Joan and I were saying what a shame it is that we haven't managed to get an arts and crafts program off the ground," Rachel said.

"Is that right?" Lisa asked cautiously, with a raised eyebrow, sensing exactly where Rachel was headed.

"Well, believe it or not, talented artists aren't exactly beating down our doors to do volunteer work," Joan explained, with a wry chuckle.

"The girls have suffered the most as a result of it," Rachel added.

"Ladies, I'm going to go out on a limb and say that I know where this conversation is going," Lisa said as she looked from Joan to Rachel, who was nearly seated on the edge of the sofa. "I've been meaning to become more of a humanitarian, but I'm not sure if I can make this kind of commitment right now."

"Perhaps not at the present moment," Joan said. "How about I give you a grand tour?" she said, stood to her feet and clasped her hands in front of her. "Shall we?"

Lisa smirked and chuckled amusedly as she stood to her feet. Genuinely flattered, she couldn't believe that she was actually being recruited as a volunteer, especially when neither of the two women had seen any of her work.

"I'm ready," Lisa said. "I'm gonna get you for this," she said to Rachel in a hushed whisper as they followed Joan out of the office.

Rachel shrugged and smiled innocently.

"Amy, if anyone calls, I'm out to lunch. I'll be back at two thirty. Oh, by the way, if Jeff Franklin from U-Tech calls, tell him I haven't forgotten about him, and I'll call him as soon as I get back," Joan informed.

"Sure thing. Have a good lunch. It was nice meeting you, Lisa. Will we be seeing more of you at the center?" Amy asked.

"We're working on that now," Joan answered before Lisa could respond. Lisa shot Rachel a threatening look.

"Just remember . . . I'm gonna get you for this," Lisa said underneath a fake smiled to Rachel in a hushed whisper.

"Uh, Joan," Rachel said as she cleared her throat, "I think it would be a good idea to first show Lisa the makeshift arts and crafts classroom."

"Good idea," Joan said and turned around to flash another cotillion smile as she sauntered toward the makeshift arts and crafts class, her heels connecting with the marble floor with unexpected rhythm as she glided down the main hall.

The study annex sat at the very end of the hall, and Lisa noticed from a distance that it was also decorated with a number of colorful pictures.

"You're going to love this," Rachel sang in Lisa's ear as they both tried to keep up with Joan.

"Here we are," Joan said as she entered a room that had been transformed into the makeshift arts and crafts class. We conducted a pilot arts and crafts class in here just yesterday evening, and I must say that it was a huge success. The girls loved it. We even left some of their work on display. What do you think?" Joan asked and looked to Lisa.

Lisa started to answer and offer some general compliments, but something caught her attention on a particular easel at the front of the class. She squinted as she tried to gain better focus across the room. Both Rachel and Joan stood back and watched, as Lisa seemed to be pulled toward the painting by some invisible magnetic force.

"I can't believe you have this!" Lisa said in a surprised tone as she stood honed in on the displayed painting.

"I thought you'd recognize it," Joan said.

Lisa continued gazing at a painting that she'd produced almost five years earlier. It was one of her many works that she had sold out of at local arts festivals and expos that showcased local talent. The rest of her work, she had sold at cultural arts festivals and exhibitions. Lisa was just absolutely speechless.

"Look around, Lisa," Joan said as she and Rachel joined Lisa in front of the easel. "The paintings displayed were inspired by your very own work."

Lisa had realized that the paintings, matted and neatly hung on the walls were all interpretations by her own work. Amazed, she walked around the room and paid special attention to each one, still not fully believing her eyes.

"They're remarkable!" Lisa exclaimed as she walked from painting to painting.

"The girls found inspiration in your painting, Lisa," Rachel said.

"How did you come across this particular painting? Lisa asked. "I parted with it years ago," she said and walked up to Joan and Rachel who were still standing toward the front of the room, near Lisa's painting, which portrayed a picturesque countryside, done in acrylics.

"I can only assume it had become a part of my collection shortly after it left yours," Joan said and tilted her head to the side as she studied the painting.

"I don't know what to say," Lisa said. "This is quite a surprise. Actually, I'm shocked.

"Say you'll lend these girls your creative spirit. It'll only be once a week. *Please!*" Rachel pleaded.

William Jaman Taylor

Lisa looked back at the artwork that adorned the walls one last time. After a moment of consideration, she nodded and smiled. "All right, you got me. I'll do it," Lisa said and threw up her hands in surrender. "By the way, who conducted the pilot class yesterday?" she asked.

"A student from The Metropolitan Art Institute," Joan said. "She was only available for that one time, which was why we presented the session on a trial basis."

After seeing how much the girls enjoyed it, we knew we had to find someone who could do it on a regular weekly basis."

"I guess that would be me," Lisa said.

"Well, we had our fingers crossed," Rachel said.

"I must say, you two definitely know how to drive a hard and convincing bargain," Lisa chuckled as they'd begun to exit the class.

"Let's discuss this further in details over lunch. My treat," Joan said.

They retraced their steps down the main hall and soon ended up outside beneath the Chicago mid-day sun.

At a nearby Italian restaurant, Joan, Rachel and Lisa had discussed plans for the new arts and crafts program. Although the food was very good, they'd done more talking than eating for much of the hour. After which, Lisa was almost as excited about lending her expertise as they were. Scheduled once a week, it wouldn't demand too much of her time, and she would have the opportunity to share her passion for art with young impressionable minds. Lisa agreed to take over the class in a week.

* * *

"Hey, Mike, check your fax machine. I've faxed you a copy of the firm's RFP. It was just released this morning," Tom said as he used his speakerphone. Mike listened on the other end.

"Thanks. I'll look for it," Mike said. "What do you suppose our wives are up to?"

"That depends . . ." Tom said. "If Rachel's behind the wheel, there's no telling."

Chapter 6

Saturday evening had marked the end of the Taylor's first week in Arlington Heights and they had gotten through it without a hitch. Surprisingly, Lisa had found, through the course of the week, that Rachel was a very interesting woman, despite her usual cheerful demeanor. They spent much of the week talking and getting to know more about each other, while their husbands were at work, and their sons were at school. The two women shared a lot in common in regard to their interests in music, movies, and even the qualities of men. The latter was a shock to them both, but they'd realized that once you gotten past the issue of color, women on both sides of the spectrum were looking for the same in a man, love, compassion, romance, sensitivity, her own personal knight in shining armor.

"How did you and Tom meet?" Lisa asked.

"Well, we met during my visit at the annual Water Festival in Beaufort, South Carolina. Tom was working toward his undergraduate degree at the University of South Carolina. He was working behind a seafood concession stand, to gain community service points for an academic business fraternity. As I walked by, Tom just insisted that I sample a shrimp and crab stuffed bell pepper, which I'd never heard of. I told him no, but he was so persistent. As I tried to walk away, Tom had stepped from behind the stand and followed me down the waterfront, explaining to me that he was getting community service credit for each one sold, and that he really needed the credits to get into a fraternity. Well, I ended up walking back with him to the concession stand. I purchased one of the stuffed peppers, after he'd promised to leave me alone. Needless to say, he didn't leave me alone. Tom also purchased a stuffed pepper. It turned out that he made up the whole thing. It was Tom's way of meeting me, and having lunch on an impromptu Dutch date. I must say, he was very convincing and creative. He got major points. We'd kept in contact. We visited each other as often as we could. And eventually, we started dating seriously. Tom had gotten accepted into the University of Chicago School of Law. After he completed grad school, and passed the bar exam, we took a trip back to the waterfront. That's where he got down on one knee, professed his undying love and proposed to me. I moved to Chicago. The star aligned, and our whirlwind romance culminated into a marriage. We had a beautiful wedding and a fabulous honeymoon in Hawaii. We made passionate love for hours every single day. That's when I got knocked up."

"How romantic," Lisa laughed as she'd begun to tell Rachel how she and Mike met.

"Well, Mike and I met during our sophomore year at the University of Chicago. During our senior year, he was voted the class president. After delivering his graduation commencement speech, Mike proposed to me. The following spring, we got married on the same day that he first met my parents. It was a small and simple wedding. We honeymooned in the Caribbean. One year later, on our wedding anniversary, I surprised Mike and told him that I was pregnant. He was so excited. We've been happily married ever since," Lisa said.

"Aww! That's so sweet," Rachel said as they enjoyed each other's stories of romance.

* * *

Jason and Brad were bonding on a similar level. His family's move to Arlington Heights was not as much a culture shock as it was an abrupt change of scenery to Jason. Brad's color was of very little issue, being that he was just as equally "hip" as some of the friends that he'd left behind at Fitzgerald High. They were already planning on trying out for Arlington's baseball team in mid-September, which still remained a few weeks away. In the meantime, the two were spending the majority of their after school free time playing video games or cruising around aimlessly in Brad's Car. Wednesday evening, Jason and Brad ended up on the baseball diamond at the nearby Lloyd Meyer Field Recreational Park. Jason had offered to give Brad a few crucial batting pointers.

"When you swing, man, think of the ball as a burglar's head, and you're trying to take it off," Jason said. "You have to put some force behind it, that way when you connect you know you're sending it all the way outfield."

"All right, I got it," Brad said with a nod, having paid close attention to Jason's careful instructions.

Jason offered Brad the baseball bat that he had been demonstrating with, and then headed toward the pitcher's mound to throw him a couple of practice balls. After Brad sent the first ball soaring, with a sharp whacking sound, over second base and straight into the outfield, Jason got the feeling that his advice had actually paid off. Another practice pitch assured them both.

"Did you see that?" Brad shouted excitedly, and jumped up and down. "*I got game! I got game!*" he chanted triumphantly.

"You've gotten the hang of it," Jason laughed as Brad started dancing, doing the cabbage patch, and then the running man.

Jason and Brad had become "thicker than thieves," as Mike had joked, over the course of their first week. Lisa and Mike were both relieved, because adjusting to the move didn't appear to be much of an issue anymore with their son.

As for Mike and Tom, they'd managed to lay a pretty sturdy business foundation for their friendly interaction. By Thursday, Mossberger, Weinstein and Stewart had received Drake and Nash's bid proposal for the planned renovation project. Friday evening, Mike received a phone call from Tom, personally congratulating Mike's division for being granted the bid.

Finally, another weekend was at hand, and Mike and Lisa were preparing for Jon and Madeline LaRue's visit. Jon and Madeline had phoned earlier in the week and informed them that they would be able to visit for the weekend. Nonetheless, Lisa was up making sure that the guest bathroom downstairs was stocked with all the essential toiletries and so forth when her parents arrived.

"Hey, babe, Jon and Maddie are here!" Mike yelled from the foyer, after he had answered the doorbell.

"Lisa, baby, where are you?" Madeline called as she walked into the living room, followed by Jon's hearty laughter.

"You're early," Lisa said and greeted her parents with a hug and kiss.

"I told Jon that we had to leave early enough for me to make groceries for my favorite grandbaby," Maddie explained and looked to her husband for confirmation.

"Dad, is she serious about cooking breakfast?" Lisa asked.

"You know your mother. She's spoiled him rotten," Jon said with a grin.

"How was the drive here?" Lisa asked as she took her mother's sweater and hung up on a coat rack.

"It was just fine, child," Maddie said as she looked around the spacious living room, and then crooked her neck to the side to take a sneak peek into an adjoining room.

"Yeah, she took a nap during the drive here," Jon said, giving Lisa a wink, knowing his wife would retort swiftly.

"Hush now, husband. I wasn't sleep. I was praying. Child, your father drove all the way here like a mad man. He knows his eyesight ain't what it used to be," Maddie protested as Mike and Lisa snickered at her animated candor.

"That's all right, baby," Jon chortled as he leaned over and planted a kiss on his wife's cheek. "I think you make the best car companion when you're asleep."

Maddie dismissed her husband's playful comment, with a flick of her wrist. "Make yourself useful, go find the kitchen, and put the bag of groceries down," she said.

"Follow me, Jon," Mike said and led the way toward the kitchen.

"Lisa, where's my grandbaby?" Maddie asked.

"Jason and Brad are at the park. They're practicing for baseball tryouts," Lisa said.

"Practicing? Since when does my favorite grandbaby need practice?" Maddie asked skeptically, and placed her hands on her hips.

"Actually, he's giving Brad some pointers. I didn't tell Jason that you two were coming. I wanted to surprise him," Lisa said.

"Are you ready for the grand tour?" Mike asked and rubbed his hands together as he and Jon exited the kitchen.

"*Ready!*" Maddie said excitedly, and hugged Jon.

The tour had begun upstairs, showing the bedrooms, bathrooms and closet spaces. Next, everyone headed downstairs and toured the basement. Finally, they headed back upstairs onto the main floor and toured the garage, another guest bedroom, living room, half bathroom, den, backyard and finally with the tour ending in the kitchen. Jon and Maddie voiced their approval in every room. Lisa and Jon left Mike and Maddie in the kitchen to prepare breakfast as they made their way into the den.

"This is a mighty fine house y'all got here," Maddie said proudly, and cracked an egg into a bowl, while Mike opened a package of bacon.

"Yeah, we lucked up on this one," Mike said.

"And then, Lisa just about talked my ear off the other day about your neighbors, and how nice they were. I told her, child, if they're that nice, I expect to see some wings attached to their shoulder blades," Maddie said.

"They're good people. In fact, Tom and I have been doing quite a bit of networking," Mike said as he reached above the central island that's faced into the center of the kitchen, to retrieve a ceramic sauté pan and skillet from a hanging rack.

"What about their son? I won't have him corrupting my grandbaby with all of that Generation X nonsense," Maddie said.

"Well, I don't think we'll have to worry about that. They're both good kids," Mike said.

"My grandbaby will be walking through that door any minute now," Maddie said.

"Maddie, how are you so sure?" Mike asked, preparing to hear about her gut instinct.

"When he smells his Grandma's cooking, no matter how far, he'll come home. You'll see," Maddie said matter-of-factly. "I don't need a crystal ball, when it comes to family. I know ya'll too well," she said and looked to Mike.

They both shared a laugh with Maddie revealing a sparkling set of teeth, which always seemed to add a mystic air of character to her smile.

Every aisle on the stovetop was occupied by ceramic cookware, and Maddie had just put a metallic non-stick pan of homemade biscuits into the oven. Although it was Mike's intention to help out with the breakfast as best he could, he spent most of the time seated on one of the kitchen stools chatting and laughing with Maddie. At the same time, he sat in awe of how that little woman could come into anyone's particular kitchen space and transform it as if it's was her own. Approximately twenty minutes later, just as Maddie removed the hot and flaky biscuits from the oven, they both heard the front door open and close. Maddie removed her apron, hung it back on its hook, and flashed Mike a knowing smile.

"What did I tell you? I knew he'd be here," Maddie said and walked out of the kitchen, left Mike dumbstruck as he shook his head.

Chapter 7

Sunday afternoon, Lisa had returned home from teaching her first arts and crafts class at the center and felt all warm and fuzzy inside. She felt that sharing the joy of art with young impressionable minds was very rewarding and elicited some natural high for her. Lisa walked into the kitchen for a bottle of water and noticed a note on the fridge, scrawled in her husband's nearly illegible handwriting. Apparently, he and Jason had decided to take her parents and Brad to a matinee movie. That left only Rachel to share the details of her first class with. Lisa retrieved the bottle of water from the fridge, and then walked into the den to dial Rachel's number.

"Hello," Rachel answered on the first ring.

"Hey, it's me," Lisa said. "I just got back from the center."

"How did it go? Rachel asked excitedly.

"It was great. I really enjoyed it," Lisa said.

"Does this mean you'll continue to volunteer on a weekly basis?" Rachel asked hopefully.

"Of course," Lisa chuckled.

"I'm so glad to hear it. Thank you so much, Lisa," Rachel said.

"Don't mention it. Those girls were like sponges. It was evident that they paid very close attention and absorbed every word I spoke. And the natural talent! I can't even describe the talent that I'd witnessed today. I can't wait until next Sunday. So what are you up to?" Lisa asked abruptly, changing the subject.

"Nothing much," Rachel said. "I just got back from the grocery store not long ago. Tom went to the office to pick up a file and do a little work. And Brad went to the movies with Mike and Jason.

"My parents have tagged along as well," Lisa said.

"Oh, so your parents are still here?"

"Yeah. You know, I was hoping we could all have dinner

tonight before they leave. Mike has been dying to fire up this barbecue pit out back. It's a perfect day for it."

"That sounds like a good idea. I don't know how long it's been since I've had some really good barbecue."

"What time do you expect Tom home from the office?" Lisa asked as she walked back to the kitchen to survey the selection of meats in the freezer.

"No later than two," Rachel said as she glanced around the kitchen at a wall clock, and realized that her husband would be home in about an hour.

"Then let's make dinnertime around 5:30," Lisa suggested. "I'm going to take the meats out now, so they can start defrosting. I sure my mother will come and whip up a bowl of potato salad."

"And I'll be over in a second to help out," Rachel said. "Do you need me to bring anything?"

Lisa laughed at Rachel's eagerness. "No. I seemed to have just about everything. For the moment, just bring your helping hands."

"All right, I'll be right over," Rachel said and hung up the phone.

A few minutes later, Rachel was in the Taylors' kitchen, helping Lisa select and retrieve meats from the freezer.

"You guys have a lot of breakfast food in here," Rachel said.

"That's courtesy of Madeline LaRue. My mother is a firm believer that breakfast is the most important meal of the day, and swears we only get a decent meal when she's here to cook it."

"Well, I'll have to tell Mother LaRue that I can attest to the fact that you all had a better-than-decent meal just last Saturday," Rachel said with a chuckle.

"Ooh, modesty is so becoming of you," Lisa joked. "I must admit, you do make a mean roast. I'll give you that."

They both shared a laugh as Lisa tried to figure out if they had forgotten to take anything out. "I think our job is done in here.

I'm sure Mike and my mother will take care of everything else."

Lisa exited the kitchen with Rachel following close behind her with an expression of confusion and disbelief.

"We're done? Rachel said.

"Yes. I'll have you know that Mike has the culinary expertise in this union. Together, he and my mother make one heck of a cooking team," Lisa said.

"Lucky you," Rachel said and took a seat on the sofa in the den as Lisa searched under the armchair's cushions for the remote.

"Well, I am still the reigning dessert diva. And besides, I do my real cooking in the bedroom anyway," Lisa boasted and found the television remote.

"You're bad," Rachel blushed. You know, you've just given me an idea. How about we plan a bake sale as a fundraiser?" Rachel beamed; her new idea seemed to brighten her expression.

"Joan has definitely picked the right person for her planning board. You are just so full of ideas," Lisa said with a chuckle.

"I'll just take that as a compliment. You just start thinking about what you're going to bake," Rachel said.

"Wait just a second. Oprah's on," Lisa said with a raised finger. She turned up the volume on the 32" TV, before returning the remote to its rightful place on the cocktail table. The two women listened intently as a reporter offered an update involving the lawsuit brought against Oprah by members of the Texas cattle farming industry. Lisa was instantly a devoted fan since Oprah had first come onto the Chicago talk show scene and her movie debut left her even more in awe of the celebrity's charisma and talent.

"Oprah is simply phenomenal," Rachel said, once the news broke for commercial. "I just loved her in *The Women of Brewster Place.*

"Get out of here!" Lisa exclaimed, surprised that Rachel was a fan as well. "That's one of my favorites as well, but I think *The Color Purple* was the absolute best," she said.

"Hey, I'm going to go call Tom and tell him to come over once he gets home," Rachel said.

"You'll probably find the cordless phone in the kitchen. I think I left it on the counter, but you'd better hurry before Oprah comes back on," Lisa advised. She readjusted her position in the armchair, and pulled her bare feet up beneath her bottom.

Just as Rachel exited the den, Lisa heard the ADT unit chime, as Mike opened the front door. He entered the foyer with the rest of the moviegoers close behind.

"*Leese!*" Mike yelled from the foyer.

"I'm in the den!" Lisa yelled and thought how they never had to yell to communicate at their former home. They all walked into the den telling Lisa about the great movie she missed. Rachel had finished making her phone call and re-entered the den, with the cordless telephone in tow.

"Mom, Dad, this is Rachel Martin, our new friend and next-door neighbor," Lisa said.

"So you're the one I've heard who cooked that great dinner last week," Maddie said.

"Well, I guess I shouldn't take all the credit. My mother taught me everything," Rachel said. "Nice meeting you," she said cordially and shook both Jon and Maddie's hands.

"Likewise," Jon and Maddie chorused.

"We thought maybe we should all barbecue this evening," Lisa said and kissed Mike on the cheek.

"I was just telling Jon how I couldn't wait to test the barbecue pit I had recently built," Mike said.

"Yeah, he told me all about those two grueling evenings he spent slaving over those wet bricks and mortar, using precise measurements to make sure the brickwork would be strong enough to support the rods that held the double grill and the cinder tray," Jon said. He then peeked through the window to get a look at the new barbecue pit, situated on the leveled concrete ground in a right corner of the backyard away from fences, overhead trees, wires and the structures around the house.

"Dad, don't let Mike fool you. I'd hardly say it was a grueling task for him. He does this for a living, you know" Lisa said as she playfully slapped Mike on his chest.

"See, what did I tell you, Jon? No sympathy," Mike said with a grin.

In true Madeline LaRue fashion, Lisa dismissed her husband's comment with a flick of the wrist, before redirecting her attention to Jason and Brad.

"I hope you two didn't pig out too much on popcorn and sodas," Lisa said as the two had plopped down on the sofa. Jason picked up the remote and changed the channel to *MTV*.

"We have room," Jason said and rubbed his stomach. Brad nodded in agreement.

"Good. I hope everyone is ready for my authentic Louisiana-style barbecue," Jon said and informed every one of his intentions of preparing his special and secret recipe for his barbecue sauce.

"You better go in the kitchen and make sure they have all the ingredients you're going to need," Maddie said and quickly ushered her husband toward the kitchen. "I'll throw together some potato salad and also fix some home-made soft rolls. Mike, I need you for a second," she said.

"I'm right behind you," Mike said and winked at Lisa as he followed his in-laws into the kitchen.

"That's my mother, take charge Maddie. You gotta love her," Lisa said and shook her head.

"She's quite a character," Rachel said.

"You don't know the half of it," Lisa said and turned her attention once again to Jason and Brad on the sofa. "Rachel, these two have just taken over the television," she said.

"I guess we can let them relax for now," Rachel said. Guess which two teenagers get to clean up after dinner?"

Jason and Brad exchanged a quick look, before searching their mothers' faces for a hint of a joke, which they did not find.

"Actually, we were just about to go upstairs and listen to some new music," Brad said, nudging Jason for confirmation.

"Uh, yeah, here you go," Jason said and changed the channel back to *CNN*, and then handed his mother the remote.

"And don't have that music up too loud!" Lisa called out as Jason and Brad rocketed from off the sofa and bolted upstairs.

"Those two are something else," Rachel chuckled as she resumed her position on the sofa.

"Why can't they just stay babies forever? Once they reach the terrible twos, it's all over with from that point on," Lisa said in overly dramatic melancholy tones as she shook her head. "Oh, by the way, have you been able to contact Tom?" she asked.

"I got him on his cell phone just as he was leaving the office. I asked him, once he gets home and changed into something comfortable, to go downstairs to the wine cellar and bring a couple bottles of red wine over," Rachel said.

"You all have a wine cellar?" Lisa said. "Mike and I don't have enough will power to keep a wine cellar fully stocked. Between the two of us, we would've drunk so much wine that we might start speaking with a French accent," she joked and turned her attention back to *CNN*.

Tom arrived shortly afterwards, and almost three and a half hours after his arrival, the picnic bench outside was set. In addition to bringing the wines, Tom brought three backyard lanterns that sat atop 5-foot wooden poles. The Taylors, Martins, and LaRues all had a delicious barbecue dinner in the Taylors' backyard, which was enclosed by a wooden privacy fence. Of course, Jason supplied the music, and Madeline LaRue supplied the majority of the dinner conversation. Tom marveled over the brick barbecue pit, and commended Mike on the craftsmanship, which yielded barbecued baby-back ribs, chicken, pork chops, and hamburgers. Tom had also followed up with Mike regarding the renovation project that one of his clients was contemplating. Tom thought it would be a good opportunity for Mike, since it would be a very big contract, and the client he referred him to had not planned on renovating until the following spring. Tom had already figured that would give Mike's division more than enough time to finish the firm's renovations. They discussed the new possibilities briefly, and then Tom promised to give Mike a call at work, in the morning, once he'd found out more details.

Lisa shared with everyone the details of her first day of teaching the arts and crafts class at the center, before she and Mike discussed their plans of hosting a house-warming party in a couple of months. Shortly after dinner, Maddie and Jon excused themselves to start preparing for their trip back home. Lisa and Mike had managed to talk them out of their plans of staying at a hotel the night before, but they were unable to talk them into staying any longer than the weekend. However, the LaRues did promise to pay another visit soon.

Once Jason and Brad realized there wouldn't be a great deal of work involved, they volunteered to clear the picnic bench, clean up around the area, and brought the dirty dishes to the dishwasher. Everyone said their goodbyes. Lisa advised Jon to drive carefully and pleaded with Maddie to stay awake and make conversation.

"I done told y'all, this woman can sleep all she wants, as long as I have some Zydeco music, my Coltrane and Gillespie jazz cassettes, I'm good," Jon said and waved the cassette tapes in plain view as he put the car in reverse.

"You all take care! Love you!" Maddie called out and blew kisses as Jon backed the car out of the driveway. As Jon put the car in drive, he slowly inched forward as he put a cassette in the cassette tape deck. A total of thirteen black crows had swooped down and landed on the hood of the car, cawing. Jon hit the brakes in front of the Martin's home. Maddie screamed, and the black crows took flight. She had clutched her chest and quickly noticed that the Martin's street number address '12613' ended in thirteen and added up to thirteen, as well, was posted on the mailbox, and that Brad's license plate number also ended in thirteen. Still clutching her chest, she gasped and looked to Jon.

Jon put the car in park, with both hands firmly gripping the steering wheel. "Maddie, I know what you're about to say, about what happened in the past and all," he said and released a deep sigh. "Just remember what the doctor told you," he said as he put the car back in drive and sped off.

Chapter 8

Mike sat at his desk, mulled over the progress report that he had recently received from his lead foreman. His division had been working on the expansion project for Tom's firm for almost three weeks, and according to the report, they would be wrapping everything up by week's end. It was Wednesday, and he really wanted to give Tom and his co-workers some good news.

September had given way to October, and the temperature in Chicago had dropped significantly. One of the reasons why Mike was thankful that he'd worked in interior development and renovations, for the most part, was simply because the work wasn't impeded by the weather. He'd remembered how boring and uneventful the fall and winter seasons were, when he had worked in construction for a previous employer as a contractor. Back then, he had been fortunate enough to have had his pay prorated for those seasons when working outside seemed nearly impossible, but he still didn't feel right just sitting at home and waiting for the snow to thaw and the warmth of Spring to return. Mike always enjoyed the extra quality time the situation would allow him to spend with Lisa, but he needed to be involved in building. That was his passion; being able to stand back, with his arms folded across his chest as he marveled the completion of the project, which in most cases were office buildings or apartment complexes.

It was actually the fall season that drove Mike to Drake and Nash. He had applied for a temporary position, during one of his waiting periods, and found out that renovating yielded a very different experience. He had the opportunity to stand back and admire the transformation that he played a part in, and for him that was more rewarding than building from the ground. He'd started out working at Drake and Nash as a foreman, and eventually moved up to a corner office that he now occupy as a

Regional District Manager. Although much of his work was office work, he'd spent a great deal of his time on-site and in the field. As a result, he earned a great deal of respect from his co-workers. It was never his intention to be the type of supervisor or manager who would disassociate himself from the team.

Later that morning, after mulling over the progress report, Mike had planned on visiting the site to see if he could give Mossberger, Weinstein, Stewart and Martin a definite completion date. As he organized the paperwork on his desk, the phone rang. The large display screen on the phone flashed Tom Martin's office number. It had been three weeks since Tom had first mentioned a pretty big renovation project that one of his clients was looking into. The week before, Mike had sent Robert to meet with Mr. Burkeman, Tom's client, so that Robert could get an idea of what layouts Mr. Burkeman favored for his place of business. Mike obtained the information from Robert, compiled it, and immediately started working with his presentation team on producing a winning proposal.

"Hey, Tom, how's it going?" Mike asked and pushed the speaker button.

"It's going great. How's it going on your end?" Tom asked as he leaned back in his leather chair and spoke into his own speakerphone.

"I was hoping to get over there this morning and see if I could get my crew out of there by Friday."

"I'm crossing my fingers as we speak," Tom said with a chuckle. "I have most of my work space packed up."

"Well, it looks like you may be in your new office as soon as Monday morning. Hell, you might even be able to move some of your things in this weekend."

"I can't wait. Oh, before I forget what I called for in the first place, I got a call from Vince Burkeman this morning. He said he's looking forward to Drake and Nash's bid proposal."

86

"Sounds like Robert made a good impression," Mike said.

"Robert must be the 'red-haired kid' that Vince kept referring to," Tom said, which made Mike laugh at the thought of Robert's red hair.

"That's my right-hand man, Rob," Mike confirmed with a laugh. "He's new blood, a sharp kid fresh out of college."

"Well, Vince was very impressed. Be sure to give Robert a pat on the back," Tom said.

"Will do. He and the rest of the projection team had been hard at work on the proposal details," Mike said.

"Sounds good. If I were hear anything else soon, I'll let you know," Tom said.

"Thanks," Mike said. "I'm going to wrap up a few things here, and then I'll make my way over to the site."

"All right. Make sure you stop by my office," Tom said.

"I will. I'll see you soon," Mike said.

Jason and Brad met up in the student parking lot after school. Baseball tryouts were to begin in a week, and they had spent a great deal of time trying to prepare. The time that they didn't spend practicing, they were doing homework, studying or hanging out at the restaurant where Shauna worked. Since the first day of Spanish class, Jason had been interested in getting to know her. Eventually, he got the idea that the feeling was mutual and that she was just not making things easy for him because that's just something that girls do. They play hard to get. That was the rationale that his eighteen-year-old psyche followed. Shauna had actually found Jason interesting, especially for his charm and persistence. The times that Jason and Brad visited the restaurant where Shauna worked, she would be sure to give them special attention, and stop by every now and then to engage in some general conversation. If nothing else, they had definitely become friends.

* * *

The following day, school had ended. Jason and Brad were sitting on the hood of the Monte Carlo, shooting the breeze and making plans for the evening when they noticed Shauna walking out of the double doors.

"Hey, there goes your girl," Brad said and nudged Jason.

"Chill out, man, before she hears you," Jason said and nudged Brad back. He kept his cool as Shauna walked toward them.

"Hey, guys," Shauna said.

"Hey," Jason said, leaning forward.

"Hi, Shauna," Brad giggled.

"What are you up to?" Jason asked.

"I'm headed to work," Shauna said. "Are you going to stop by?" she asked.

"Definitely," Jason said and nodded as he slid down from off the hood of the car.

"Are you two still preparing for baseball tryouts?" Shauna asked.

"We have one week before tryouts," Brad said.

"Are you trying out for the cheerleading team?" Jason asked.

"What's the point? Cheerleading didn't help the team last year," Shauna said.

"Hey, I was part of that team last year," Brad said.

"Perhaps your good looks would make the team play harder by trying to impress you," Jason said as he poured the charm on thick.

"You're such a charmer," Shauna said with a laugh. "And besides, between school and work, my schedule is too hectic," she added.

"It's a shame though, because I would be so motivated. I'd be hitting home-runs left and right," Jason said, still pouring it on thick.

"Whatever!" Shauna said and blushed noticeably, which was all the more encouraging to Jason.

"Yeah, and we have to talk about that hectic schedule of yours too," Jason said.

"Huh?" Shauna said.

"I want you to pencil me in every now and then," Jason said as he stepped closer to her.

"I'm sure you do," Shauna giggled as she playfully pushed him back. "Brad, get him so you two can go to practice. I'm late for work. See you guys later," she said and scurried off.

"Will do," Brad said.

"See you after practice," Jason yelled as Shauna blushed again as she looked back at him.

Jason stood there in front of Brad's car and watched as Shauna strutted toward her car. Her long jet-black hair swept back and forth across the back of the slightly faded blue denim jacket. Jason slowly shook his head in admiration.

"You ready, man?" Brad asked as he stepped inside the car.

"I'm ready to make her my woman. No doubt," Jason said and shook his head.

"In your dreams," Brad said. "Let's go."

Brad and Jason left the student parking lot and headed toward the park, where they had been practicing. At the park, they pulled the baseball bats and balls Jason had supplied from the trunk. His past success had been phenomenal so Jason thought it would be a good idea to use the very same bat in conditioning with Brad.

"I see you've turned out to be a pretty good batter after all," Jason complimented and handed Brad one of the bats.

"I owe it all to you," Brad said.

"Actually, not to sound cliché, but you pretty much had it in you all along.

"You helped me out a lot. And this bat is awesome," Brad said and swung the bat forcefully against the light breeze. "I've got to get one just like it."

"Keep it. It's yours. Consider it your diploma. I've been

schooling you in Batting 101 for the past few weeks. I think you've earned it."

"Thanks, bro'," Brad said as he took another crack at an imagined pitch.

"Don't mention it. *Whoa!* Watch where you're swinging that bat," Jason warned, giving Brad a slap on the chest with a baseball glove. "Just make sure you incorporate everything you've learned during our practice sessions. Hopefully, we'll make it to the playoffs this season." He said as he walked toward the pitcher's mound.

"I will. That's a promise," Brad said.

Chapter 9

Mike and his assistant, Robert, met with Vince Burkeman and his son, Vince Jr., to discuss the renovation plans for the new restaurant. They were actually meeting inside the future restaurant, seated in folding chairs, situated around a rectangular wooden table. Aside from themselves, the table, and the chairs, the future restaurant was completely gutted. It was Mike's idea to meet there, as opposed to inside a conference room, so that he wouldn't have to have the Burkeman's to call upon memory when he tried to explain specific detailed plans. He could simply point or walk them over to the area in question and begin explaining. It was a practice that had worked quite remarkably well in the past.

Neither Vince Burkeman nor his son wasted time with pleasantries. They were staunch businessman. Mike wondered how Robert could have ever survived the meeting he had alone with the two. According to Tom, Robert had turned out an impressive performance. Apparently, Robert had answered a great deal of their questions during that first meeting, because the two men had very little to say in regard to Drake and Nash's projections.

"Gentleman, please feel free to review the projections we've provided you with. We are really looking forward to doing business with you," Mike said, after completing his presentation.

"Of course you are," Vince Burkeman said flatly. He and his son stuffed all of the paperwork they had been reviewing inside the manila folders that Mike and Robert had provided them with.

It was easy to see the family resemblance, with similarities in the Burkemans' manner of speaking to their facial expressions. However, Vince Burkeman, in his sixties, a bald man in which the hair on one side of his head has grown long and then combed over the bald area, had actually spoken only a total of three times during the entire meeting.

"We'll be in touch," Vince Burkeman informed them as he backed his chair away from the table.

"Do you expect to make a decision soon?" Robert asked and gathered his own paperwork.

"Well, we have quite a few proposals in front of us. We don't expect to make a hasty decision, but as my father said, we'll be in touch either way," Vince Jr. said. He stuffed the manila folder into his leather briefcase, before he re-buttoned his navy blazer.

"If you have any further questions, just feel free to contact my office," Mike said as they all headed toward the door.

"If one should arise, we will do just that," Vince Burkeman assured. He locked the door behind them and turned to walk toward the black Lincoln Continental parked at curbside.
Mike and Robert crossed the street and walked toward Mike's car that was parked on the opposite side.

"I don't know what to make of that meeting," Robert said as they stepped inside the car.

"Nor did I," Mike said, with a number of unspoken questions racing through his head. "I guess we'll hear something in a few weeks. Tell me again how the first meeting went."

"The first meeting went well. Mr. Burkeman was quite responsive, inquisitive, and there was no dead silence at all. I just don't get it," Robert said apprehensively.

"I see. Well, don't worry about it. You'll learn that some people will flip the script on you just as the Burkemans have done today, and as O'Hare's Chairman Anderson had done a month ago. Perhaps it's just their business tactic, to see how well you'll hold up under pressure. If you don't go into panic mode, and keep your cool, then that could be taken as a sign of confidence and in our favor in their decision process," Mike rationalized.

"Oh, so I guess it's one of those 'never let them see you sweat' type of deal," Robert said.

"My point exactly. Hey, it's almost lunchtime. How about we

stop and get a bite to eat?" Mike suggested.

"Sure," Robert said.

They'd agreed on a Chinese restaurant and headed in the direction of a nearby location.

Despite the advice Mike had given Robert, he was still uncertain about the Burkeman deal. The two had hoped to hear a favorable response soon.

* * *

Rachel was over at the Taylor's home. She and Lisa were in the kitchen, seated at the two-tiered peninsula and central island with its prep sink. They sipped tea and skimmed over the entertainment section of the newspaper.

"What about the new James Bond movie? There's a 2:45 p.m. matinee showing," Rachel suggested.

"A James Bond movie," Lisa repeated.

"James Bond," Rachel said in her best British accent.

"I'm not a big fan of the modern James Bond movies," Lisa said.

"Neither am I, but Pierce Brosnan is a totally different story," Rachel confessed. Lisa agreed and gave a thumbs-up.

"Hey, Rachel, do you know if Joan had ever thought about implementing a fitness and wellness program or an aerobics class at the center?" Lisa asked.

"I'm not sure if she'd ever thought about it. I know we've never had one," Rachel said.

"*Hmm!*" Lisa pondered the idea and sipped her tea.

Rachel looked up from the newspaper, and stared in contemplation at Lisa for a moment.

"What?" Lisa asked.

"You know, that's a great idea!" Rachel said and hopped off of the stool.

Lisa studied Rachel's enthusiastic expression. "Don't you even think about it," she said.

"And why not? It was your idea," Rachel said, her Southern accent coming through strong. "And besides, you are a certified aerobics instructor. I just think it would be a great idea to have a fitness and wellness program or an aerobics class at the center."

"I wasn't asking because I was interested in taking on another class. I simply asked because I feel that health and fitness should be part of a woman's daily lifestyle. I'm sure you'll be able to find a volunteer. Chicago is full of humanitarians, you know," Lisa said.

"Lisa, I know you can do it," Rachel said.

"I know it too, but I'm already teaching arts and crafts, and I'm only one person. I still have my own art and family to tend to," Lisa explained, hoping that Rachel would understand.

Rachel's shoulders dropped as she plopped down onto the stool, stuck out her lower lip, which also caused Lisa to laugh. Snapping out of her mock pouting mode, Rachel resumed her posture before speaking. "You're right. I shouldn't be getting all worked up about it anyway. You haven't even taken the idea to Joan yet."

"Hello. That's why you're on the planning committee, right? I presented the idea to you, and then you present the idea to Joan," Lisa said.

"Well, my suggestion to you is that you should be the new coordinator of the center's fitness and wellness program or an aerobics class. My guess is that I think you want me to present the idea to Joan."

"Never mind, I'll do it myself," Lisa said as she finished her tea.

"What made you think of it anyway?" Rachel asked.

Lisa shrugged. "I don't know. It just seemed odd not to have one or the other in place," she said.

"Well, when you put it that way, I suppose you're right. Leave it to Joan, she probably has a very good reason for not having a fitness and wellness program or an aerobics class already in place," Rachel said.

"Well, Joan is a pretty fit woman. She can't be against fitness and health.

"Oh, I can assure you, Joan is all for sex-ercise, if not exercise. I'm telling you, that Joan Grutner is a real firecracker, and her husband is barely fifty," Rachel revealed and sipped her tea.

"Girl, you need to stop," Lisa said with a chuckle. "All the same, I'll run it by her to see what she thinks."

"She'll love the idea. In fact, let's go to the center right now.

"Uhh, no, we can't," Lisa said, knowing that they couldn't just go to the center without Rachel wanting to hang around for hours.

"Why not?" Rachel asked.

"Don't you remember? We have a date with Bond . . . James Bond, that is," Lisa reminded Rachel, in her best British accent, of their prior engagement.

"But I thought--" Rachel said and abruptly cut-off.

"Let me grab my purse. I don't want to miss the opening credits," Lisa said as she stood and rushed out of the kitchen.

Chapter 10

Jason and Shauna sat inside Shauna's car, parked in Arlington High's student parking lot. They were waiting for Brad to get out of his last class so he and Jason could go to baseball tryouts. They had the windows rolled up and the heat turned on low.

"I hope Brad does well," Shauna said as she toyed with the radio dial.

"What about me?" Jason asked.

"How could you not do well?" Shauna said.

"I could be too busy thinking about you and miss every single pitch," Jason said and raised his left hand to massage the back of Shauna's neck.

"I guess you should be thankful that I'm not a cheerleader."

"It doesn't matter. I'm going to think about you no matter what."

"I have to watch out for you," Shauna said with a grin. "With all this charm and flattery, you could make a girl drop her guard."

"I'm offended," Jason pouted playfully.

"Why is that?" Shauna asked and folded her arms.

"You didn't even mention my good looks," Jason said shyly and smiled as Shauna looked at him straight in the face.

"You're all right," Shauna joked before giving him a quick kiss on the lips. "That's for good luck."

Jason leaned over and gave her a longer, more passionate kiss, which took Shauna by complete surprise, but she didn't pull away.

"Thank you," Jason whispered as he pulled his lips away from hers.

Shauna took a deep breath. "Gratitude. I like that," she said and used her right index finger to wipe smudged lipstick from off Jason's lips.

Just then, Brad walked up and tapped on Jason's side of the window, startling them both. Shauna giggled and pushed the power window control button to roll down the front passenger's side window.

"Whassup, man? You ready?" Brad asked as he leaned over to look into the car. "Hey, Shauna."

"Hey," Shauna smiled and waved.

"Yeah, I'm ready. I was waiting on you. What's more important is whether you're ready," Jason said.

"Hey, I'm as ready as anybody can be," Brad said.

"Well, alrighty then," Jason said with a nod, before he turned to Shauna. "We'll have to continue our conversation a little later. I'll call you tonight."

"Okay," Shauna said and nodded. Jason puckered his lips and blew a kiss in her direction before opening the door and stepping out.

"All right, let's do this," Jason said as he and Brad walked in the direction toward the gymnasium.

Once inside the gymnasium, there were at least forty guys already lined up on the bleachers, and there was a batting cage erected in the corner of the gymnasium. Brad knew most of the guys from the previous school year and introduced them to Jason. A few of them recognized him from the games Arlington had played against Fitzgerald. Most of them were a little nervous, others were just anxious for their turn so they could get it over with.

As each hopeful individual was called one by one to the batting cage, Jason and Brad looked on and waited patiently.

"These are only the preliminary tryouts," Jason said. "The coach is not putting anyone up against anything too difficult. I guess he just wanted to see who can hit a simple pitch and who can't."

"Yeah, I was wondering about that. The pitching machine used seemed as if it's aiming perfectly for the bat," Brad observed.

"Have you noticed the number of guys who nearly struck out?

Jason said. "Coach Kirkpatrick is narrowing it down in phases. This must be the elimination process for those who can hardly bat at all."

"So we're cool, right?" Brad asked nervously.

"Of course we are. Look at those pitches coming from the pitching machine. Before we even started practicing, you were connecting with pitches like that," Jason reassured Brad.

"Brad Martin," Coach Kirkpatrick called.

"Well, wish me luck," Brad said and released a deep sigh.

He jogged toward Coach Kirkpatrick who was standing with his clipboard. Brad received his instructions, and then proceeded to the batting cage.

Brad positioned himself over the in-door baseball plate, took his proper stance and gripped the bat just as Jason had coached him. He sent three out of five of his pitches soaring as far as the batting cage would allow. Coach Kirkpatrick nodded in Brad's direction to signal that his evaluation was completed, before pointing to Jason. Jason turned out an excellent performance, connecting with each of his pitches with force and sending all five of them into the far upper corners of the batting cage. After his evaluation was completed, he met up with Brad, who was waiting for him on the opposite side of the gymnasium.

"Good job, man," Jason complimented and slapped Brad on his backside.

"Yeah, thanks. You did great," Brad said.

They exited the gymnasium over an hour later, and returned to the student parking lot, where Brad was parked. Coach Kirkpatrick had informed them that there would be a list outside his office the next day showing the names of everyone who should return to phase two of the three-phase tryouts.

"I hope I can make it through Wednesday," Brad said as he sped out of the parking lot.

"You will," Jason said, leaned back in his seat and allowed his thoughts to drift to Shauna. He couldn't wait to continue his conversation with her. In fact, he was planning on calling her as soon as he got home.

Chapter 11

A few weeks have passed and the Martins were having Christmas dinner at the Taylors, since Thanksgiving was celebrated at the Martins. The snow drifted. Thick plumes of whiteness blanketed the frozen subdivision. Layer upon layer of soft-packed snowflakes settled in near silence, forming a quilt of feathery ice crystals.

A traditional Christmas wreath hung from front doors. For some, windows and rooflines sported strings of Christmas icicle lights. Lisa's parents were also visiting for the holiday.

Mike still haven't received a response from the Burkemans, but Tom had pretty much assured him that a final decision would be rendered shortly into the New Year. Caught up in the Christmas spirit, the Burkeman bid had been temporarily filed in the back of Mike's mind.

As an early Christmas gift, Mike presented Lisa with a check for $17,000 thousand dollars, a grand for each year of marriage, to budget any way she wanted. Of course, Lisa had her mind set on some brand new furnishings for their new home.

After enjoying the elaborate Christmas feast, compliments of Maddie, everyone sat around in the living room mulling over New Year resolutions and drinking an ice cube-filled highball glass of non-alcoholic eggnog.

A seven-foot Fraser Fir Christmas tree, adorned with ornaments, candy canes and mini lights, which stood directly centered of the living room's three-paneled custom bay window, a safe distance from the crackling fireplace, had several brightly colored wrapped gifts beneath the tree limbs. Christmas stockings were pinned to the mantel.

Jason suddenly stood up and politely excused himself from the ongoing mundane conversation.

"Son, where are you going?" Mike asked and sniffled from a cold that he was trying desperately to get over.

"I just remembered that I have this Christmas song that's dope. And since family and friends are all here, I thought it would be appropriate enough to play," Jason said as he stood near the stairway.

"I hope it ain't none of that hippity-hop gangster rap," Jon blurted.

"Hush, husband, and let my grandbaby go play his Christmas song," Maddie said.

"It's not hip-hop or gangster rap, Grandpa," Jason chuckled and shook his head.

"Thank the Lord!" Jon said with a sigh of relief.

Rachel and Tom laughed as Lisa and her mother exchanged knowing glances, having already heard Jon's personal opinion on most of today's music.

Mike let out a sneeze that demanded a "bless you" from everyone in unison before Jason bolted upstairs to play the song. He pulled one of his stereo speakers into the hall and projected it in the direction of the stairs. Just as he returned to the living room, the house was filled with a very catchy modern Christmas jingle, with a holiday message, rhythmic grooving beat with infectious jingle bell riffs.

"This is nice," Maddie said, clapped her hands and rocked to the rhythm of the beat.

"Yeah, It's very nice," Rachel agreed and rocked her head to the rhythm of the beat.

"What's the name of it? I never heard it before," Lisa asked curiously.

"I've had it a few years. It's called *My First Christmas With You,* by Joi Cardwell," Jason said as strong and soulful female vocals drifted over the rhythmic grooving beat.

"That's tight," Brad said.

"Now I can deal with this," Jon said with a huff before he completely changed the subject. "Jason, have you decided on a college yet?" he asked.

Maddie interjected almost immediately, "Speaking of going off to college . . ."

"Ma, I know where you're about to go. We have guests. This isn't the place or time to voice any of your superstitions. We're going to let Jason make his own decision on where he's going to attend college," Lisa said matter-of-factly.

"Well, it's just that I have the strangest gut feeling that--"

"Ma, we've just enjoyed the fabulous Christmas dinner that you've prepared. Let's just continue with our festive evening, okay? And besides, we have plenty of time to discuss Jason's future college plans," Lisa said.

Maddie and Lisa had already had the discussion about Jason's college plans too many times. Her mother claimed to have a strange feeling that Aurora University would not be a good choice, but Lisa was convinced that Maddie's gut feeling was due to the fact that she really wanted Jason to go to Xavier, located in New Orleans. Lisa and Mike both agreed that the decision was solely up to Jason. The important thing was that he was going to college, and it had just so happened that Aurora University had caught his interest.

"Speaking of festive, what are we going to do for New Year's Eve?" Mike asked, between sniffles, sensed it would be a good time to change the subject once again.

"I know!" Brad blurted out and leaned forward as he sat on the very edge of the loveseat and offered his suggestion. "How about we all bring in the new year at The Sanctuary? My boy here got his first DJ gig, so we all can go hear him do his thing," he said.

"Man, I haven't even told them yet," Jason said and rolled his eyes in disgust.

William Jaman Taylor

"Oh, my fault," Brad apologized.

"Care to tell us now?" Mike asked.

Jason sighed after he glared at Brad one last time. "You see, Romeo is the resident DJ at the club, and now that I'm 18, he was able to hook me up with a gig there," he explained.

"Have you committed to doing this gig?" Lisa asked.

"Well, yeah," Jason said.

"You've made a commitment without first asking for our permission?" Mike asked.

"I was going to. I had to commit to it. I didn't want Romeo to give it to someone else. As a matter of fact, I had planned on discussing it with you both tomorrow, but someone beat me to it," Jason said and looked to Brad.

"Man, I said it was my fault," Brad said.

"Son, we have no problem with you doing this DJ gig at the club. You should have brought it to our attention when you first learned of it," Mike said understandably, seemingly deep in the Christmas spirit.

Jason was shocked. He looked to his mother, who appeared to be as equally understanding. They were both usually pretty good about being in agreement on most family matters.

"What's this club like?" Tom asked.

"It's off the charts, I'm telling you," Jason said as his grandparents looked at each other in total bewilderment, not hip at all.

"It's party central all the way. I've compared it to The Warehouse—an after-hours, alcohol-free club for teens, and a counter to the legendary Studio 54 in New York," Brad said.

Tom and Rachel looked at each other and wondered how he'd known specific details about the club.

Tom gradually lifted his hand, as in extending an accusatory finger. "Have you frequented these clubs in the past? he asked, with a straight face.

103

"I plead the fifth," Brad said and dropped his head.

"Maddie and I appreciate the invitation. We'll leave the partying up to you young people," Jon said.

"You know, I was thinking the exact same thing," Tom chuckled.

"Nonsense," Maddie said. "There are only two old people in this house. You all go on out and enjoy yourselves."

"Jason, would you mind if we tagged along," Rachel asked, clearly interested in the idea.

"Of course he wouldn't mind if the adults tagged along, since we're allowing him to do this DJ gig," Lisa said.

"I don't mind," Jason said.

"Well, then, it's settled. The Sanctuary it is," Mike said and raised his glass, suggesting another toast.

"Party over here!" Lisa blurted out.

Everyone made a toast, including Jon and Maddie.

CLINK!
CLINK!
CLINK!
CLINK!
CLINK!
CLINK!
CLINK!
CLINK!

"Now that the rest of our holiday plans are set in stone, how about we open some gifts," Mike said as he stood up, walked over to the Christmas tree, picked up an envelope from atop a wrapped box and handed it to Jon and Maddie.

Maddie squealed excitedly, and grabbed the envelope, ripping it open to examine its content. She extracted a Christmas card with two round-trip airline tickets to New Orleans.

"Look, husband," she said and handed Jon the tickets.

"We know it's been a while since you two have visited New

Orleans," Mike said and sniffed.

"Mom and Dad, I know how much you two love being in the thick of the city's culture and shopping that the French Quarters has to offer," Lisa said.

"Well, we thank you both kindly. We will definitely put these to good use for Mardi Gras," Jon said. Maddie nodded in agreement.

"Jason, this big heavy box is for you," Mike said.

Jason took the big heavy box from his father, and carefully placed it on the floor and started to unwrap it for everyone to see. The box contained a Roland VS-880 Digital Studio Workstation and a Hammond keyboard. Jason had been throwing hints at his parents about purchasing him some additional DJ equipment, but he never thought they'd actually know what to get without his input.

"This is exactly what I wanted! Thanks, Mom and Dad. How did you know what to get?" Jason asked.

"You have Romeo to thank. He knew exactly what you wanted," Lisa said.

"I knew it," Jason said.

"We didn't forget about our new friends from across the lawn either. Brad, this is for you," Lisa said and handed him a neatly wrapped box as he looked from her to his parents, very surprised.

"Thanks, Mr. and Mrs. Taylor," Brad said.

"Clearly, I must be in the wrong profession," Tom joked.

"You guys didn't have to go to such great lengths," Rachel said, noticeably touched by the kind gesture.

"Yeah, you should have told us. We would have gotten more than just Christmas cards," Tom said.

"That would've defeated the purpose of the Christmas spirit. Don't worry about it," Lisa said. "It's just our way of saying thank you, for welcoming us to the neighborhood."

"That's so sweet of you," Rachel said softly and hugged Lisa.

"*Ladies*! Now let's not get all mushy and teary-eyed here,"

Mike said. "Brad, it's your turn to open your gift."

Brad ripped away at the wrapping paper, opened the box, and removed an All Star Black and Tan 33 ½" Baseball Catcher's Mitt and a pair of professional-quality Nike Low Metal Baseball Cleats. "These are phat!" he said excitedly and displayed his gifts to everyone.

"And right on time, might I add," Lisa said.

"Now, let's see if you, Jason and Arlington's baseball team can win the championship," Mike said.

"Thanks Mr. and Mrs. Taylor," Brad said, still admiring his gifts. Jason was still busy examining his new equipment.

"You're welcome," Lisa said with a warm smile. Mike smiled and nodded.

"We saved the best for last," Lisa said as she handed Rachel and Tom a beautifully wrapped box from underneath the Christmas tree.

"You guys," Rachel said and shook her head as she started unwrapping the gift box. Inside, she found his and hers chef's aprons and hats, and a set of high-end restaurant-quality barbecue utensils. "These are so nice," she said.

"You guys really didn't have to go all out," Tom said politely, somewhat confused about the gift.

Lisa and Mike just looked at each other and smiled.

"When was the last time either one of you looked in your backyard?" Mike asked.

"It was shortly before Thanksgiving. Brad and I raked the remaining leaves and bagged then up," Tom said with a shrug.

"Why don't we go take a look now? Shall we?" Mike said.

Rachel and Tom looked at each other and shrugged as they got up and followed Mike and Lisa to the window in the kitchen, with everyone else following close behind them.

"Do you see that big pile of snow over there in the corner?" Mike asked and pointed his right index finger toward the Martins'

William Jaman Taylor

backyard.

"Yes," Rachel said and looked at Mike and Lisa who were smiling anxiously.

"Well, when the snow has thawed out, you'll both find that you have your very own brick barbecue pit, much like the one that's under the pile of snow in our backyard," Mike said.

"You guys. I don't know what to say," Tom said as he continued staring in the direction of his backyard.

"Say you'll invite us over for the very first barbecue," Mike said.

"How did you manage to find the time to build it in the winter in a short period of time?" Tom asked skeptically.

"It was easier than you could've imagined. With the help of a co-worker, we assembled it together in our garage and then we fork lifted it over into your backyard. The only thing we had to do then was to clear the foundation and secure the mounting. Luckily, the heavy snow storm the past few days covered the tracks from the forklift and the pit itself," Mike explained and sneezed.

"Bless you," Lisa said. "He did manage to catch a cold in the process. And by the way, Jason and I were in on the surprise as well. While Tom was working hard and long hours the past few nights, it was our job to get you and Brad out of the house and to the mall two nights in a row."

"I was wondering why we were going to the mall in almost two feet of snow. You guys are too much," Rachel said.

"Let me pay you for the labor and materials. I insist," Tom said.

"No, Tom, it's our gift to you and your family. Enjoy it," Mike said.

Tom shook his head, and placed both hands on his hips. "You guys are really something. Thanks," he said, shook Mike's hand and hugged him. Rachel and Lisa hugged each other.

"You're welcome. Now let's get away from this drafty window," Lisa said as everyone retreated to the living room. They all sat down and resumed their conversation with Maddie and Jon discussing their plans to use their tickets to visit New Orleans during Mardi Gras. They both promised to attend the Martins' first barbecue in the spring. Afterwards, Rachel proposed a toast to health, happiness, and a long-lasting friendship. Everyone raised their glasses of eggnog, made a toast and continued celebrating the Christmas holiday.

Chapter 12

It was almost eight in the evening, New Year's Eve, when Rachel was carefully walking down the stairs in an elegant designer one-shouldered, sheath neckline hunter green evening gown, black purse and shoes. Tom was waiting patiently in the living room in a black tux, with Brad dressed more casually in a black wool turtleneck sweater and blue jeans, sitting in a living-room chair, lacing up a pair of black boots. Just as Rachel made her way into the living room, the doorbell rang.

"I'll get it," Brad said and jumped to his feet to answer the door.

"Looking good, honey," Tom complimented as he stood behind Rachel, and helped her into her full-length black mink coat.

"Thanks. You're looking quite dapper yourself," Rachel said.

"Whassup, yo?" Brad asked Jason, who was standing on the other side of the door with Mike and Lisa. "You ready to tear the club up?"

"You know it, kid. When the clock strikes twelve, that's all she wrote," Jason replied with a grin.

After clearing his throat, Mike stated, "Brad, it's freezing out here. Aren't you going to invite us in?"

"Oh, I'm sorry," Brad apologized. "Come in," he said.

"Are Tom and Rachel ready?" Lisa asked as they entered the foyer. Brad closed the door once everyone was inside.

"Yes. We're right here and ready to go," Rachel yelled cheerfully as she and Tom turned the corner and joined everyone in the foyer.

"Don't you two look absolutely drop-dead gorgeous," Lisa said and beaming.

"Why thank you, Lisa," Rachel replied. "I love your fur coat."

"Thank you," Lisa said as she looked down at the black fur coat that covered her elegant designer black halter evening gown.

"I was just admiring yours too."

"This old thing?" Rachel chuckled.

"I hate to interrupt this female bonding moment," Tom interjected, "but we've got to get going."

"Good idea," Mike agreed.

"Lisa and Rachel both rolled their eyes playfully.

"Did we forget to tell the men how impeccably dressed they were?" Rachel said.

"Oh, I'm sorry. Tom, you look absolutely dashing," Lisa said in her best British accent.

"And Mike, you look handsome as always. Armani suits you well," Rachel said. Both men smiled and shook their heads before leading them out the door.

About forty-five minutes later, the Taylors were passing the Johnson Publishing Company on South Michigan Avenue, a major north-south street, sometimes referred to as The Magnificent Mile, known for its high-end shopping and nightlife. The Martins were following in their car close behind them.

"*Wow!* Look at all these people waiting in line to get inside the club," Lisa said, in awe.

"Yeah, it seems as if half the city of Chicago's elite will be bringing in the New Year here," Mike said as he looked at the shivering patrons who stood in line that extended from the Johnson Publishing Building and snaked around the corner.

"There might be a few celebrities here," Jason said. "And I know the music will definitely be off da' chain too," he said and pointed out the club to Mike, who brought the car to a stop in front of the valet parking area and unlocked the trunk.

"Are you nervous, Jason?" Lisa asked as a valet parking attendant opened the door.

"No," Jason said confidently as he stepped out of the car, and removed his crate of records from the trunk. The Martins were getting out of their car directly behind the Taylors.

110

"Hey, Rachel, are you ready to get your dance on, girl?" Lisa said, trying to be hip as Jason and Brad burst into laughter.

"What is so funny?" Rachel asked.

"Mom, let me just warn you that dancing has changed quite a bit since your time," Brad said.

"What's your point, young man?" Rachel said.

"I'm just saying . . ." Brad said.

"Hey," Jason interrupted. "I think that's Romeo at the door. We'd better go catch him," he said and led everyone to the front of the line, where Romeo stood, chatting with a bouncer.

"Hey, how's everybody doing this evening?" Romeo asked enthusiastically.

"Cold," Mike and Lisa said almost simultaneously.

"Romeo, you do remember Brad, right?" Jason asked.

"Yeah, I remember him. Whassup, man," Romeo said.

"Whassup," Brad replied.

"These are Brad's parents, Mr. and Mrs. Martin," Jason introduced.

"Nice to meet you both," Romeo said and instructed the big straight faced bouncer, in a full-length black leather coat, who worked the door, to checked them all off on the guest list.

"Follow me," the bouncer said in his bass voice.

Once inside the sleek modern nightclub, they were all surrounded by the thumping surround sound of Chicago-style house music. The nightclub delivered the ultimate musical and visual experience, and served as a modern canvas for nightly entertainment ranging from nationally and internationally renowned DJs to the best in local talent. Also, the nightclub maintained a constant element of superior audio sound and quality. Jason and Brad's parents simply took in the festive scene, watching the partygoers dancing on the packed dance floor, which was surrounded by a flutter of wealthy individuals, local and well-known celebrities, dressed in formal attire, occupied the VIP sections as well as sectioned-off tables and plush booths with bottles of champagne flowing. All of the partygoers appeared to be really enjoying themselves, and some of them were even dressed in elaborately festive costumes, 1999 New Years Eve party hats and glasses. Others were casually dressed, dancing, twirling noisemakers and blowing horns.

"Look, I have to get back to the DJ booth," Romeo yelled to Jason over the loud music. "I'm gonna turn it over to you right before the countdown, so you need to be up there about ten minutes before midnight. Then, it's gonna be on you to tear the club up. It's your world, my brother!"

"It's my world, huh? Thanks, man," Jason said and grinned as he and Romeo exchanged a hip-hop handshake.

"No problem. See you all later," Romeo said and waived as he walked in the direction toward the DJ booth.

After the Taylors and Martins checked in their coats at the coat check, they managed to find a table reserved for them with a perfect view of the dance floor. Jason and Brad almost immediately excused themselves to have a look around the club. Moments later, a waiter walked up to their table, leaned in.

"Good evening, and welcome to The Sanctuary. My name is Trey, and I'll be your waiter for the evening," he greeted and placed napkins on the table in front of each of them. "Can I take your drink orders? he asked and retrieved a pen and pad from his apron.

"I'll have *Tanqueray* on the rocks," Mike ordered.

"I'll have a *Fuzzy Navel,*" Lisa ordered.

"I'll have what she's having," Rachel said.

"I'll take a shot of *Bourbon*," Tom ordered.

"Thank you. I'll return shortly with your drinks," Trey said before he turned and walked off toward the bar.

After an hour or so, both couples had loosened up a bit from the cocktails. Lisa and Rachel had managed to convince their husbands to accompany them to the dance floor.

Approximately eleven forty-five, Romeo was still putting it down on the 1's and 2's. The Taylors and Martins had returned to their table, when Jason brought Shauna over to introduce her to his parents and the Martins.

"Hey, everybody, I'd like for you to meet Shauna," Jason shouted over the loud music and noise.

Everyone smiled and greeted Shauna, who waived and flashed her sweet school girl smile.

"I'm about to be on in a few minutes, so I need to get to the DJ booth," Jason said, realizing that it was now fifteen minutes to mid-night. "Look, I need everyone's support. I want you all to chant 'go Jason, go, go Jason, go'."

"Son, just get to the DJ booth before you miss the countdown," Mike chuckled.

The wait staff had already begun coming around and offering the partygoers a plastic flute of complimentary champagne.

Brad finally made his way back to the table just in time to wish Jason good luck.

"Don't hold back, man. Do your thing," Brad encouraged, giving Jason a hip-hop handshake and hug.

"Thanks, man. Wish me luck," Jason said as he and Shauna, who waived politely to everyone, pushed through the dancing crowd and toward the DJ booth.

A few moments later they all heard Romeo's voice as he introduced Jason to the New Year's Eve crowd.

"May I have your attention, please? Now, it's almost that time, so I'm gonna turn it over to DJ Jammin' Jason as he takes us into 1999. Show some love, and let me hear y'all make some noise. Somebody scream!" Romeo said, getting the crowd hyped up.

The crowd cheered, clapped, whistled, screamed and shouted as Jason's voice replaced Romeo's.

"Chi-Town's in the house. Are y'all ready to party?" Jason said as the crowd screamed and shouted. "Y'all don't hear me. Are y'all ready to party?" he said as the crowd screamed and shouted even louder as some partygoers started wildly twirling their noisemakers while others were blowing their party horns. "All right, y'all had me scared for a minute. We have a few more minutes before midnight, so let me drop a classic house track before the countdown."

Jason started with the intro to a familiar dance track that immediately sent the hyped crowd into a dancing frenzy, cheering and blowing their party horns, clapping their hands and stomping their feet to the beat. Looking down at the sea of partygoers, he spotted his parents and the Martins back on the dance floor again. Jason was trying to spot Shauna, but the dance floor had become too crowded. He knew that she had to meet up with some of her girlfriends, to attend another party, but was hopeful that she would have at least hung around until after the countdown.

"All right, Chicago, we have less than a minute to go," Jason said. "If y'all are ready to bring in the New Year, let me hear you make some noise!" he said. The partygoers collectively yelled in a state of frenzy. Finally, it was just seconds away from midnight.

"All right, here we go! *Ten, nine, eight, seven, six, five, four, three, two, one! Happy New Year!!!*" Jason announced as a large balloon drop nets suspended above the dance floor were released, sending an assortment of colored balloons and metallic confetti down on the partygoers. Appropriately, the first song that Jason played was *1999*, an apocalyptic yet upbeat party anthem by Prince, the title track from his 1982 enduring hit album of the same name.

The entire club, in a partying and dancing frenzy, yelled and cheered as everyone converged upon the already packed dance floor. He looked down on the sea of partygoers and spotted Shauna, who had stood on top of a chair waving her arms to get his attention. Once she realized that he had finally spotted her, she

114

blew him a kiss and waved goodbye. A grin spread across Jason's face as he waved back and watched Shauna exit the club to the beat of Prince's ultimate sing-along dance anthem.

A few hours have passed, and the club's party vibe was still going strong. Jason was so caught up in mixing just the right tracks to keep the crowd hype that he almost didn't even notice Brad as he entered the DJ booth.

"Happy New Year, man!" Brad shouted before giving Jason another hug. "I had to come and tell you that you are really putting down some slamming house tracks. Just look at the floor, man."

Jason followed Brad's finger as he pointed down toward the dance floor.

"Look at that fine young lady in the black dress," Brad said.

"Man, you are seriously trippin'. That's my mother," Jason said.

"I know," Brad laughed. "Look at our parents, bro. They're acting as if the complimentary champagne had come from a fountain of youth or something. Just look at them," he said and shook his head.

"They're really enjoying themselves," Jason smiled and nodded. Romeo stuck his head inside the DJ booth.

"Hey, Jay, fade out the music in the next ten minutes," Romeo said.

"What time is it?" Jason asked.

"It's four forty-five. We close at five," Romeo said.

"I guess time does fly when you're having fun," Jason said.

"You did a good job. I'm proud of you," Romeo said and pulled his head out of the DJ booth. Jason nodded and smiled proudly.

Approximately fifteen minutes later, Jason ascended the stairs, from the DJ booth, carrying his crate of records, with Brad following close behind. Romeo was standing at the foot of the stairs talking to the club manager.

"Jay, this is my boss, Jack Russo," Romeo introduced.

"Nice to meet you," Jason said and shook Jack's hand.

"Same here. Actually, I told Jerome here that I wanted to meet and personally thank you. I think you did an excellent job," Jack said.

"Thank you, sir. That really means a lot, since this was my first real gig," Jason said proudly.

"A bedroom DJ, huh? I never would have guessed this was your first time spinning in a club. Well, here's your pay, and thanks again," Jack said as he handed Jason an envelope and walked off.

Jason opened the envelope and thumbed through ten fifty dollar bills. "500 dollars!" he exclaimed.

"DJs get paid big bucks," Romeo said and walked off.

"I need to invest in a pair of turntables," Brad joked as he and Jason made their way over toward the table where their parents were sitting and waiting.

"What did y'all think? Jason asked excitedly.

"You were great. You kept the dance floor packed. I'm proud of you," Mike said.

"So am I," Lisa agreed and hugged her son. "Putting up with your countless hours of practicing was well worth it," she added.

"You did an excellent job," Tom said.

"You were magnificent," Rachel said.

"Thanks. How about we all go to breakfast? My treat," Jason suggested as he showed everyone the money that he was paid. They all agreed, exited the club, and headed toward a nearby 24-hour restaurant. The evening had been a success, starting the New Year off just right.

Chapter 13

Tom sat on the edge of the bed, close to the TV, wearing a pair of prescription glasses. He attempted to divide his attention between his wife's voice emanating from their master bathroom on-suite, as he flipped through the channels. Tom had already gotten ready for bed and left Rachel in the bathroom, who wore a sexy red silk nightgown, brushing her hair. She was telling Tom how much she loved her Valentine's gift, a 14K yellow gold 3-carat tennis bracelet, and a bouquet of two-dozen red roses that set on a bedside dresser. When Tom did not respond, she cut off the bathroom light, walked into the bedroom, only to find him staring intently at the television. Realizing that she was unintentionally being ignored, Rachel shook her head and stepped between Tom and his view of the television, which displayed what he recognized to be one of the most gruesome scenes from the movie *Rosewood*. She frowned at the image of a black man being lynched, before turning off the television.

"Tom?" Rachel called curiously as she looked at him. Tom seemed to be very pensive as he stared blankly at the television with a glazed over look in his eyes. "Hey, Earth to Tom!" Rachel said and snapped her fingers to get her husband's attention. "What were you thinking about?"

"Huh?" Tom said absent-mindedly. He suddenly snapped out of his deep thought and noticed Rachel staring at him. "Oh, uh, I was just thinking about how lynchings and other types of hate crimes were so commonplace back then. Just the thought of it makes me sick to my stomach."

"Well, it wasn't all that long ago," Rachel said as she pulled the covers back on her side of the bed, tucked herself in and turned off a bedside lamp.

"Yeah, I know," Tom said as he stood and walked over to his

side of the bed, took off his glasses, placed them on the a bedside night table, pulled the covers back on his side of the bed, and crawled into bed next to his wife, who was tucked under the covers. Rachel had given him a kiss on the forehead before resting her head on his muscular and hairy chest. Moments later she quickly dozed off peacefully, but Tom was unable to find sound sleep, his head tossing on a rumpled pillow with racing thoughts as the night wore on. Rachel was purring gently, sensuous little snores, her body curled up beside him, one arm dangled loosely over his chest. She stirred, adjusted her pillow. "*Hmm.*" Rachel stretched long, languid legs under the covering sheet before turning onto her right side with her backside now toward Tom. For an hour or two, Tom's constant tossing and turning had given way to an engaging dream, mumbling incoherently but not loudly enough to awaken Rachel.

Tom's dream took him back to his childhood, as a ten-year-old kid. He gathered his fishing pole and a pail, and headed into the woods, taking a shortcut to a nearby lake. He noticed light clouds of dust and heard men laughing. As he walked deeper into the woods, the laughter had become more audible as the clouds of dust thickened. Gradually, the clouds of dust thinned out. Tommy Ray witnessed a group of white men who were all wearing black sweatshirts with big red letters K T N on them. Tommy Ray noticed bloodstains on most of the men's sweatshirts.

As he inched closer, he heard someone crying out in agonizing pain. He'd hidden behind a tree, seen one of the men standing over the body of a badly beaten black man. A second or two later, the man stomped on the black man's chest. The black man curled up in a fetal-like position and coughed up blood.

Stan had thrown a half-eaten apple to the ground. He picked up the black man's severed right arm, positioned it to his right shoulder, took his hunting knife and then stabbed the black man, attaching it to his shoulder. The black man let out an agonizing

118

scream. Tommy Ray jumped to his feet, his eyes widened, mouth agape, trembling with fear. The hairs on the back of his neck stood up. A patch of hair on the left side of his head had literally turned white. Tommy Ray was scared out of his wits.

Stan had thrown the end of a hangman's noose over a low-hanging tree limb. Two other frat members hoisted and stood the black man up on the back of one of the trucks, and placed the noose around his neck. Amazingly, somehow, the black man spotted Tommy Ray. He mustered the strength to pantomime calling out a heart-wrenching plea, "Help me, please!"

Tommy Ray, paralyzed with fear, looked at the badly beaten black man and realized that he was the same man who had eaten supper and entertained his family. His shaky right hand slowly moved to his shirt pocket and felt for the harmonica. The white men observed Tommy Ray's presence.

"Hey, Stan, do you want me to go get the little bastard? Andy asked.

"Naw! Stan said and yelled, "Hey, boy, you let this be a lesson to you. Niggers ain't welcomed in this here neck of the woods. You got that?

Tommy Ray stood numb, as Stan rushed and hopped inside one of the trucks, started the engine, slammed on the gas and drove a yard or two before coming to an abrupt stop, with its wheels generating thick clouds of dust. The black man dangled at the rope's end, flailing and kicking his feet violently. His head snapped back with a sickening crack, his body swung rhythmically as a pendulum from the tree.

Tommy Ray was trembling with fear. He slowly shook his head, then faster. Still trembling in total disbelief, he took slow steps walking backwards. He almost tripped, knocking over his fishing rod and pail. Suddenly, he turned and begun to run home as fast as he could, and heard the white men as they chanted, "K T N! Kill The Niggers! K T N! Kill The Niggers!" fade away behind him.

Tom's face contorted in deep sadness as he spoke incoherently in his sleep. "K T N!"

He bolted upright in bed in a cold sweat, his heart racing. The clock radio on the bedside table said 3:13 a.m. He's panting. He turned on the light. Rachel woke up and turned on the light on her nightstand and clutched her chest.

"Tom, it's okay. You were just having another one of your bad nightmares," Rachel said.

"K T N," Tom whispered.

"What are you saying, Tom? You're starting to scare me," Rachel said and placed her left hand on his right shoulder. Tom flinched. He flung back the covers, swung his legs over the side of the bed, jumped up, stumbled into the bathroom, flicked on the light, and stared at himself in the medicine cabinet mirror hanging over the sink. He dropped his head over the basin and turned the cold water faucet on, cupped water in his hands and splashed his face.

Rachel got out of bed and stood in the doorway of the bathroom.

"Tom, are you all right? Rachel asked worriedly.

"Yeah," Tom nodded.

"I'll go get you a glass of water," Rachel said and headed downstairs.

Tom stood up straight and stared at his blanched face in the mirror, running both hands through his hair. He opened the medicine cabinet and picked up a medicine bottle. It read: VALIUM (DIAZEPAM) TAB 5MG TAKE ONE TABLET 2 to 4 TIMES DAILY.

Tom opened the bottle and shook two pills in his right hand. He closed the medicine cabinet and saw the reflection of the ghost in the mirror, hanging from a noose, swinging as rhythmically as a pendulum, in the middle of the bathroom doorway. Tom heard the shrill whisper, "Help me, please!"

Tom closed his eyes, lowered his head over the basin, and yelled, "What do you want from me?"

"Tom, who are you talking to?" Rachel asked, visibly nervous as she held the glass of water in her shaky right hand and clutched her gown with the other.

"Nobody. I was talking to nobody," Tom said as he slowly raised his head and seen his wife's reflection in the mirror.

Rachel walked with caution toward Tom and handed him the glass of water. Tom popped the pills in his mouth, and washed them down with the water. He set down the glass on the basin and walked past her, detached, expressionless.

Rachel wrapped her arms around her shoulders, and stood motionless as her eyes followed Tom into the bedroom. She noticed her breath formed a tiny cloud in the air. Rachel shivered and rubbed her arms and shoulders.

"I felt a draft," Rachel said as she walked into the bedroom and seen Tom standing in front of an open drawer to the nightstand. Rachel turned, leaned over the thermostat and turned up the heat.

Tom noticed the harmonica given to him, as a present, nearly forty years ago, was placed next to his glasses on top of the nightstand. Tom did not remember removing the harmonica from the top drawer. He picked up the harmonica in his right hand, glanced at it briefly, looked to his wife, turned around, and placed the harmonica back in the drawer.

Chapter 14

"*Yes!* An aerobics class sounds like a great idea!" Joan said ecstatically as she leaned forward in the large leather chair.

Rachel smiled and looked at Lisa.

"Now, all we have to do is find an instructor who would be willing to volunteer his or her time," Lisa said.

"Even though we have a certified aerobics instructor sitting right here in our mist," Rachel muttered.

"What was that, Rachel? Joan asked. Lisa shot Rachel a threatening look, determined not to allow them to talk her into taking on yet another class at the center.

"Well, I was just agreeing that finding a qualified aerobics instructor shouldn't be a problem at all, since Lisa has valuable experience in that area," Rachel acknowledged.

"I don't quite understand," Joan said, with a perplexed look, covering her surprisingly youthful face.

"Well, Lisa is a certified aerobics instructor. I'm sure it will be fairly easy for her to recognize a qualified instructor, if she were to come across one," Rachel explained, looked and smiled at Lisa in spite of Lisa's blank expression.

"Why, Lisa, I had no idea!" Joan said.

Lisa cast a wry glance and smile at Joan, fully aware of what would come next.

"Maybe you can take on the class, just on a trial basis," Joan suggested hopefully.

"I don't know, Joan," Lisa said and shook her head reluctantly.

"Why not? I've sat in on your arts and crafts class and seen enough to know that you'd make a wonderful instructor," Joan said.

"Actually, Rachel and I have already toyed with the idea and concluded that it would be best if we were to find someone else. I haven't taught an arts and crafts class in quite a while, and don't want to commit to another class at the present moment."

"That's understandable," Joan said regrettably with a sigh. "Do you have anyone in mind?" she asked.

"Well, I can contact a friend of mine who is an aerobics instructor. She also trains aspiring instructors. I'm sure she might have a couple individuals who wouldn't mine doing some volunteer work to gain the experience," Lisa said.

"*Great!*" Joan said with her enthusiasm restored. "You know, it would be great if we can get this program off the ground as soon as possible. It's already mid-February, and I'm afraid people will start to get discourage or simply lose interest and won't stick to their New Year's resolution to get back in shape or lose weight."

"Amen to that," Rachel chuckled, patting her own thighs.

"You know, Joan, I wondered why the Women's Center never had a fitness and wellness program or an aerobics class in place to begin with?" Lisa said.

"That's a really good point, now that you've mentioned it," Joan said. "Fitness and health are very important, and I wish the idea would have come up much sooner."

"Joan, how have you managed to stay so fit?" Rachel asked and winked at Lisa.

"Well, Rachel, as you already know, I'm married to a younger man who has a very high sex drive. Need I say more?" Joan said without hesitation.

"I knew it," Rachel said, trying to hold in a giggle.

"I eat right, and have great sex daily. Yes, ladies, I'm trying to hold onto youth as long as I can. There ain't no shame to my game," Joan said in hip-hop fashion.

"I heard that," Rachel chuckled.

"Unlike Stella, I never lost my groove. Okay," Joan said and chuckled.

"You go, girl!" Lisa said and joined Rachel in a giggle.

"Oh, before I forget, Lisa, I have a really big favor to ask,"

Joan said.

"I'm all ears," Lisa said, with a slight giggle lingering from Joan's previous statement.

"First, do you have any experience with cheerleading?" Joan asked.

Lisa smiled as she reminisced about her high school and college years as a cheerleader. "Well, I've done a little cheerleading back in high school and college," Lisa said.

"*Perfect!* My granddaughter, Wendy, is really in a jam. She's captain of her cheerleading team. The flu bug has bitten their coach as well as half of the cheerleading squad. My granddaughter was just telling me the other day that they desperately need someone to help them to go over a few of their routines with them, and to offer some constructive criticism."

"Is this just a one-time thing?" Lisa asked.

"That's correct. Hopefully, their coach should be back on the job within a week or so. In the meantime, the girls have a basketball game coming up, and I don't think she will be fully recovered by then. I told Wendy that they could use the gymnasium here, to practice, if needed. If you could help them out with their routines, I'd really appreciate it," Joan said.

"Well, have they scheduled a practice date?" Lisa asked.

"Not yet, so that means the date can be totally up to you, as long as it's before next Monday," Joan replied.

"Well, Saturday afternoon would be perfect for me. How does four o'clock sound?" Lisa asked.

"I'm sure four o'clock will be just fine. I'll pass the good news on to Wendy," Joan said.

"I guess that will give me tomorrow afternoon to do a little preparation," Lisa said. "It has been a while since I've done a cheer."

"I'm sure you'll do just fine. The girls are pretty much stuck between a rock and a hard place, so I know they will be grateful for whatever guidance you can offer."

"Well, it's a date. C'mon, Rachel. We still have a date with the mall," Lisa said as she rose to her feet.

"We'll see you later, Joan," Rachel said as she stood and led the way out of the office.

"Bye! Don't you ladies spend too much money. Thanks again, Lisa," Joan yelled.

* * *

Tom returned home around noon to retrieve a couple of court documents that he had inadvertently left behind earlier that morning. When he saw the empty driveway, he knew that Rachel and Lisa were still out and about, more than likely at the Women's Center. As Tom walked down the hallway, the closer he got to his office, the more audible a male's voice had become. Realizing that it was someone, perhaps from the office, attempting to leave a message on the answering machine, which sat on the corner of his mahogany desk, he scurried into the office, hoping to intercept the message before the caller on the other end hung up.

Tom's hand was hovering right over the receiver when he recognized the male's voice as that of Vince Burkeman. The message had ended. He had assumed Vince was returning his call from earlier in the week. Tom was curious to know if Vince Burkeman had made a determination in regards to which company he would be granting the bid to for the church and restaurant renovations. What Tom had gathered from the message that was left, a decision still had not been made, but Vince promised to have a final determination by the first week of March.

Tom was about to hit the replay button when he heard just a single click from the machine's speaker. This was very unusual since messages that would normally be left would always be followed by a distinctive long beep and then a click. Suddenly, Vince Burkeman's voice returned to Tom's office through the answering machine speaker. This time, it was accompanied by another male's voice, which Tom hadn't immediately recognized. He figured that the men had been on a three-way call when Vince left the message, and hung up, so he thought, but failed to successfully do so. What Tom had overheard undoubtedly shed some light on Vince Burkeman's delay in potentially awarding Drake and Nash the winning bid for the church and restaurant renovation projects.

"Now, all I have to do is make sure Tom Martin will continue to take on my wife's case by the first of March," Vince said to the man on the other end of the phone. "I have already called Tom's office, and his secretary said that he's as Tom, with a glazed expression on his face, took a seat in the leather desk chair, leaned back and listened intently as the two men continued their discussion.

"Why did you agree to meet in the first place," Joe asked.

"Just listen to me, Joe. I didn't know this contractor was some fancy nigger. During the initial meeting, I met with a redhead kid fresh out of college. Look, I know how these lawyers operate. I only agreed to hear the bid on the church and restaurant renovations, so he'll be more apt to vigorously defend my wife's robbery and sexual assault case," Vince explained. "Hey, one hand washes the other. If you know what I mean."

"What exactly are you saying?" Joe said.

"I'm telling you that I don't care if that uppity nigger has the lowest bid, he won't get the contract," Vince said.

"That's good to hear. Because if you had any intentions on giving the winning bid to that spade, you can kiss the bank loan goodbye," Joe said sternly.

"I'll call Tom's office and set up a meeting with his secretary," Vince said.

"You do that. The last thing we need is for that spade to get the contract. The next thing you know, he'll start recommending soul food dishes for the restaurant's menu," Joe said.

Both men laughed uncontrollably as Tom rocked back and forth in his plush leather chair with his hands fused at the fingertips. His forehead showed crinkles of deep contemplation. Suddenly, Tom recognized the second voice as that of Joseph Dobbs, a prominent banker.

"Oh, oh! I almost forget about the dessert menu," Vince said.

"What's that?" Joe asked.

"Watermelon!" Vince said.

The men laughed harder as Tom reclined in the chair, his hands still fused at the fingertips.

"Well, I hope you're right about this Tom fella," Joe said.

"Of course I am. Trust me on this one. I'll give him a call tomorrow and follow-up with him," Vince assured.

"All right. Just let me know what happens," Joe said.

"Will do. Don't worry, everything will be just fine. Give that pretty wife of yours my love," Vince said.

"I will. Talk to you later," Joe said before hanging up. That click was followed by another click that indicated Vince had hung up as well.

Tom leaned forward in his chair and hit the rewind button on the answering machine. After the mini-cassette had been rewound completely, he carefully removed it and placed it in a business-size manila envelope, which he dropped into his bottom desk drawer. Tom then focused his attention on the rolodex open rotary business card file that set next to the phone and answering machine. He flipped through it until his fingers landed on the page that displayed Vince Burkeman's office number. Tom picked up his phone and dialed the number.

"Burkeman and Son, this is Stacey, how may I help you?" she answered.

"Hello, Stacey. This is Tom Martin," he said.

"Hi, Tom. How are you?" Stacey said.

"I'm just fine. How are you? Tom said.

"No complaints here. How can I help you?" Stacey said.

"Listen, I need to schedule a meeting with Mr. Burkeman as soon as possible," Tom said.

"Sure thing," Stacey said as she checked Vince Burkeman's schedule. "Let's see here, I can squeeze you in tomorrow at two," she said.

"That'll be fine," Tom said.

"I have you down. We'll see you then," Stacey said.

* * *

The next day, Tom was at the office of Burkeman and Son, Inc., promptly at two. Stacey had allowed him to have a seat in Vince's office, while he finished wrapping up a meeting with his son across the hall. Tom sat in the chair directly in front of Vince's desk, picked up a beautifully framed photo of his daughter, as he waited patiently. He had been in the very same office a number of times before, but all of those times were strictly regarding business. This time, things were a bit personal.

Tom heard the door open behind him. He placed the framed photo back on the desk, turned around and stood to greet both Vince Burkeman and his eldest son, Vince, Jr., as they entered the office. Vince took his seat behind the desk, as his son sat in a chair beside Tom.

"She's pretty," Tom said.

"That's my angel. Well, this is indeed an unexpected visit. I suspect you have some good news for me. Hopefully, the police have caught the scumbag," Vince said as he picked up the humidor chest that sat atop a credenza behind his desk and offered Tom a Stradavarius Churchill Cigar.

"No thanks," Tom said.

"When we go to trial, I want you to fry that scumbag who robbed and sexually assaulted my wife. She still has nightmares, you know," Vince said as he sat the cigar box back on top of the credenza.

"I know that you are both very busy men, so I'll cut straight to the chase," Tom said as he opened his briefcase, extracted the micro-cassette and manila folder, withdrew a document from it, signed it in front of the Burkemans. They both looked at each other curiously as Tom slid the document across Vince's desk in front of him and placed the mini-cassette on top of it.

Vince's initial reason for Tom's visit went awkwardly awry. "What's this?" he asked and looked puzzled as he stared at the document and mini-cassette, then up at Tom.

"That, Mr. Burkeman, is a legal and binding document acknowledging that I am here by withdrawing my services as legal advisor."

"What's the meaning of this?" Vince said gruffly.

"With all due respect, sir, I suggest that you immediately seek legal representation elsewhere," Tom said as he watched both of their faces turned slightly red. There followed an awkward silence as they all stared at each other for a moment. "Oh, and by the way, here's a piece of advice, free of charge. Should you decide not to grant Drake and Nash their bid on the renovation projects for your church and restaurant, be prepared to defend your decision in court," he said as he stood and picked up his briefcase. "You gentlemen have a good day," he said.

"You can't do this to us," Vince Jr. said.

"Shut the fuck up and get the hell out of here!" Vince Sr. yelled, and pointed toward the door as his son looked stunned by his father's outburst.

Just as Vince Jr. was about to leave, Stacey had tapped on the door and stuck her head in cautiously. "Is everything all right?"

she asked.

"Everything is goddamn hunky-dory. Get out! Both of you," Vince yelled, rocketed from his chair, stepped from behind his desk, and stood face-to-face with Tom. "You listen to me you goddamn nigger lover! Who in the hell do you think you are coming into my office threatening me, and telling me who I can and cannot do business with?" he vented.

"Of course I can't, but let me just simply remind you that racial discrimination is against the law. You better have a good reason other than the fact that Michael Taylor is African-American. According to the message laden with racial expletives and slurs you inadvertently left on my answering machine, and not to mention calling me an 'N word' lover to my face, Mr. Taylor's race is the only reason why you are denying Drake and Nash's bid. But, of course, that's my take on it. Let's see how the court system would perceive this matter, given the evidence. A taped confession can be very persuasive in court," Tom said.

"You would actually bring a lawsuit against me?" Vince said, a hint of anxiety had crept into his voice.

"No, Mr. Burkeman. I'm pretty sure Drake and Nash have their own corporate attorneys. Good day, sir," Tom said and walked toward the door. He paused, not looking back. "Give Anne my regards. I can sympathize with her when it comes to nightmares," he said in a monotone, opened and closed the door behind him.

Vince walked back to his desk and dropped in his chair, looking dumbfounded as he stared blankly at the document and mini-cassette.

As Tom was about to exit the office suite, satisfied with his performance, he looked at Stacey and flashed a pleasant smile. He anxiously looked forward to what would follow. Stacey's eyes followed him, mouth agape, to suggest, "What just happened in there?"

130

Chapter 15

As Lisa entered the front door, she wondered why her hunter green 1995 Acura Legend was parked in the driveway. She was greeted by the enticingly delicious smell of something simmering on the stove. Lisa and Rachel had spent a few hours at the mall, but surprisingly she left with only a couple of shopping bags. She set the bags on top of the stool before tiptoeing over to the stove to try to sneak a peek inside the pots. It looked as if Mike, who had made it home before her, went immediately to work on dinner. Whatever it was that he was preparing, it reminded Lisa of how hungry she was from skipping lunch. Just as she was about to lift the lid off on one the pots, Mike entered the kitchen with an expensive bottle of a German Riesling wine and a corkscrew in tow.

Mike cleared his throat. "What do you think you're doing?" he asked as he walked up behind her and pulled her away from the stove and closer to him.

"I was just making sure the food wasn't burning," Lisa said as Mike planted a kiss on her lips.

"You are a terrible liar," Mike said with a smirk.

"It smells delicious. What is it?" Lisa asked.

"Just a second ago, I thought you suggested something was possibly burning. Now, which is it?" Mike joked.

Lisa playfully pushed him away, determined to find out for herself.

"It's a surprise," Mike said and pulled her away from the stove once again before she was able to look into any of the pots. "Why don't you go put your bags away and get ready for dinner? It'll be ready in a minute," he said.

Lisa smiled, kissed him again, grabbed her bags, and headed out of the kitchen. When she returned, she found two place settings arranged on the table, complete with soupspoons and napkins. A footed soup tureen was placed between the two place settings. The bottle of wine sat off to the side by Mike.

"Is my mother hiding somewhere in the house?" Lisa asked and looked at the two bowls of Gumbo, served over rice.

"No, but I did call her for a refresher course," Mike said.

"Well, you've certainly outdone yourself. It looks just as good as it smells. What's the occasion?" Lisa said as Mike pulled the chair back from the table for her before taking a seat across from her.

"We've sealed the deal, and landed the Burkeman contract," Mike said as he poured wine into each glass, and then set the bottle down on the table.

"Congratulations," Lisa praised. "*Cheers!*" she said, raised her glass. She and Mike made a toast.

CLINK!

"Thank you for eighteen wonderful years of marriage," Mike said.

"You remembered our anniversary," Lisa beamed.

"How could I forget? It was the same day that I met your parents for the first time. I remember when I walked into their living room, candles were burning everywhere. Maddie and Jon walked in. Your mother was wearing this voodoo priestess-like dress and matching head wrap. She looked at you and said, 'he's the one. He's going to marry you.' Then she turned to me and said, 'since you're the one who'll marry my daughter, you must learn to make gumbo.'

"That's tradition. My father did it for my mother," Lisa said.

"I remember asking myself . . . what did this voodoo witch say? I had to learn how to make Louisiana-style gumbo," Mike teased as Lisa's mouth was agape, hands on her hips.

Lisa simulated shock. "*You said what?*"

"Hell, I was scared. Thought she was going to lure me into the kitchen, turn me into large chunks of sweet, succulent crabmeat,

132

and add me to that big old witch's pot she had bubbling up on top of the stove." He leaned in close. "Have you ever told your mother that I called her a witch?" Mike asked, a slow grin splitting his face as his gaze met hers.

"Of course I didn't. Why do you thing you didn't get any that night?" Lisa said and rolled her eyes. "Calling my mother a witch," she added.

"Where's Jason?" Mike asked, changing the subject as he placed the napkin on his lap.

"He left a message letting us know that he, Shauna and Brad were going out for pizza," Lisa said.

"How was your day?" Mike asked.

Lisa let out a sigh. "I somehow let Joan talk me into helping her granddaughter's cheerleading squad with their routines."

"Joan and Rachel know how to take the 'volunteer' out of volunteer work," Mike chuckled as he brought a spoonful of Cajun cuisine and rice to his mouth.

"Well, she promised that it would be a one-time thing. Their cheerleading coach has been out sick, with the flu, for a while, so they just need some help with some new routines for an upcoming basketball game."

"In that case, Joan asked the right person. If I remember correctly, you were a damn good cheerleader in college. I loved seeing you in that little red, white and blue pleated skirt," Mike said.

Lisa laughed out loud and shook her head. "A little red, white and blue pleated skirt, huh?"

"Yeah, baby. That little red, white and blue pleated skirt," Mike reminisced with a nod and smile.

"My college cheerleading outfit was maroon, white and black," Lisa reminded as she relished the look on his face. Mike realized that he'd put his foot in his mouth. "Don't get it twisted," she said.

Hesitantly, Mike released a nervous chuckle as he searched

desperately for a response. Lisa studied his expression. "What do you mean?" he asked.

"Well, if my memory serves me correctly, you and every other hard-up male on campus were drooling over little Ms. what's-her-name," Lisa said and snapped her fingers as she desperately tried to think of the rival cheerleader's name.

"Tiffany Jones," Mike recalled.

Thank you. Tiffany Jones, a student at DePaul who flaunted her scantily-clad butt around in that little red, white and blue outfit that you seemed to remember so fondly."

"Maybe so, but you saved me from all of the insanity," Mike replied.

"I saved our future marriage," Lisa said and took a sip of wine. "Anyway, I'll be at the Women's Center helping the girls tomorrow evening for a couple hours."

"Well, how about you show me some new moves tonight," Mike suggested seductively.

"You sure you don't want Tiffany Jones?" Lisa joked as she raised a steaming spoonful of gumbo to her lips.

"I'm sure," Mike said and shook his head, trying not to laugh. He had regretted ever mentioning the red, white and blue cheerleading outfit by mistake, but he knew that his wife's attitude was all in fun. She knew better than to ever feel insecure or threatened, especially in regard to college memories. He was all hers . . . mind, body, and soul.

"How was your day?" Lisa said finally.

"Busy," Mike said simply.

"Sounds like job security to me," Lisa said.

"I guess you can look at it that way, but the constant turnover of business, and the rise in real estate sales equal job security. Renovations are running neck and neck with construction, and our work does not drop off in the winter months which are a good thing," Mike said.

"Well, we both know how much you love your work, so don't even attempt to complain," Lisa said.

"True. I'd rather be busy than bored any day," Mike said.

"Exactly," Lisa remarked.

"By the way, Tom wants me to go look at a building with him tomorrow afternoon. The firm is planning on purchasing another office, and I think they've narrowed it down to two possibilities," Mike informed.

"We better not let Jason find out too soon that he'll have the entire house to himself for a few hours. I don't want to give him enough time to make any plans," Lisa said.

"Good point," Mike said.

"So you still think my mother is a witch? I'm not letting you off the hook that easy," Lisa said.

"I'm sorry, babe. How can I make it up to you?" Mike said.

Lisa's eyes were averted. "A new Jag would be nice," she said and looked sharply to him.

"Consider it done," Mike said and smiled. He reached inside his shirt pocket and handed Lisa a set of car keys to the new Jag. *"Happy Anniversary!"* he said.

"Happy Anniversary!" Lisa said and licked the spoon provocatively. How about I take you for a nice long ride? And I'm not talking about in my new car," she said. Mike drooled as he slowly moved his bowl of gumbo aside.

"Finished," Mike said as they locked their eyes on each other. After a moment, they both jumped up from the table and made a quick dash out the kitchen, upstairs and to their bedroom.

* * *

Lisa had pulled into the Women's Center's parking lot just as the cheerleading squad spilled out of a Dodge Grand Caravan and a mid-sized sedan. She counted eleven girls in all as she walked

135

across the parking lot and greeted them with a duffel bag and boom box in tow.

"Hi, I'm Lisa," she said. "Which one of you is Wendy?"

"I'm Wendy," one of the girls said and stepped forward to greet Lisa personally.

"It's nice to finally meet you. Your grandmother has told me so many good things about you," Lisa said.

"Thanks. This is Anna, Marie, Tonya, Kim, Nikki, Tracie, Robyn, Lynn, LaKeisha, and Vanessa," Wendy introduced as each girl waved at the mention of their name.

"Well, if you girls are ready to get started, follow me into the gym," Lisa said.

Lisa started walking toward the gymnasium with Wendy alongside her rambling on about how glad she was that she could help them out. Wendy had begun to describe some of the new cheerleading routines to Lisa when she heard giggling from behind.

"What are you girls giggling at?" Lisa asked as she turned around to face the rest of the cheerleading squad.

"Don't mind them," Tonya said and rolled her eyes.

"We were just telling Tonya that she has a secret admirer hiding over there," Nikki said and pointed near the rear of the building. "He was right there just a second ago."

"I saw him too. He looked old," LaKeisha said.

"Yeah. An old weirdo," Kim added.

"Ladies, let's be nice. That was probably Old Man Preston. He's the custodian. And besides, with eleven beautiful young girls parading through the parking lot, who could blame him for peeping around the building," Lisa said.

"There are twelve of us, including you," Vanessa corrected as the girls all giggled once again.

Once inside the gymnasium, Lisa led them directly to the locker room, where they could change into their cheerleading outfits.

"Here, this is for you, "Wendy said and handed Lisa a gift bag.

"What's this?" Lisa asked curiously.

"Open it and see," Wendy said anxiously.

Lisa opened the bag and pulled out a cheerleading outfit.

"Nanna told me you could probably fit it, so we thought maybe you'd like to wear it and have some fun with us."

"*Power colors!* Thanks, girls," Lisa said and held the red, white and black skirt up to her waist.

A few minutes later, they were all in the gym, going through routine after routine. For the most part, Lisa was just looking on from the sideline, but she also found herself demonstrating quite a few cheers from back in the day. The girls loved them and ended up incorporating some of the old with the new, coming up with fresh new routines. Two hours later, they were all exhausted and sprawled out on the floor catching their breath. Lisa, a fan of all aerobic activity, had actually enjoyed herself. It brought back fond memories.

"Hey, I think we may have some bottled water in the fridge," Lisa said and rose to her feet. "I'll go check. I can't have you girls getting dehydrated on me."

"I'll go with you," Tonya volunteered. She and Lisa started walking toward the direction of the center's faculty lounge.

Lisa pulled an opened case of bottled spring water out of the refrigerator. Conveniently, there were twelve bottles packed in the cardboard and plastic. They returned to the gym to find the girls huddled in one big circle, talking and giggling.

Lisa and Tonya passed the bottles of water around and joined the circle, while they all cooled down from their practice.

"Lisa, we can't thank you enough for helping us out," Wendy said.

"You already have," Lisa replied. "I've enjoyed taking a stroll down memory lane."

"You still have it, and you looked fabulous in the cheerleading outfit," Wendy complimented as the other girls nodded in agreement.

"Thank you. I wonder what my husband would think," Lisa said and smiled at the thought as the girls giggled and blushed with embarrassment. "Okay, ladies, why don't you go hit the showers while I trash these water bottles."

The squad stood up, filed out of the gymnasium and headed toward the locker room.

Lisa wiped some perspiration from her brow with one side of a white towel wrapped around her neck. She swallowed the last of water from her own bottle before collecting the empty ones, which were staggered across the floor like a set of discombobulated bowling pins. Lisa used the same cardboard box they were packed in to taxi the empty bottles.

Lisa exited the gymnasium and walked past the locker room, where the sound of giggling teenage girls was clearly audible. After exiting the double doors to the back hallway, she made a mental note to be sure to have the custodian, Old Man Preston, as he's commonly known and referred to, whose real name was Harry Preston, to apply some WD-40 to the door's squeaky hinges that whined so miserably behind her as she ascended down the dimly lit corridor with her box of recyclables. Trying to maintain her balance, she shifted the weight of the gym bag back up on her right shoulder as she emptied the box's contents into the bin marked "RECYCLABLE PLASTICS." After the last bottle fell into the recycle bin, she heard a shuffling noise coming from a dark corner at that the end of the corridor. Now with dread and shuddering from the thought of a mouse or, even worse, a rat, Lisa quickly tossed the empty box in the bin that collected paper and cardboard. She turned around and walked briskly toward the squeaky double doors and away from the idea of a rat in a nearby pile of large garbage bags.

Out of nowhere, Lisa was abruptly lifted from behind, and then thrown onto the pile of large garbage bags near the wall. She was being attacked. Although she tried to scream, nothing had come out but muffled groans, as a result of the coarse hand clamped tightly over her mouth. Lisa could not make out her attacker, but she was assured that it wasn't a mere prank or joke when she saw a glistening blade from what appeared to be a knife put to her throat.

"Shut the fuck up and do exactly what I tell you! Hell, you just might enjoy it," a silhouetted figure said, his funky breath hot on her ear. He looked over his shoulder toward the double doors to make sure nobody had witnessed or heard anything.

Lisa's resistance subsided as she shook her head from side to side, pleaded silently with the threatening figure. All she could think of was the fact that she was about to be raped, and stabbed to death. With the attacker's filthy hand pressed tightly against her mouth, she tried her best to think of something to do. With the knife still at her throat, an overwhelming feeling of helplessness caused tears of rage and anger to well up in her eyes. She ceased resisting completely, but continued thinking frantically.

"Yeah, now that's the idea. Be a good girl, and you won't get hurt," the attacker said and moved his face into a stream of light just enough for Lisa to make mental note of his rugged Caucasian features. His face made her stomach clench even tighter in a knot, but she swallowed and shook free of the attacker's silencing hand.

"If you scream, bitch, I'll cut your fuckin' throat. You got that? the attacker threatened and forcefully jerked Lisa by the neck.

Lisa coughed and nodded, giving an okay sign. She tried her best to offer up a reassuring smile, while attempting to bide a little more time.

"Is it true?" the attacker asked with a sly grin.

"Is what true?" Lisa said.

"The darker the cherry--I mean berry, the sweeter the juice?" the attacker chuckled at his non-accidental Freudian slip as he secured the knife and put it in his back pocket with one hand, while using his other hand to restrain her by both of her wrists above her head.

"My husband thinks so," Lisa said in a surprisingly calm voice that even shocked her attacker who took a moment to look her in the face as if he couldn't believe that she'd actually spoken so calmly.

"Is that right? Well now, my little sexual chocolate fantasy, there's only one way to find out," the attacker whispered as he'd begun to unfasten his pants.

More tears had rolled down Lisa's face at the thought of being raped, but she quickly shook the thought out of her head and tried to stay focused.

"L-let me help you with that," Lisa stuttered as she peered down at her attacker's crotch.

The attacker thick and bushy eyebrows arched in great suspicion as he squinted through his gray eyes, as if to detect a trick of some sort. Lisa tried to reassure him with a forced smile.

"Didn't you tell me to be a good girl?" Lisa said in a more cool, calm and collected voice. "Honestly, I've been curious to know what it's like to be with a bad boy, a rugged white man, and have his sweet cream in my steamy hot cup of black coffee."

"Now that's what I'm talking about," the attacker said as he retrieved the knife from his back pocket, freed Lisa's hands and waived the knife in her face. "Don't try anything funny, you hear?"

"Yeah, baby, I hear you," Lisa said calmly. "I'm a good girl," she said seductively as she pulled down his pants and dingy white boxers to his knees.

Somewhat suspicious of Lisa's willingness to fully cooperate, the attacker laughed excitedly, but remained cautious or on guard as she had taken his semi-erect penis into her left hand and begun to gently strokes it.

William Jaman Taylor

"Tell your sexual chocolate fantasy what you desire," Lisa asked, still in a seductive voice as she felt that she had gained some control over the situation, but still fully aware that her attacker had a knife. Lisa had no intentions of allowing him to rape and leaves her for dead.

The attacker laughed more excitedly. I want some of your chocolate kitty cat," he said.

Lisa was trying her best to maintain her composure, but she feared she couldn't go on with the charade too much longer, and she knew she had to do something fast.

"So you want some of my chocolate kitty cat, huh?" Lisa asked and noticed that her attacker had allowed his hand brandishing the knife to drop to his side. The attacker's smile grew wide and curious, his excitement holding him in a state of near hysteria.

"Oh, yeah," the attacker said excitedly as he nodded.

"I just want you to know that this is going to be the fuck of your life. One you'll never forget," Lisa said and stepped out of her panties, lowered her body to the floor, spreading her legs, exposing her chocolate kitty cat. In her same soft and seductive voice, she said, "Come and get it!"

"Kitty cat, kitty cat, here I come," the attacker said and drooled as he pulled his pants and boxers down to his ankles, and was about to step out of them.

The attacker's expression barely had a chance to change to confused bewilderment before Lisa got a good grip on his fully erect penis and tried her best to cause serious injury. The attacker immediately keeled over, released an agonizing howl as he tightly clutched his aching groin area with both hands. Lisa's adrenaline was rushing, with the thought of fiercely fighting off her attacker, she quickly pulled up her panties, and followed up with a forceful kick to his already throbbing groin area that sent him doubling over. The attacker's howl had now suddenly changed to a choking and gurgled cough that made him sound like a farm animal being slaughtered. Lisa had leaned back on her elbows and managed to propel herself to her feet, never once took her eyes off of her attacker, who was now against the opposite wall curled up in a fetal-like position.

"You dirty son-of-a-bitch!" an enraged Lisa shouted before she spat on her attacker as he howled and rolled around in pain. Out of breath, adrenaline still rushing, Lisa issued a number of angry vulgarities. Her words were followed by a muffled thud as her right Nike sneaker connected with the attacker's stomach.

"You crazy bitch, I'm gonna --"

"Do what? Rape me? Cut my throat? You have some nerve, you fucking lowlife. I'm about to show you a crazy bitch," Lisa interjected as she spun around, searched the shadowed floor for the attacker's knife, leaving him trying desperately to pull himself up against the wall.

Once Lisa found the knife, she spun around once again, brandishing the weapon that had been used to subdue her a few minutes earlier. Whatever her intentions, they were thwarted when she spotted the attacker's silhouette figure stumbling clumsily, but quickly out of the exit door where she had previously heard the shuffling noise.

"Just as I thought, a big fuckin' rat," Lisa said, short of breath.

Lisa let out an angry cry as she pressed her back against the wall and slid down it.

Seconds later, another strange man appeared.

"Ma'am, are you all right?" the strange man asked and placed a hand on her left shoulder.

"Get the fuck away from me," Lisa cried out in a crazed tone and swung the knife aimlessly and wildly into the air.

"Everything's fine now. I'm Preston . . . the janitor here. I'm here to help you," he assured in a calm and caring voice.

"He tried to rape me," Lisa cried out as she tried to stand up.

142

"Here, let me help you," Old Man Preston offered in a caring and sincere voice, extended his right hand and helped Lisa to her feet. Afterwards, he carefully and gently removed the knife from Lisa's shaky right hand.

After retrieving her gym bag from the nearby pile of garbage bags, Lisa straightened out her clothes and brushed herself off and begun walking angrily toward the double doors, heading into the gymnasium. She knew she looked a mess, and she could still smell the stench of her attacker on her clothes and skin, but she knew she had to go check on the girls. On top of that, she had a pulsating headache that would not stop. Lisa had unzipped and reached into the bottom of her gym bag for her cellular phone, which she found just as she entered the gymnasium. She pressed down the red "9" button until "911" appeared on the display screen.

"Oh, God! What happened, Lisa? Wendy screeched and clutched her face, with both hands, as she exited the locker room with the rest of the cheerleading squad close behind.

Lisa raised a finger to quiet the panicking girls, but her hand seemed to go automatically to her throbbing temples. Just then, the 911 operator answered as the cheerleading squad surrounded her, murmured and chattered amongst themselves.

"My name is Lisa Taylor, I'm at the Women's Center off Goebbert Road, and I was just attacked. Please send the police here as soon as possible," she said in a trembling voice.

Looking down at her shoes, and massaging her right ankle with her other free hand, Lisa quickly forgot that the girls were all standing around until she heard about eleven separate gasps, followed by hushed-panicked chattering.

"No, he got away, and aside from a sore ankle and headache I'm fine. I want this bastard caught and off the streets, before he attacks someone else. Please hurry!" Lisa said in a commanding manner so loud that the girls continued their gasped.

Lisa thanked the 911 operator, and then pressed the "End" button a split-second before being bombarded by a litany of questions and concerns from the cheerleading squad.

"Girls, girls, girls . . . I'm fine. I just need a moment to make another phone call, so just stand here for a moment until I'm done," Lisa said and offered a reassuring smile that caused her temples to ache even more. "There's absolutely nothing to worry about, but I appreciate your concerns. I do think you all should wait here until the policemen arrive before any of us leave," she added.

"Lisa, I am so sorry," Wendy said, with the rest of the girls joining in consensus.

Lisa shook her head and attempted another reassuring smile as the girls stood and chatted. Lisa quickly dialed Mike's cellular phone, but she ended the call when she heard his familiar voice mail greeting.

"How in the hell do I put this in a voice mail?" Lisa mumbled to herself, her eyes averted. She stuffed the phone back into her gym bag.

Less than five minutes later, two uniformed police officers found their way into the gymnasium, followed by a female detective, butch, fortyish, stocky build, short-cropped haircut with strong features and dressed in a masculine business suit. Lisa started walking in their direction as the girls had become silent and attentive.

"Are you Mrs. Lisa Taylor?" the detective asked.

"Yes," Lisa replied.

"Mrs. Taylor, I'm Detective Sharon Stephens," she said, flashed a badge, showed her credentials and tucked it inside her jacket pocket. "And these are officers John Patrelli and Frank Rosario," she introduced the two uniformed officers and produced a pen and small pad from her jacket pocket. "I have a few questions to ask. This may be difficult for you," she added.

144

"Okay," Lisa sighed and nodded.

"Were you sexually assaulted? Detective Stephens asked bluntly.

"No." Lisa said and shook her head. "It happened so fast," she answered, before relaying the entire story to the detective, who jotted down some notes, then requested to see the areas or locations the assault had occurred. A forensic evidence technician walked up and proceeded to check for any potential evidence. The two officers stood by as the forensic evidence technician dusted the exit door in the corridor for fingerprints. Old Man Preston stood nearby as well as the detective questioned and spoke further with Lisa.

"I must say, you're a lucky woman. Five other women were recently attacked in the area. They were not so lucky.

"That's comforting to know," Lisa said as she rubbed her arms.

"I need you to come to the station and look at some photos, to see if you can make a positive ID," Detective Stephens said.

"Right now! Can't this wait until in the morning? I want my husband there with me," Lisa pleaded.

"I'd rather you come now while the perpetrator's face is still fresh in your mind. I want you to meet with a police sketch artist," Detective Stephens suggested.

"I can assure you, detective; I'm like a super recognizer. I don't forget a face. I'm also an artist. I can produce a sketch and have it for you first thing in the morning," Lisa said.

The detective looked reluctantly down the corridor toward the officers, then back to her and handed her a card.

"Tomorrow it is. I want you and your husband at the station first thing in the morning. Nine o'clock sharp!" Detective Stephens said.

"Thank you, detective," Lisa said and released a sigh of relief as she looked at the card.

The detective looked Lisa up and down, produced a lecherous

smile. Lisa looked up, does a double take at the detective.

"Be sure to bring your sketch, and we'll see what we can do with it. We've already registered an APB, so we'll be on the lookout for the perpetrator. I'm going to see if my officers are almost done so that everyone gets escorted safely to their vehicles," Detective Stephens said, turned and walked toward the officers.

"Thank you, detective," Lisa said as she walked with a slight limp back into the gymnasium and noticed the girls had become silent once again. "All right, ladies, we've all had an eventful evening. Let's get ready to leave," she said and limped slightly toward the girls with her hands clasped in front of her.

"Lisa, he didn't . . . you know? He didn't do it, did he?" Wendy managed to ask skeptically as the other girls seemed to have leaned in closer for the answer.

"Nothing happened," Lisa said and rolled her eyes playfully.

"This is our fault," Kim said.

"What? Why would you say that?" Lisa said in a concerned maternal tone.

"I mean, if we didn't have cheerleading practice, none of this would have happened," Kim explained.

"Look, girls, you mustn't go blaming yourselves. It's not anyone's fault," Lisa assured. "Understood?"

"Yeah," the entire squad mumbled and nodded in apparent agreement.

"I hope all of this excitement hasn't caused you all to forget the new routines that I've taught you," Lisa said and looked at the entire squad, feeling their acceptance as they smiled.

"Thanks again, Lisa," Wendy said as she and the entire cheerleading squad hugged Lisa. They were all still engaged in a group hug when the whining double doors announced the return of the detective, the two police officers and the forensic evidence technician.

"Okay, ladies, your escorts have arrived. Make sure you have all of your belongings," Detective Stephens said.

The entire cheerleading squad had begun filing out as Detective Stephens stopped Lisa and reiterated how important it was that she come to the station first thing in the morning. They all walked outside to the parking lot together. As Lisa stepped into her car and closed the door, she released a sigh of relief, realizing that the worst part was over. She pulled out of the parking lot and headed home. Old Man Preston closed and locked up the building for the evening.

Chapter 16

Approximately thirty minutes later, Lisa had returned home. Although her body seemed to ache for her husband's comforting embrace, she was a bit relieved to find their driveway absent of his vehicle. Lisa had planned on taking a shower immediately, followed by a hot bath. Even though she had not been raped, she couldn't imagine feeling any filthier if she had been. It seemed as if every time she turned slightly to the left, she would get an overwhelming whiff of her attacker's scent.

"Is the smell also in my hair?" Lisa wondered as she sucked her teeth, irritated by the thought that she had run out of shampoo a few days earlier, and had not had a chance to replace it yet.

Lisa stepped out of the car, with her duffel bag in tow, into the crisp night air, which was a welcomed relief to her nostrils that had been tortured by the lingering musty odor hiding in and around her clothing. She had to hit the shower quick. In fact, that was the first place Lisa headed after she'd stopped in the kitchen long enough to open a door that lead down to the basement, and tossed the duffel bag down into the dark depths. She'd planned on laundering everything, including the bag itself, the very next day. Lisa stripped down to her underwear and tossed the cheerleading outfit down to the dark depths to accompany the banished duffel bag. She raced upstairs to the master bedroom and then straight into the bathroom, making sure not to look at her reflection in the mirror. She didn't care to see herself at that moment. Lisa was sure the mirror would reveal a thick layer of filth that she had convinced herself her attacker had left on her. Everything would be better after the shower and bath combination.

Lisa opened the closet behind the bathroom door and searched for a bottle of shampoo that may have been overlooked a few days earlier. To her surprise, her hand fondled a half-used bottle of herbal shampoo, part of a gift basket that Mike had surprised her with some three or four months ago. The discovery of the shampoo bottle warranted a smile, which was followed by another smile brought on by the thought of how easily a simple thing, like a bottle of shampoo, could make you smile at the worst of times.

Lisa stepped out of her panties and wiggled out of her bra before sticking one arm into the shower stall to start the cleansing stream of hot water. She adjusted the water to just the right temperature, and stepped into the shower stall with the shampoo bottle in tow. Lisa allowed the water to run down her cocoa skin, dancing off the top of her head and hurdling over her brow, skiing down on her nose and lips. She set the bottle of shampoo next to a bottle of body wash that sat on the toiletry rack on the wall. Lisa had begun to lather her body almost violently, trying her best to scrub herself clean. She then retrieved the shampoo and massaged a generous amount of the soothing aromatic gel into her hair. Lisa soon thought about how wonderful Mike's hands felt massaging her scalp whenever he would treat her to one of his personal shampoos. She also thought about how she would tell Mike and Jason what happened, knowing that she couldn't possibly keep something like this from them. Not that she even wanted to conceal it, but she feared that it would enrage them even more than it had enraged her, and there was nothing she hated more than seeing the two upset. Too many worries invaded her shower, which was supposed to be a step toward relaxation. Lisa simply focused on rinsing her body and hair and prepping them both for a second lather.

When Lisa washed and rinsed once again in the shower stall, fit for and most comfortably utilized by two, she exited and quickly tip-toed across the bathroom floor toward the antique cast iron slipper claw foot bathtub. Instantly, she'd begun running the water a few degrees warmer than the preceding steamy hot shower into the tub. The bath was to replenish the moisture that her hot shower took away. She added some vanilla bath oil to the water before stepping in and sitting down. Lisa leaned her head back against the rim of the tub and closed her eyes, as the running water slowly envelope her body. The soothing vanilla aroma helped to relax her more, and she was then able to give some thought to how she would disclose the eventful evening to her family without her two men going ballistic and organizing their own vigilante manhunt. That thought brought to mind her very own composite sketch that she was supposed to produce for tomorrow morning's meeting with Detective Stephens. She allowed her body to sink a little deeper into the tub.

Lisa already felt a lot cleaner and she successfully managed to get her attacker's stench off of her body. She especially wanted to be clean when she informed Mike and Jason. The idea that another man had breathed and nearly drooled all over her body made her skin crawl. Not to mention the fact that she had stroked his penis. Lisa shuddered at the thought and once again sunk her body a little deeper into the tub. The water was up to her neck when she raised her foot to turn the knobs to cut off the water. Lisa leaned back and thought long and hard. She was proud of the way she handled the situation and was very thankful that she wasn't raped or even killed for that matter. Replaying the scenario in her head over and over, she found herself giggling out loud as she remembered her attacker thought he was about to get some. It was small and shriveled like a Vienna sausage. Not a foot-long hot dog.

"I haven't seen a pee-wee like that since I stopped bathing and dressing Jason," Lisa thought as she giggled some more, with her giggling eventually turning into a poker face followed by a deep sigh.

Lisa soaked for about ten more minutes before releasing the water from the tub and stepping out onto the plush bathroom mat, reached and grabbed a thick mint-green bath towel from a wall mounted 2-Tier wooden cabinet with an attached hotel style towel shelf rack complete with robe hooks.

After toweling herself dry, Lisa retrieved a silk kimono-style robe from off a hook. Ready to face herself, she wiped the condensation from the mirror, combed her hair and smiled at her reflection before leaving the bathroom and returning to the kitchen.

While making a calming cup of tea, a gentle blend of chamomile, lemon balm, and peppermint, she heard Mike pulling up in the driveway.

"Well, here goes nothing," Lisa mumbled.

Mike entered the kitchen and found Lisa, who sat numb at the breakfast table waiting patiently for the teapot to finish its task.

"Hey, babe," Mike said and planted a kiss on her lips. "*Mmmm!* Damn, you smell good."

Lisa produced a wry smile. "I knew you wouldn't come near me with a stench from helping the girls with their cheerleading routines."

"If you had on one of those cute little cheerleading outfits, it wouldn't matter what you smelled like," Mike said.

"Well, go take a whiff of my honorary cheerleading outfit, now residing in the basement, and then tell me if you want to reconsider," Lisa joked. "Hey, do you think Jason and Brad have made it back yet?"

"His car was parked in the driveway. I'm sure they're back and he's just hanging out over at the Martins," Mike said.

"Be a sweetheart and go get Jason for me. I need to have a talk with you two," Lisa said.

Mike was taken aback. He'd raised an eyebrow curiously as to what it could be, and used his hands to motion for her to give him a hint or a little more information.

"I want to tell you both at the same time. Please, you know how much I hate repeating myself. I just want to kill two birds with one stone. Would you go get Jason, please? This is very important,"

Lisa said, with a serious face.

"Is everything all right," Mike asked.

"Everything is fine; now go," Lisa commanded and nudged Mike forward.

All right, all right, I'll go get Jason," Mike said. He walked slowly as he looked back curiously at his wife, and then exited the kitchen.

A few minutes have passed. After taking a sip of tea, Lisa walked into the living room and assumed her most comfortable position on the sofa. She heard a series of beeps from the ADT unit door chimes to indicate that Mike and Jason had entered the foyer, and then into the living room.

"Pops said you wanted to talk to us," Jason said as he picked a throw pillow. He plopped down in the chair and hugged the pillow in front of his chest.

Hey, baby, how are you?" Lisa asked as Mike sat beside her, waiting patiently to hear the news.

"I'm fine. I think. So what is it that you want to talk to us about? Mike asked impatiently.

Lisa sighed and placed the mug on the coffee table. She looked visibly nervous as she looked to Jason, and then to Mike.

"You're pregnant? Jason asked.

"No, silly. Now don't you two get upset when I tell you this," Lisa said, took a deep breath and exhaled. "I was attacked at the Women's Center today," she said and noticed Mike and Jason with shocked faces. "I'm fine. It's no big deal."

"*What!*" Mike exclaimed, obviously very upset, and rocketed from off the sofa. "Attacked? What do you mean attacked?" he yelled." Are you all right?" he asked and plopped down next to his wife.

"Mike, baby, please calm down. I'm fine. Really, I'm all right," Lisa reassured him and grabbed his hand in hers to keep him from rocketing to his feet and raging on any further.

"No, Mom, it's not all right. Where's his punk-ass? I'll fuck him up," Jason mouthed and rocketed to his feet.

"Jason Lamar Taylor!" Lisa exclaimed sternly.

"Who is he? Where's the bastard?" Mike spouted off again.

Lisa squeezed his hand a little tighter and answered, "He's probably still somewhere with a bag of ice in his groin area," she said jokingly.

"Mom, this isn't a joke. It's serious. You could have been raped, seriously hurt or even killed for that matter," Jason said.

"And asking if I was pregnant wasn't a joke, huh?" Lisa said.

"That was before I knew the situation was this serious," Jason said.

"I know, baby. I'm sorry. Sometimes you have to laugh just to keep from crying. I know this is serious. I'm just so thankful that he was the one who injured instead of me," Lisa said.

"Why am I just now hearing about this?" Mike asked.

"I tried calling you, but I got your voicemail. I didn't know how to leave you a message. I didn't even know where to begin," Lisa said as she searched her husband's eyes for a hint of understanding.

"How about 'Mike, baby, I was attacked, and I need for you to come to the Women's Center'," Mike said angrily, as an example.

"Mike, now that's not fair, and you know it," Lisa said.

"Dad, Mom's right. The important thing is that she's all right. Mom, you have to be more careful. There are a bunch of weirdoes out there. Pops and I won't always be around to protect you. We love you," Jason said with a serious face, his eyes welled up as he leaned over and hugged his mother.

"I know. I love you both. And I'm not letting either of you go. Maybe you, Jason, but this one here," Lisa said and tugged Mike's hand, "he's here for life. No matter how mad he gets at me."

"That's all fine and dandy, but I don't want you going to the Women's Center anymore. I don't want anything to happen to

153

you," Mike explained.

"I don't want anything to happen to any of us either. My "Danger Stranger" instincts kicked into high gear, and if I have to scream, scratch, and kick some butt every now and then, so be it," Lisa said, making light of the situation, at the same time, meant every word of it. "By the way, does this mean I won't be getting my own art gallery?"

Jason sighed and shook his head. "Pops, she's all yours," he said and bolted upstairs.

"It's a crying shame," Mike said and dropped his head.

"What's that?" Lisa asked.

Mike looked up sharply. "We moved to this nice neighborhood only to have my wife attacked," he said, released a deep sigh and shook his head.

"All right, all right," Lisa said. "I see I'm going to have to put you to bed right now."

"Lisa, please be serious about this. Stop acting like it was nothing. Do you realize how serious this could have been? I don't know what I would do if something were to ever happen to you. I love you, Lisa. I don't want to lose you," Mike had confessed his dying love, his voice cracked with emotion.

With that being said, Lisa's eyes welled up. She cuddled into her man, buried her face into his chest, and cried herself a good cry. Mike accepted her onto his chest and gently massaged and rubbed her back. He decided not to say anything else. Mike was just glad she was all right.

Moments later, Mike took Lisa by the hand, and escorted her upstairs. They leaned against the banister, their left hands on the smooth polished oak as they scaled the staircase.

At the top of the stairs, they went left to their bedroom. Mike and Lisa sat on the bed. He held and reassured her that his duties as a husband were to be a provider as well as a protector. After Lisa's sobbing had subsided, she told Mike all about Detective

Stephens, and their nine o'clock appointment in the morning. They made plans to leave out as soon as she produced the composite sketch. Even though Mike tried to convince Lisa to sketch it that night, while the attacker's face was still clear in her head, she was able to assure him with the same response she gave to Detective Stephens. The attacker's face would be fresh and clear, in her mind, for quite some time.

Chapter 17

Since Lisa's attack, time seemed to have just flown by. She tried to get her life back to normal by staying very busy, in an attempt to keep her mind off of what had happened. In addition to working with Rachel to prepare for their sons' graduation, Lisa also preoccupied some of her free-time by helping the cheerleaders prepare for a citywide cheerleading competition. When Lisa would walked in or out the door of the Women's Center, she took particular notice of two small nails positioned vertically on one of the tall white pillars that made up the building's Greek Revival façade. The nails themselves seemed to be simple and harmless enough; showing speckles of rust, but Lisa looked at them and allowed her mind to present something more in depth. The nails to her were a constant reminder of the reason they had been hammered into the cylindrical wooden posts in the first place. They once held up a copy of the police notice regarding her attacker, complete with her very own composite sketch. Joan had pleaded with Lisa to have the composite sketch posted somewhere else so it would not be a constant reminder every time she'd come to the Women's Center, but Lisa could think of no better place where it could serve its purpose better, so it stayed. The nails remained and served as a constant reminder to her, and as a warning to others.

As for Mike, weeks after finally receiving word that his division was granted the Burkeman contract, he'd been very busy, aside from all the other projects that he and his division were working on. Burkeman and Son, Inc. went as far as surprising Mike with a very hefty bonus, which Mike had put toward the new Jag, for Lisa's anniversary gift. Almost five months after she and Mike made their early morning trip to the police precinct to deliver Lisa's sketch and speak further with Detective Stephens, she received a phone call that presented a bitter-sweet relief to the

156

small element of fear she had not been able to shake from the back of her mind. Lisa recognized Detective Stephens' matter-of-fact tone almost immediately. She said that a man, closely fitting the description of the composite Lisa had drawn, was struck and killed by a tractor trailer as he tried to evade two police officers on foot. Detective Stephens went on to disclose that the man had been pursued in connection to another female attack, which took place at a rest stop, in Elk Grove Village, less than twenty minutes away from the Women's Center. She asked Lisa to come to the morgue to identify the man. Lisa's mind was set to rest as she identified the man, William Jack Smith, as her attacker.

On June 4, 1999, Lisa and Mike sat proudly beside Rachel and Tom as they all watched their sons' high school commencement ceremonies. Both sets of parents shared a feeling of great accomplishment as they watched Jason and Brad receive their diplomas. At that time, Lisa was dealing with her anxiety about sending her son off to college, but Mike had tried his best to reassure her that Jason would be just fine. The ensuing rainstorm that had provided several inches of water over the metropolitan area had forced the outside ceremony, intended for the stadium, inside the much smaller gymnasium. Being that the gymnasium offered limited seating, in respect to the city's fire code, all family aside from parents were accommodated in a nearby auditorium, which displayed the ceremony on a giant-screen television. Of course, Maddie and Jon were watching their grandson walk across the stage, looking ten feet tall on the big screen. Although Lisa wished that her parents could have been seated inside the gymnasium with them, she was thankful that she would be spared her mother's continuous discussion of how attending Aurora University would be an outright mistake. Still, she offered no other substantial reasoning outside of her gut feeling. It turned out that both Jason and Brad decided on attending Aurora University, which was a welcomed decision for Lisa who felt a little more at ease knowing her "Pookie," as Jason was affectionately called, wasn't going to be far away from home.

* * *

Months later, now in the middle of their sons' first semester as sophomores, the Taylor and Martins had planned a trip to the campus to visit them. Lisa was deep in thought about their afternoon trip as she left the Women's Center. Still, she did not cease her volunteer work there. But instead, Lisa took on an additional load. She agreed to instruct an aerobics class as well, in spite of the attack. Lisa wanted to prove to herself that she was strong enough to handle it and she did.

Jason and Brad's parents arrived in front of their dorm apartment around five. They all left Arlington Heights as soon as Lisa returned from dropping off some new art supplies at the Women's Center. Then of course, she had to quickly get Jason's care package together, making sure all of his favorite goodies that would help him get through the late night cram sessions for exams and finals were packed.

The trip usually took a little over an hour, but with Tom behind the wheel, they made it to the campus in record time forty-five minutes flat.

"How fast were you driving? Lisa asked.

"I was going the speed limit, of course. You know, as a lawyer, I am sworn to uphold the law," Tom joked.

Tom arrived on campus and immediately looked for Marseillaise Place, building 13. Once he found Jason and Brad's apartment, Tom parked; everyone exited the car and headed directly to the apartment. They didn't even have a chance to knock before Brad swung the door open and greeted them with a welcoming smile and hugs. Jason, engaged in some last-minute tidying up, soon joined them.

"This is an unusual layout," Lisa said as she looked around the apartment.

Everyone stood in the middle of a large bedroom, the right side being obviously occupied by Jason with baseball caps adorning the wall, DJ equipment and records stacked in the corner.

"I don't know why you two didn't get a two-bedroom dorm apartment," Rachel said.

"Well, it was first come first serve," Jason replied.

"Yeah, Mom, the two-bedroom apartments went to the students who pre-registered," Brad added.

They all followed Lisa as she walked further into the apartment toward the study area directly behind the bedroom.

"Has anyone tried to pry this sliding door open?" Lisa asked as she examined the study quad's glass door that lead outside.

"Nope," Jason answered.

"If anyone tried to, that's what my baseball bat is for," Brad said and picked it up, swung it wildly through the air.

"This is my bat. The one I gave you has my initials 'JT' on the bottom of it. Where is it?" Jason asked.

"It's in the trunk of my car, "Brad said.

Mike looked at Brad and Jason. "Are you guys hungry?" he asked.

"A little," Brad said. Jason nodded in agreement.

"If you guys can lead the way to a good restaurant, then we'll follow you. Our treat," Tom suggested.

"We can take one car," Brad said.

"Who drove?" Jason asked.

"I did," Tom said.

"Dad, your car is more-than spacious. It can easily seat six passengers very comfortably," Brad assured.

"Y'all are on campus now, so we have to travel college style," Jason said.

"What's college style?" Rachel shrugged.

"That's when everyone has crammed into one car like sardines," Brad said as he and Jason laughed.

Moments later, everyone was seated comfortably into Tom's car, with Tom, Brad and Mike in front, Rachel, Lisa and Jason in the back.

Minutes later, both families arrived at Red Lobster. An hour or so had passed, and everyone had enjoyed a pretty good seafood dinner. During dinner, Lisa and Rachel had managed to talk their husbands into going shopping at the nearby Westfield Fox Valley Mall. Brad and Jason were given credit cards as graduation gifts and had proven to be surprisingly responsible with their spending. So after dinner, they all ended up at mall, buying Jason and Brad new sneakers. By the time dusk approached, the parents were ready to say their goodbyes.

Once Tom drove off, Jason and Brad dashed into the apartment.

"Man, I thought they'd never leave," Brad said as he grabbed an iron and begun to press the wrinkles out of a white bed sheet.

"Yeah, I know," Jason agreed and frenetically stripped down to his underwear.

"We've only missed about thirty minutes of Toga Jam 2000," Brad said.

"We're sophomores. And you know what that means . . . no more curfews!" Jason exclaimed.

"You know it," Brad agreed and gave Jason a hi-five.

"*Ouch!*" Jason exclaimed and winced after he stubbed his toe painfully on the bedpost.

"Damn, man, you all right?" Brad chuckled. "That's the second time this week you've done that," he said.

"Shut up and go take a shower," Jason said, still wincing.

Jason and Brad took turns taking quick showers before trying to come up with their own unique toga designs. Upon arriving at the student union, which was reserved for Toga Jam 2000, they both noticed that out of the two hundred or more students, very few were actually dancing.

"What's with this? Everyone's just standing around looking bored," Brad said over the loud music.

"That's because we have an unskilled DJ in our midst," Jason said and immediately looked for the DJ booth.

"Luckily, the boring party hasn't driven the ladies away," Brad said and smiled as two females walked by.

"Hold that thought," Jason said as he spotted the DJ booth, and made his way through the meandering crowd.

"I don't take requests," the DJ said before Jason could get a word out.

"I didn't come to make a request. I'm a DJ as well. I was just wondering if I could spin for . . . let's say an hour or two. You know . . . give you a chance to mingle with some of these fine ladies just standing around," Jason said.

The DJ looked at Jason skeptically for a moment before looking past him into the meandering crowd, and realized that many partygoers were not dancing.

"You have your own music?" the DJ asked.

"I can run back to the dorm and get some. I'm just a couple minutes away," Jason said.

"That's cool. As you can see, this crowd isn't in much of a party mood," the DJ said.

"Well, I'll see if I can do something about that," Jason said.

The DJ grinned and shook his head. "Good luck. Where are you from?" he asked.

"I'm from Chi-Town," Jason said. "I'm Jason. Where are you from?" he asked and extended his hand.

"Chris Brooks. I'm from St. Louis," he said and shook Jason's hand.

"Oh," Jason said with a 'that explains it' expression on his face.

"Well, you can go get your music. Perhaps I've been keeping the lovely ladies waiting too long," Chris boasted.

"Cool. I'll be back in a minute," Jason said as turned and weaved through the meandering crowd.

Within minutes, Jason returned to the DJ booth, carrying a crate of vinyl records.

"All right, my man, let's see what you got," Chris said as he leaned in closer to the microphone to announce his departure. "All right, you squares, I'm about to turn it over to DJ Jason from Chicago," he announced.

Chris stepped down from the DJ booth and handed Jason a pair of headphones. Jason dug through his crate of music, pulled out a 12 inch record, put it on the turntable, cued and blended in a slamming house track, with a 4/4 or four-on-the-floor kick, a snare drum sound on beats two and four of every bar, and a booming bass line that brought the partygoers instantly into hysterics. Everyone moved in sync to the rhythm, as they flocked to the dance floor.

Approximately thirty minutes later, Jason was in the process of blending in another track when a male and two females approached the DJ booth.

"Thanks, man," the male said.

"What for?" Jason said.

"You saved my party. The Lamda Fraternity, Incorporated, has a reputation to uphold on campus. I haven't heard house music like this since I left my hometown, in Detroit, this past winter. I'm Eric Mitchell, president and pledge master," he introduced.

"I'm Jason Taylor," Jason replied, still preoccupied with his mix.

"Are you a sophomore?" Eric asked.

"Yes," Jason said.

"Have you considered pledging a fraternity?" Eric asked.

162

"I've thought about it," Jason said.

"Why don't you consider looking into our fraternity? By the way, these two lovely ladies are Lamda sweethearts. On my right is Tasha, and on my left is Deedra. They help out in all our fundraising events and parties," Eric said and hugged both females.

"Damn! Can I join now?" Jason joked as he surveyed the smiling beauties.

"Not until this coming fall semester," Eric chuckled.

"We're having a recruitment meeting Monday evening at six in the Smith Hall Building. Information will be provided to all of our prospective pledges for the coming fall. You're welcome to attend," Eric said and handed Jason a pamphlet. "Read over it. If you're interested, I expect to see you on Monday.

"Thanks. I'll be there," Jason said.

"Good. Hopefully, you'll make the cut and go on line in September. But for now, just keep my party jumping," Eric said as he and the two females slipped back into the dancing crowd.

An hour had passed and Jason had begun to blend in a track when a cute female walked up to him and smiled.

"Do you take requests?" the female asked.

"I do now," Jason beamed.

"I'm Janaya."

"Jason."

"Is your girlfriend here?" Janaya asked.

"Well, uh . . . yes. I mean no," Jason said.

"Which is it?" Janaya shrugged.

"We tried doing the long distant thing. I came to AU and she went to Michigan State. We were too far apart. It just didn't work out," Jason said.

Janaya slipped Jason her phone number. "Call me. I have to leave. I have a lab class in the morning. I would love to stay and dance with you, but I'll settle for a private one at a later date," she said and strutted off, exited through a set of double doors.

By now, Jason, was ready to do a little mingling himself and turned the booth back over to DJ Chris a little before midnight.

Just as he expected, the floor had become almost empty once Chris took over again, but Jason didn't care. He felt he'd done his job, at least making it known that there was some better house music other than break beats Chris had been mixing earlier that evening. Jason spotted Brad and trotted up next to him.

"Yo, Brad, man, I had the party jumpin'. Did you see that fine-ass girl I was talking to?" Jason boasted.

"Brag to someone else," Brad said dryly, shook his head and walked off. He headed toward the set of double doors, and burst through them almost collided with people entering. A partygoer had thrown up both hands to suggest, "Dude, what's your freakin' problem?"

Not feeling up to partying anymore, Jason gathered his crate of records and decided to head back to the dorm as well. Minutes later, he returned and found Brad as he sat in front of his computer, and surfed the web.

"Brad, what was that all about?" Jason asked as he took a seat on the edge of his bed.

Brad spun around in his chair. "Come on, man, don't even try to play me. You know whassup," he said.

"Well, let's just pretend that I don't. How about you try to break it down for me," Jason said.

"For one, I don't particularly like it when you started rubbing your popularity in my face. You basically ditched me as soon as we got to the party, so you could single-handedly pack the dance floor, and be Mr. DJ hero to the rescue. And, to top it all off, you just had to brag about the fine-ass girl you met. What kinda friend are you?" Brad asked, obviously upset.

"Look, Brad, you are seriously buggin'," Jason said.

"Oh, I'm buggin'? I guess since the playboy said it, then it must be true!" Brad shouted as he stormed out of the apartment, and slammed the door shut behind him. Jason stood motionless, in total disbelief.

Chapter 18

Brad walked across the college campus. It was awash with people. The campus was just as alive as on any typical Friday night, and Brad soon found himself coming on yet another fraternity party. A little mentally exhausted from his anger and frustration, he took a seat on a bench across the street from a fraternity house, watching as people filtered in and out.

A female, around twenty, strikingly beautiful, walked up to him.

"Why is a good-looking guy sitting here all alone?" the female asked.

"Are you talking to me?" Brad asked.

"There's no one else sitting here," the female said.

"I just needed some fresh air," Brad said, a little discontent.

"I'm Lana, by the way," she introduced herself, sat on the bench next to him, and offered a hand.

"I'm Brad," he said and shook her hand. "Why is a pretty girl out at night all alone?"

"I just left a rush party. I needed some fresh air myself," Lana said.

"A rush party?" Brad said.

"The frat's recruiting new members," Lana said and looked in the direction of the frat house as individual filtered in and out. Some stood and talked on the steps. Others danced and quaffed down beers.

"What fraternity?" Brad asked.

"That's the K T N frat house. I'm a sweetheart. We help them out with parties and fundraisers. Things like that. Do you belong to a frat?" Lana said.

"No," Brad said.

"Have you thought about joining a fraternity?" Lana said.

"Not really," Brad said and shook his head.

Lana paused for a moment, thinking to herself. "I have an idea! Come with me to the party? I'll introduce you to all the frat members," she said.

"I wouldn't feel comfortable," Brad said skeptically and shook his head.

Lana stood up and pulled brad to his feet. "Come on. Other sweethearts have brought their boyfriends or dates," she said and kissed Brad on the cheek. "You can be my date. Are you comfortable now?"

"You're so pretty. You can have any guy you want," Brad said.

"I want you," Lana said, grabbed Brad by the hand, and tugged him along as she walked briskly toward the frat house.

Brad stopped Lana at the foot of the steps that lead up to the frat house.

"Are you sure it's all right?" Brad said, feeling unsure as they walked up the six steps and onto the porch.

"It'll be fine. Just relax," Lana said and smiled as they entered the frat house. "I want you to meet someone," she said.

Brad turned around. His eyes widen. Ted Ralston, the frat's president looked on, with a 1959/1960 University of Fayetteville, North Carolina's Yearbook, with a pamphlet tucked inside, and a book, *Spirit of '69: A Skinhead Bible* by George Marshall in tow.

"This is Ted. Ted, this is--" Lana said and was abruptly cut off mid-sentence.

"Brad Martin," Ted said.

"You two know each other?" Lana asked, taken by surprise.

"He was like family," Ted said as Lana turned and walked off. "We meet again. So, tell me, how was the trip to South Africa? he asked.

"News travel fast," Brad said.

"I was very disappointed in you, Martin. You let me down," Ted said.

"You knew the situation with my family," Brad said.

"The organization was your new family," Ted said in a hushed, panicked tone. He looked around, careful not to make or cause a scene. "Why are you here, huh? Is it because of Lana? She's hot. Isn't she? he said.

"We just met, and she invited me to the party," Brad said.

"You want to fuck her. Is that it, Martin?" Ted said.

"I want to join the fraternity," Brad said.

Ted folded his arms, with the yearbook and book. "Is that right?" he said.

"I'm serious," Brad said.

"People don't change, huh, Martin? Ted said.

"This is where I fit in," Brad said.

"So let me get this straight . . . you want to join the frat, right, Martin? Ted said.

"Right," Brad said.

"How do I know you're telling the truth this time?" Ted said and looked at him with narrow eyes.

"This is what I want. You have my word," Brad said.

"I had your word three years ago," Ted said and looked back at the now frat members, Chad, Zack and Josh, and frat sweetheart, Melissa, whom Brad had run afoul of back in his sophomore and junior high school years.

Chad extended his arms to suggest, "You got to be kidding me." Zack and Josh cocked their heads to the side to suggest, "Can you believe this fucking shit?" Melissa had thrown up both hands, turned and walked off to suggest, "Whatever, dudes. I'm so out of here."

Ted pondered a moment, and then said, "Tell you what . . . I'll let you join as the thirteenth pre-pledge member," he said and handed Brad the college yearbook and book. Brad viewed them, looked up at him, a sigh of relief.

"Thanks, man. You won't regret it," Brad said.

"Everything you need to know is in the book. You have one

week to read it and return it to me. Read the pamphlet too." Ted leaned in close and whispered into his ear, "Don't let me down again, Martin," he said.

"I won't. I swear," Brad said and shook his head convincingly.

Ted stared long and hard into his eyes. "Let me introduce you to your future family," he said as they walked off.

Chapter 19

On July 15th, a smothering dome of high pressure from Montana to Arizona has immersed the Mid-West in record-breaking temperatures, on an otherwise picture-perfect Saturday afternoon. The City of Chicago and Mayor Richard Daley hosted the 20th annual event The Taste of Chicago, and paying homage to Jesse Saunders and the Pioneers of House Music.

Jason and Brad were home for the summer vacation, both prepared to set out and enjoy The Taste of Chicago's annual food and music festival. It's the nation's premier outdoor food festival showcasing the diversity of the city's dining community. The delicious array of food served at The Taste of Chicago is complemented by music and activities for the entire family. People from different cities and states, cultures, and all walks of life ascended upon Chicago's beautiful Grant Park on the city's magnificent lakefront to enjoy a day of good food, non-stop music, rides, and celebration.

Lisa had surprised Jason and promised to let him borrow the Acura Legend for the evening. Jason took advantage of the offer and informed Brad immediately.

"Mom, how does my new cologne smell? I know I look good," Jason said as he flashed a big smile.

"It smells good. You look good too, I must admit," Lisa complimented and smiled, closing a magazine in hand.

"You diggin' the gear?" Jason asked and modeled his outfit.

"What I am not digging is your jersey unbuttoned and your bare chest exposed. Here, button this thing up," Lisa said as she buttoned up Jason's Chicago Cubs jersey.

"Mom, no! I wanna be a hot boy. I've got to show the ladies my assets," Jason said as he stuck out his buttocks, and begun to unbutton the two buttons that Lisa had buttoned up.

DING DONG!
DING DONG!
DING DONG!

"How about you and your assets go get the door," Lisa said and looked up before returning to her magazine on the living room sofa.

"Whassup, bro? Oh hell no! Check out my boy's gear. Sweet," Brad said and complimented Jason's outfit.

"I heard that," Lisa yelled.

Brad cleared his throat and apologized. "Sorry. Hello, Mrs. Taylor."

"Damn! Your outfit is tight too," Jason said as he complimented Brad's outfit.

"I heard that too," Lisa yelled again.

"My bad," Jason apologized.

"Are we ready to roll?" Brad asked from the foyer.

"As soon as the best mom in the whole wide world hands over the car keys," Jason said, purposely loud enough for her to hear. He soon reappeared in the archway of the living room.

Lisa, still seated on the sofa, tossed him the keys without looking up from the article she was reading.

"Mom, I was just wondering, why are you letting me drive the car before my twentieth birthday?"

"I'm not going to beat around the bush," Lisa said and rested the magazine on the cushion beside her. "It's a test. Whether you pass it or not, will determine if you return to campus next semester with your own car, as a birthday gift, now that I have a new one," she said.

Jason smiled from ear to ear. He had spent the last few months trying to convince his parents into letting him use the Acura Legend while away at school. He had reasoned with himself that both parents have cars, but neither Mike nor Lisa budge on the issue.

"Mom, I know you've seen my grades. Tests don't stand a chance against the kid," Jason boasted as he walked over to his mother and hugged her. "Thanks."

"Yeah, thanks, Mrs. Taylor," Brad said from the archway.

"That's the other reason why I'm letting you drive the car. Your grades were very good, and you've proven to me and your father that you're responsible. You're both welcome," Lisa said and picked up the magazine, and resumed her reading.

"What time would you like for me to have the car back?" Jason asked.

"Have any of your professors given you the answers to the exams? Lisa asked.

"Point taken. "We'll be back home at a decent time," Jason said as he and Brad walked out the door.

"Hope you pass the test," Lisa said as she stood up and walked toward the window. "Please be careful," she whispered to herself as she peered out the living room window and watched as they disappeared out of the subdivision.

BBRRIINNGG!

BBRRIINNGG!

BBRRIINNGG!

"Hello," Lisa said.

"Hey, baby girl, how are you?" Jon asked dryly.

"I'm fine, Dad. Is everything all right?"

"It's your mother. She said that she'd dreamed about thirteen black crows cawing as they tapped on the window pane and woke up to a terrible migraine. She said it felt like somebody struck her on the left side of her head with a two-by-four. Your mother has been on edge ever since the night of the cookout. That's when she noticed the Martin's address, and Brad's license plate number. Your mother's first thought was that something terrible was going to happen to Jason," Jon said.

172

"Why would she think such a thing," Lisa hissed.

"Well, you know your mother. She's very steadfast in her superstitious beliefs. She went on ranting and raving, and then reminded me of the time when she experienced the sharp pain in her left hip and found out that Sister Edna fell down the steps and broke her left hip that very same day and died thirteen hours later. Then she reminded me of her bingo partner, Clara Mae, who had flown to Las Vegas, for a two-week vacation, and on the thirteenth day, died peacefully in her sleep while on the flight back home," Jon explained.

"What do these superstitious beliefs have to do with Jason?" Lisa said.

"Bad karma. Your mother believes something is going to happen to him in thirteen weeks," Jon said. "I guess the doctor was right," he added.

"What doctor? And right about what?" Lisa asked.

"Triskaidekaphobia," Jon said tersely.

"*What!*" Lisa said.

"Fear of the number thirteen. The doctor said your mother's fear was simply brought on by the intense negative experiences from her past," Jon said.

"Where's she?" Lisa asked.

"She's getting dressed. I tried to get her to rest, but she insisted on going to Woodfield Mall, to do some shopping. I thought about it, and maybe some fresh air would do her some good," Jon said.

"Look, Dad, I have to go. I'll call you later," Lisa said.

"Okay, baby girl, I'll talk to you later," Jon said.

"Bye, Dad," Lisa said and hung up the phone.

By now, Lisa appeared to be quite nervous. She peered out the window again, and thought aloud to herself, "Please return home safely."

The Acura Legend convertible powered down I-94, at highway

speed. Jason, in the driver's seat, drove with the top down, with the music played loudly. Brad was seated in the front passenger's side of the car. They'd found themselves attracted to a lot of attention from other cars, especially from a female driver, in a Jeep, with three other attractive female passengers, who drove onto the highway, in a lane next to them, obviously headed to the festival as well.

"Hey, Jason, check out the babes," Brad said and gawked. "Hey, Jeep girls," he yelled out the window.

The girls smiled and waved before the driver sped off.

"See y'all at the festival," Brad yelled.

"Man, forget them. This is the jam!" Jason said as he turned up the music even louder, and sang along to Kenny Bobien's remake of *You Are My Friend*, a tune fitting for their friendship, which played at ear shattering decibels.

"That's dope," Brad yelled.

After Brad had listened closely to the lyrics, for a minute or two, he leaned in and spoke into Jason's ear, and then turned and stared blankly out the window at the flowing traffic.

"Where did that come from?" Jason yelled over the loud music as he reached for the volume control button, and turned it down.

"Do you remember the night when I had flown off the handle and said we were not friends?" Brad asked.

"You mean the night when you were seriously buggin'? Yeah, I remember," Jason said.

"Well, I've thought about it, and I guess I was just a little jealous," Brad confessed.

"Jealous? What for?" Jason asked.

"All the attention you were getting. I mean, you hit a home run and girls go crazy. You were voted MVP of the year. You put a needle on a record and the girls just seem to flock to you. Then you would bring it up. Seemed as if you were always throwing it up in my face," Brad said.

174

"I know you ain't about to start buggin' out on me again," Jason said and turned the music completely off.

"I'm serious, bro. I felt as if you thought you were better than me. Like I was just your shadow," Brad said.

"The way I see it, had you not bugged out on me that night, you wouldn't have met that girl you told me about," Jason said.

"Lana?" Brad said.

"Yeah. What about her? I know she put out that night," Jason said.

Brad laughed with embarrassment and shook his head. "Well, that's where you're wrong. Lana ain't putting out until I pledge," he said.

"What? You're pledging a fraternity?" Jason said, shocked by the news.

"Yep," Brad said and nodded.

"Get out of here! I'm pledging too!" Jason said.

"You're pledging a fraternity? Why didn't you tell me?" Brad asked, equally shocked.

"How come you didn't tell me?" Jason asked.

"Which fraternity? Brad asked.

"Lamda. I go on line on September 18th, and I cross over on October 6th," Jason said proudly.

"I go on line September 25th, and I cross over on October 13th. And that's my birthday too! It's on that night," Brad said.

"With Lana?" Jason said.

"You know it. I can't wait to get into those panties," Brad said.

"You're my best friend. I would die for you too," Jason said and turned on the music again.

They continued through the thickening traffic, finally making it to a parking garage at Michigan and Randolph streets, approximately thirty minutes later. Once Jason found a parking spot, he and Brad set out on foot, sampling some of the various foods, and just enjoying the festive scene. They ended up running into Romeo, who was carrying a small stack of records.

"Whassup, Romeo?" Jason said.

"Whassup, man? Hey, Brad? Romeo said.

"Just checking out the scene," Jason said.

"Checking out the scene is right. Look at all the fine ladies," Brad added as he wandered off in the direction of a group of females.

"I heard that. Let me introduce you to my partners in crime. This is Hector, De'Montay, José, T-zone, and Meethias," Romeo introduced.

"Whassup, fellas?" Jason spoke.

"Whassup?" Hector, DeMontay, José, T-zone, and Meethias spoke collectively.

"Yo, Jason, I was gonna call you. I'm going to be djing a 70s party up on AU's campus October thirteenth. It's gonna be all of that," Romeo said.

"Word? We'll probably see flyers all over the place when we return to campus this fall. Where are you going to be spinning?' Jason asked.

"In the student union," Romeo said.

Brad returned and flashed a piece of paper. "Check it out. I got the digits!" he boasted.

"Oh, it's on now. Let's go scope out some tits and asses," Romeo said as he turned and led the way through the bustling crowd. They ended up on the lakefront or what's referred to colloquial speech as simply *The Rocks*, flirted with females and collected phone numbers. Jason and Brad joked back and forth, when Jason suddenly stopped in mid-sentence, stared over Brad's shoulder.

"What is it?" Brad asked and looked over his shoulder to see what caught his attention.

"Jason noticed that Shauna and one of her girlfriends had walked directly toward them. For some reason, Jason hadn't remembered Shauna looking so fine. She looked especially sexy in a form fitting mini-skirt and low-cut shirt combo. Jason couldn't help but to stare.

"Hello, guys," Shauna said and smiled.

Jason reached out his arms and hugged her. "You're looking good. And you smell good too," he complimented and took in a whiff of her perfume.

"Thank you. I'm sure I don't need to tell you the same," Shauna said. "Everybody, this is my roommate Jennifer," she introduced as they all exchanged pleasantries.

Jason gently pulled Shauna to the side, leaving Jennifer to mingle with Brad, Romeo and his friends.

"Hey, beautiful, let me holla at you for a minute," Romeo said to Jennifer and stepped up to her.

"I didn't expect to run into you out here," Jason said.

"Same here," Shauna said softly, taking in a deep breath of the fresh breeze blowing off of Lake Michigan.

"Now, I believe in pleasant surprises again," Jason said.

Shauna laughed out loud. "Jason, don't try to run that game on me. Have you forgotten how charming I know you can be," she reminded.

"I'm sure you do, but I'm just speaking from my heart. I've missed you," Jason said as he took her hand and placed it against his flexed chest muscles.

"That's really sweet. But let's not complicate things. I'm at Michigan State, and you're at ASU. We've thought things through, made a mature decision, and I think it was the right one," Shauna said and removed her hand from his chest.

"I was just trying to define our relationship, to know where we actually stood. So, is this what you really want?" Jason asked.

"Yeah," Shauna nodded and sighed.

Jason smiled and planted a kiss on Shauna's perfectly made up lips before he lead her back over to the others.

"You ready, girl?" Shauna asked.

"Sure. It was nice meeting all of you," Jennifer said.

"Bye," Shauna said as she and Jennifer walked off.

"Man, why in the hell did you let her get away?" Romeo asked as they all watched Shauna and Jennifer disappear into the crowd.

"She's been away for quite some time now," Jason said in a slurry voice.

The eight of them hung out a few more hours on *The Rocks*, but by nine, Jason was ready to go home. He and Brad parted with Romeo and the others, and headed back toward the parking garage. Jason figured that he would be able to have the car back home before ten that night, and thereby made a good impression on his mother.

Running into Shauna had put a damper on his mood. It had really thrown him for a loop. Jason couldn't get her off of his mind. He'd realized how much he missed her, and found himself deep in thought, and reminisced of how things were before they headed off to two different colleges.

Approximately 9:45 p.m., Jason had returned home and went directly to his bedroom. Lisa was relieved to see that he and Brad had made it home safely. She exhaled a sigh of relief, picked up the cordless phone, and dialed her parents.

"Hey, Dad, I called to check up on Mom. How's she doing?" Lisa asked.

"She's doing fine. After we returned from the mall, she said she had a slight headache and went straight to bed.

"Did she buy anything from the mall?" Lisa asked.

"She bought two black dresses; one appeared to be much smaller than the other. I guess she'd finally planned on losing some weight. Maybe the headache was brought on by her blood pressure being up," Jon said.

"Well, give her my love, and I'll talk to you tomorrow," Lisa said.

178

"Okay, baby girl, I'm gonna turn in myself. I'll tell your mother that you called," Jon said.

"Love you, Dad" Lisa said.

"Love you too," Jon said.

"Good night," Lisa said and hung up.

Chapter 20

Approximately twelve weeks have come and gone. With the spring/summer vacation over, and the summer/fall semester well under way, Jason and Brad were trying their best to uphold their duties as pledges. For Jason, he was just a few days away from crossing over into the Lamda Fraternity, Incorporated.

Jason was inside the apartment and had finished getting prepared for the annual Lamda Male Auction Review. For the past decade, the Lamda sweethearts had been hosting the event to raise money for the pledges' initiation fees, fraternity attire and merchandising. Of course, the pledges were the ones providing themselves as some of the merchandise. All seven prospective inductees were to stand upon an auction block, with a room filled with screaming females appraising their nearly naked bodies before bidding. The auction had begun at six that evening, and Jason was in his room all prepared to leave when the phone rang.

"Hello," Jason answered.

"How's my favorite son?" Lisa asked.

"I'm good. How's my favorite mother?" Jason asked, mocking her mother.

"I'm doing just fine. I'm just sitting here waiting on Rachel to stop over. I've received your mid-term report. You got three A's and two B's. Your father and I are so proud of you," Lisa said.

"When did you get it?" Jason asked.

"It arrived in today's mail. Well, are you a Lamda man yet? Lisa asked.

"No. Not yet. How did you find out I was pledging? I had planned on surprising you and Pops," Jason said.

"Romeo let the cat out of the bag. He called yesterday for your number, but I warned him that you and Brad were almost never at the apartment," Lisa said.

"I'm sure he tried to call," Jason chuckled as he pulled a Lamda sweatshirt over his head.

"Did he tell you that Brad's pledging too?" Jason said.

"Brad's pledging Lamda?" Lisa asked.

"No. Brad's pledging K T N," Jason said.

"I haven't heard of it, but I wish you two the best of luck. And I hope y'all don't let any of those frat members beat up on you. I know all about the culture and horrors of hazing," Lisa said as she twisted the cap off of her bottled water.

"What did Romeo want?" Jason asked and hoped to divert his mother's attention away from the subject of hazing.

"He wanted to know if you could fill in for him on a DJ gig on campus next Friday. He said he had sprained his right wrist while playing football so he definitely wouldn't be able to do it, but he will be there to support you if you can fill in for him," Lisa said.

"No problem. If you speak to him before I do, tell him I'll do anything for my dawg," Jason said.

"*Your dog!*" Lisa said.

"You know . . . my homeboy. Never mind. It's a generation thing," Jason said and sat on Brad's bed, putting on a pair of black boots.

"Excuse me!" Lisa said defensively.

"Mom, I'm only kidding," Jason chuckled.

"I thought so. How's the car?" Lisa asked.

"The car's fine. You just don't know how much attention an Acura Legend gets a brother on campus," Jason beamed.

"No matter how much attention you're getting, don't you even think about desecrating the back seat of that car," Lisa warned.

"That's what the apartment is for," Jason said.

"Jason Lamar Taylor," Lisa said sternly.

"I'm kidding," Jason chuckled. "But I gotta get ready to go meet the other pledges for a frat function," he said as he looked down and noticed a church pamphlet that protruded from underneath Brad's bed.

"All right, love you, Pookie," Lisa said as Rachel knocked on the door and entered.

"Mom, you promised never to call me by my nickname as long as I live," Jason reminded.

"I'm sorry. My baby's all grown up. No more nicknames. I promise. Listen, Rachel just walked in, and we're headed to the Women's Center for our aerobics class. I'll talk to you later. Love you," Lisa said.

"Love you too. Tell Mrs. Martin I said hello," Jason said.

"I will. Don't let them beat up on you. And be careful," Lisa said.

"I promise. Bye, Mom" Jason said and hung up the phone. He looked at the pamphlet. "Movement of Creativity," he said to himself as he flipped through it.

"What's Jason's nickname?" Rachel asked inquisitively.

"Come on, let's go, we're running a little late," Lisa said, avoiding Rachel's question.

"I'll tell you Brad's nickname," Rachel said.

"Nice try. Brad doesn't have a nickname. Remember? By the way, have you received Brad's mid-term report?" Lisa asked as she showed Rachel Jason's mid-term report.

"I haven't checked the mail yet. Stop avoiding my question. What's so secretive about Jason's nickname?" Rachel asked.

"Jason got three A's and two B's. Isn't that great?" Lisa said, still avoiding Rachel's question as they walked outside, closing the door behind them.

Back at the apartment, Jason was still engulfed in the pamphlet. He discovered that it was from a church known as The World Church Caucasus Preservation: Dedication to the preservation of the Supreme White Race. Small print on the bottom back of the pamphlet indicated that the church was in direct association with Movement of Creativity, The Children of the Confederacy, and the K T N Fraternity, Inc. Before Jason had read any further, there was a knock at the door.

"Who is it?" Jason asked, startled by the knock as he sprang up from Brad's bed, and stuck the pamphlet inside his book bag.

"Eric," the Lamda president said.

"Be right out!" Jason shouted as he grabbed his jacket, and headed toward the door. He was confused by the pamphlet, and why it was underneath Brad's bed.

* * *

"Ladies, I'm Tasha Morgan, a Lamda sweetheart, and I will be your auction host for the evening," she said into the microphone in front of a room filled with screaming females. "Are you ladies ready to see some fine Zulu Warriors?"

The crowd roared their unanimous response.

Tasha continued and hyped the crowd up into a more ecstatic frenzy. "I hope you ladies brought plenty of cash or your credit cards. Without further ado, here are a few words from the Lamda President, Big Brother Eric Mitchell!" she said and waved a handheld credit card machine in the air.

"The crowd continued to roar as Eric stepped out and wore only a pair of jeans and black boots as he showed off his chiseled physique. "Now, ladies, I would first like to thank you all for coming out this evening. The seven pledges we have on line will be crossing over into the Lamda Fraternity, Incorporated, within the next forty-eight hours. I know y'all are anxious to spend some money, so I'm going to turn it back over to Tasha so she can introduce the merchandise for the *LAMDA'S HOT BOYS AUCTION REVIEW 2000!*

"Ladies, prepare yourselves to see some fine bodied men that will make you weak in the knees. Get ready, 'cause they were definitely worth the wait. And remember, ladies, whomever you take home tonight will be all yours until the crack of dawn!" Tasha announced before she presented each of the pledges.

"Here's the lineup. We have Michael Bankhead, D'Shawn Williams, Tony Roehill, Raheem Nelson, Antwan Jackson, Joe Miller and Jason Taylor, representing the men of Lamda Fraternity, Incorporated," Tasha rattled off each of the pledges' names as they took to the auction block, danced and flexed their muscles before a crowd of screaming young ladies.

Thirty minutes later, six pledges had been auctioned off. Finally, it was Jason's turn. As he stepped upon the auction block, instantly, there was an initial bid of 100 dollars shouted from somewhere within the crowd.

"One hundred dollars! That sister must know something that we don't. Jason, what are you packing in that thong?" Tasha teased. "Do I hear $125?" she said.

"$250!" another female shouted from within the crowd.

"Girlfriend, please step forward," Tasha urged. "It seems as if you will be taking him home with you tonight."

Janaya stepped forward and waved a Visa card in the air.

Jason smiled and winked at her from the auction block.

"Damn, girlfriend, you must've had it already. It was good, huh?" Tasha said as she taunted the hyped crowd. "$250 going once . . . going twice . . ."

"$500!" still another female shouted from deep in the crowd. Everyone gasped and looked back.

The crowd seemed to part as the female made her way to the front of the auction block.

"I'm sorry, can you repeat that?" Tasha said.

"Five hundred dollars," the female said she as she'd slowly come into full view of both Jason and Janaya. It was Shauna.

"Excuse me, who the hell are you?" Janaya asked with her arms folded across her chest.

"I'm Shauna, and if Jason hasn't spoken of me, look forward to seeing a lot more of me," she said.

All the females in earshot gasped, including Tasha.

Jason just looked on in total bewilderment.

"I believe you belong to me for the evening," Shauna said to a still bewildered Jason as she reached for his hand. She politely passed Tasha her credit card as Jason stepped down from the auction block. Tasha quickly swiped Shauna's credit card and handed it back to her.

Janaya cut her eyes and sucked her teeth loudly before she pushed her way back through the crowd. The room seemed to stand perfectly still.

* * *

Shauna and Jason returned to the dorm apartment after having dinner at a nearby Italian restaurant. Shauna drove all the way from Michigan State to make a surprise appearance at the auction, which she learned through Jennifer, who heard about it from none other than Romeo. Jason had not realized that Jennifer and Romeo exchanged telephone numbers the day they'd met at The Taste of Chicago.

"Here we are. Welcome to our cozy little place," Jason said as he led Shauna into the apartment. He had assured her that Brad would've most likely spent the night at the K T N frat house or snuggled up next to Lana at her apartment.

"It's cool in here. Turn on the heat," Shauna said as she rubbed her shoulders.

"How about our bodies joined together, making some friction to generate body heat," Jason said as he grabbed Shauna by the waist, and pulled her close to him.

"Is that right?" Shauna said with an agreeing smile.

"Yeah, that's right," Jason said and kissed her on the lips.

"Well, I'm going to hold you to it," Shauna whispered softly into his ear. "But first, I need to freshen up. Where's the bathroom?" she asked and removed Jason's hands from her waist.

"How are you going to just break off a brother's mack?" Jason said. "It's right there . . . the first door on your right," he said and pointed toward the study quad area.

"I'll be right back," Shauna said and blew him a kiss.

"I'll be right here," Jason said and grabbed Shauna's invisible kiss.

As soon as Shauna disappeared into the bathroom, Jason turned on the heat, and quickly stripped down to his underwear. He pulled back the covers on his bed, and jumped on it.

"*Aah!* These sheets are cold," Jason said as he sprang up off the bed.

He quickly pulled his iron from the top shelf of his closet and plugged it into a nearby wall socket. The iron was hot in no time, and Jason had run the iron over the sheets. After he'd warmed the sheets, Jason put the iron up and hurried back to get in bed. In the process, once again, Jason stubbed his toe on the side of the bed.

"Ahhh! Fuck!" Jason grimaced in agonizing pain as he dove into his bed and grabbed his left foot.

"Did you say something?" Shauna yelled from the bathroom.

"No. That's the radio. I'm trying to find some slow jams," Jason responded with slight pain lingering in his voice as he turned on the radio, and flipped through the dials.

Shauna returned to the room, wore only her bra and panties, and joined Jason in bed. "The bed is nice and warm," she said as she slipped under the covers.

"I told you our bodies would generate heat," Jason said.

"Right. You're just hot and horny as hell for some sex," Shauna said as she maneuvered her body under the cover.

"I'm hot and horny as hell only for you," Jason said in a sexy voice.

"But what about little Miss--" Shauna said and cut off in mid-

186

sentence.

"*Ssh*," Jason silenced her question with his index finger against her lips.

"How do I know that I'm the only one?" Shauna asked.

"Because you're here and she isn't," Jason said as he climbed on top of Shauna and looked at her, his eyes staring into her glistening eyes. He kissed her softly, as if he'd gradually become emotionally reacquainted with her through the taste of her mouth.

Jason opened his mouth slightly and allowed his tongue to trace the outside of her mouth. Shauna opened her mouth. Hungrily, his tongue sought hers, and he kissed her with desperation. Shauna wrapped her arms around Jason's back, and clung tightly against him.

As their tongues danced and twined, Jason grabbed her hips. He groaned audibly as her pelvis brushed against his groin and her breast pressed against his chest, both actions teased his growing erection. Slowly, Jason's hands traveled freely up to the rounded curves of her breast; cupped them in the palm of his hands. Shauna moaned as he gently rubbed and squeezed them.

Again, Jason captured her mouth with his as their tongues danced and twined. One hand supported her back, while the other found its way down the front of her panties. He slid his hand underneath the band of her panties, circled it till he'd found his target—her nest of black hair. As his fingers traced circles around her labia, Shauna withered her vagina against his hand. Jason took this as an unspoken command to move in for the kill. Soon, his index and middle fingers rubbed back and forth against her very sensitive clit. As Jason did this, her hands clawed at his back. Finally, he removed both their bottom layers of clothing and entered her. Inside, she was hot and wet, and despite her brief moans, she squeezed her internal muscles around his thrusting penis. Jason nibbled on her earlobe and kissed his way down her neck.

Shauna's orgasm came in a continuous wave, crashing and breaking; her moans filling the apartment. The loudest part of the climax hit when he licked the cleft of her breast.

"Oh, God . . . Jason," Shauna screamed, arched her back regally, and showed that she wanted him.

Jason looked into her eyes as he was slowly and methodically thrusting in and out of her. Shauna's legs were opened wider for him as her internal muscles closed in on him. This drove Jason crazy, and sent an electric shock from his head to his toes and back up to his groin. He impaled his entire penis insider her, thrust wildly; flexed his muscled thighs and she went wild, roared like a feral lioness, her hands clutched his shoulders, rocked against him, and matched him stroke for stroke.

Caught up in the moment of pure ecstasy, neither one of them heard Brad, in a drunken stupor, stumbled as he entered the apartment through the sliding glass door in the study quad. Brad had been partying quite a bit lately, and that night he had consumed more than his share of booze and drugs, and almost fell out flat on his face at the frat party he had attended. After Brad heard the moans from the bedroom, he was drawn to the doorway by curiosity. There, he watched as the two silhouetted bodies continued with their passionate lovemaking. After a moment of entertainment at Jason and Shauna's expense, Brad had quietly wandered back into the quad area and collapsed onto the sofa, fantasized about a night of passionate lovemaking with Lana before he drifted off to sleep.

Chapter 21

A blinding stream of sunlight had somehow maneuvered through the closed window blinds and awakened Jason shortly after nine that morning. His bed was empty, and had it not been for the lingering scent of Shauna's perfume that reminded him of her early morning departure, he surely would have thought that their intimate sexual encounter was merely a dream. They said their goodbyes a few hours earlier, as she set out in time to make it back to MSU to meet with a study group.

Brad dragged himself into the bedroom from his drunken stupor, and started fumbling through the closet for a clean bath towel. Obviously, he suffered from a hangover.

"Good morning. Man, you look like crap. You okay?" Jason asked as he stood, yarned and stretched.

"Ask me after I've taken a dump, shaved and showered," Brad mumbled and wiped away dried rheum from his eyes as he walked back out of the room.

Jason simply shook his head, and wondered when Brad had come home. Suddenly, he remembered the pamphlet that he had tucked away inside his book bag, and went to retrieve it. Jason sat down on his bed and examined the pamphlet more carefully, read over all the ideology of the World Church Caucasus Preservation. Many questions raced through his mind as he focused on Brad, and the possibility that he could've been involved in any or all of the organizations.

Approximately twenty minutes later, Brad walked back into the bedroom, freshly showered and wore only a pair of white briefs.

"*Whew!* I feel a whole lot better now," Brad said as he pulled a pair of socks, jeans and sweatshirt from his closet.

"Was that Janaya in here last night, 'cause, man, you were banging the hell out of that ass," Brad said.

"If you really must know, that wasn't Janaya. It was Shauna.

"Obviously, I hadn't realized you were home. So what time did you get in?" Jason asked as he folded his arms, with the pamphlet in his right hand.

"I would've assumed shortly after you'd gotten inside her," Brad said and laughed as he dropped the jeans and sweatshirt on the floor, sat on the edge of his bed, and put on the socks.

"In addition to being a voyeur, you're a racist too, huh?" Jason quipped.

"What are you talking about?" Brad asked nonchalantly as he picked up and put on the jeans, and stepped into a pair of tennis shoes.

"This is what I'm talking about," Jason said and tossed the pamphlet onto Brad's bed. "Are you part of this racist church?" he asked sternly.

"I've visited the church with Lana. It's not like I'm a member. Relax, bro, it's no big deal," Brad shrugged and chuckled wryly.

"I'm sure your membership would become official once you've crossed over into K T N," Jason retorted. "It's a big deal to me when the frat's name is also on the back of the pamphlet."

"At times, the church would help us out," Brad said.

"How? By conditioning y'all to be virulent Neo-Nazis," Jason said.

"Are you jealous? Look, they're my friends. Regardless of whom they are or what they believe shouldn't concern you. Have I ever imposed anything on you? Have I? *Huh!*" Brad exclaimed in a snippy voice.

"Is that supposed to be a fucking consolation to me? And to just think, all this time, I thought we were friends. I guess it was all just a sham. In the past few weeks, you've turned into a totally different person. I don't know who you are or what you've become, "Jason vented as he paced the floor.

"*Boo hoo!* Cry me a river. Please! I didn't start buggin' when you told me you were going to join an all-black fraternity," Brad

190

tried to justify as he picked up the sweatshirt.

"It's not racist. And besides, the reason why I joined an all-black fraternity is because fraternities like K T N don't want people like me to join or be around them," Jason said.

"You see, that's why I didn't tell you in the first place. I knew you'd get all hostile on me," Brad said as he quickly pulled his sweatshirt over his head.

"That's bullshit! And you know it. Let me tell you something . . . African-Americans had to put up with this racist nonsense for centuries, and still to this very day. You're damn right I'm hostile. I've earned the right to be this way," Jason lashed out in anger as he got closer toward Brad.

"Don't blame me for the misdeeds of the past," Brad said.

"That's hard to do. Instead of turning a blind eye, you've associated yourself with these sick-minded people; therefore you've become part of this growing problem by perpetuating the misdeeds of your forefathers."

"I don't have to stand here and listen to this crap. I'm out of here," Brad said as he grabbed an electric razor, and hurriedly stuffed some clothes inside a duffel bag.

"Brad, you need to wake up! Can't you see that you've been brainwashed? And if you've done all of this just to sleep with Lana, you need to pull her fucking panties from your nostrils and realize that she's the one who lured you into this *Children of the Corn* cult shit," Jason pleaded.

"Don't you drag Lana into this? Don't you even say her fucking name! This is between you and me. And as far as I'm concerned, the church was right about everything it preached about you people. I guess I done seen the light," Brad fumed as he continued to stuff more clothes inside the duffel bag.

"You people, huh?" Jason said and released a deep sigh. "Look, perhaps we just need to chill out a minute and discuss this later," he suggested calmly.

"You chill the fuck out, bro! I'll be back later for the rest of my things. I'm moving out," Brad said, flung the duffel bag over his right shoulder, and stormed out of the room in a fit of rage.

Jason, with an incredulous look on his face, plopped down on his bed, and shook his head.

* * *

"Honey, take a look at Brad's mid-term report. I'm a little worried," Rachel said as she handed Brad's mid-term report to Tom.

"One B, three C's and a D. This isn't like Brad. He'd made the Dean's List his entire freshmen year, and the first semester as a sophomore," Tom said after he perused the mid-term report, took off his glasses and hand wiped his face.

"Perhaps he's just experiencing a case of the sophomore slump," Rachel said.

"I'll have a talk with him, and see what's going on," Tom said.

"I'm sure this is just a one-time thing. Maybe this pledging thing has him stressed out . . . trying to keep up with his studies and all," Rachel speculated.

Awe struck, Tom looked up sharply. "I didn't know Brad was joining a fraternity," he said nervously as he sat Brad's mid-term report down on his desk.

"I thought you knew. As a matter of fact, both Brad and Jason are joining fraternities. Jason is pledging Lamda, and Brad's pledging K T N. Here's an old college yearbook from our hometown that Brad left here. I found it under his bed while cleaning his room," Rachel said and handed the yearbook to Tom.

"*Oh, God!*" Tom said frantically.

A second or two later, a disconcerted Tom feverishly flipped through the yearbook until a particular page caught his immediate attention. His flustered gaze at the K T N fraternity photo turned to a shock of recognition. His jaw dropped.

"What is it, Tom? Rachel asked nervously as she watched Tom jumped to his feet and slammed the yearbook to the floor. He hurriedly searched for his car keys on his cluttered desk.

Tom had planned on working from home that day, since he had no scheduled client visits or meetings. Rachel looked puzzled as he located his keys, stormed past her, and grabbed a jacket from a coat rack by the door. She was unaware as to what had just happened or why, and scurried after him.

"Tom, what's going on? Where are you going?" Rachel asked nervously.

"I'm going to the university," Tom said before he rushed out of the front door, and left it ajar.

"What for?" Rachel asked as she stood in the doorway. "Tom, answer me?" she pleaded.

Tom stopped dead in his tracks. He looked back at her, said nothing, hopped into the car and sped off.

Still unaware as to what had just happened, Rachel closed the door, walked across the lawn, next-door, and rang the Taylor's doorbell.

DING DONG!
DING DONG!
DING DONG!

"*Coming!*" Lisa yelled and walked briskly toward the door as she stuffed popcorn in her mouth. She opened the door.

"Hey, Rachel said dryly, no cheer in her tone.

"Hey, come on in. Was that Tom I just heard drove off like that?" Lisa asked.

"That was Tom all right," Rachel huffed.

"Wanna talk about it?" Lisa said and ushered Rachel into the den, where she watched her favorite movie, *The Color Purple*.

"Did Mike get upset when he found out that Jason was pledging a fraternity?" Rachel asked.

"No. Why?" Lisa asked.

"Well, I told Tom that Brad was pledging a fraternity. He'd lost his cool and become enraged. That's when he stormed out of the house and sped off like a madman. *Hmm*! Just last night, Tom had another one of his typical nightmares, and now Brad's mid-term report. I just don't understand," Rachel said and shook her head.

"Well, did he say anything?" Lisa asked.

"Nothing. We were just talking about Brad's mid-term report beforehand. Now that I've thought about it, perhaps that had something to do with it," Rachel surmised.

"How were Brad's grades?" Lisa asked as she munched on popcorn.

"Terrible. It's not like him," Rachel said.

"Well, I'm sure Tom went to the university to get to the bottom of it. Maybe he wanted to have a face-to-face talk with Brad about his grades. Don't you worry, by the time Tom made it to the university, he would've cooled down."

"I hope you're right," Rachel said.

"Of course I am. Here, have some popcorn. The least you can do is stay and watch the rest of the movie with me," Lisa said as she handed Rachel the large bowl of theater-style buttered popcorn.

"Oh, I can't resist. This is a classic!" Rachel said and stuffed popcorn in her mouth.

"You know, I've cried every time that I've watched this movie," Lisa confessed.

"The scene where Celie and Nettie were separated has always brought me to tears," Rachel said.

"I know. I mean, I don't have a sister or brother, but I can only imagine how that must've felt," Lisa said.

"Well, you're pretty much the closest thing to a sister I've ever had," Rachel said.

"*Aww!* That's so sweet," Lisa said.

194

"What if Tom hadn't made partner and a big-time New York law firm recruited him, and we had to relocate, would we still be best friends?" Rachel asked?

"Of course we would," Lisa said and grabbed Rachel's hand, and mimicked their dramatic modern rendition of that scene.

"I guess we could write and call each other," Rachel said in a timid voice.

"And we can e-mail each other too," Lisa said.

"I don't know the first thing about computers," Rachel said.

"Then I'll teach you. That way, if either one of our husband's jobs were to ever separate us, we can write, call, and e-mail each other!" Lisa said excitedly before they both laughed at their performances, having a little *Color Purple* moment there before they turned their attention back to the movie.

* * *

"Mr. Martin," Jason said, surprised to see him as he stood on the other side of the door. He watched as Tom barged in, absently walked past him, and into the apartment.

"Where's Brad?" Tom demanded, with both hands on his waist.

"C'mon in, why don't you?" Jason muttered and closed the door. "We had a disagreement earlier this morning. He'd gotten upset, stuffed some clothes into a duffel bag and left. Said he was going to move out. I haven't seen or heard from him since," he said and shrugged.

"I've always admonished Brad and instilled in him to never walk away from a problem. Instead, deal with it, and make things right," Tom said.

"Well, like I said, Brad was pretty upset when he left. He said he'd be back for the rest of his things," Jason said.

"Do you know where he went?" Tom asked.

195

"I guess he'd gone to Lana's apartment or the frat house," Jason said and shrugged.

"The K T N fraternity house?" Is this what sparked the disagreement? Tom asked.

Jason nodded. "You knew about this fraternity?" he asked.

"More than I care to," Tom said simply.

"Are you for or against Brad pledging this sick fraternity?" Jason asked and folded his arms.

"Of course I'm against it. I'd just learned of Brad's involvement in this fraternity just within the past hour. That's why I'm here. I'm on my way to the fraternity house. If Brad comes back here, tell him to stay put," Tom said as he walked toward the door.

"Do you know where the frat house is located?" Jason asked as he watched Tom open the door.

"I'll find it," Tom said and closed the door behind him.

Jason picked up his book bag from off his bed and headed to his computer lab class.

Moments later, Tom located the K T N fraternity house. He quickly exited the car, entered the frat house and found Brad lounging on a sofa smoking pot along with a few frat members as they watched music videos blaring on a Toshiba 50 inch color TV that sat in the corner of the living room. As soon as the frat members heard the door being slammed shut, they'd seen the father-figure, rushed to make a last-ditch effort to get rid of their illegal drug paraphernalia. Brad, undaunted, tilted back his head, closed his eyes and took another drag from the joint. Tom stepped in front of him and slapped the joint from his thumb and index fingers to the dirt-stained carpet, and extinguished it as he ground it with his right foot.

"What in the hell do you think you're doing?" Tom shouted.

Brad, noticeably high, cocked his head to the side as he attempted to look beyond his father, and maintained his focus on the music videos.

"Have you heard a word I've said?" Tom yelled angrily.

In a fit of rage, Brad jumped to his feet, scowled and grunted under his breath like a raging bull as the frat members stood numb.

"This is my life, so just get the fuck off my back!" Brad shouted.

"What the hell has gotten into you? You went behind my back and got involved with these sick-minded people when I had explicitly warned you not to. And now you've turned into a drug addict. What's next, huh? A lynching?" Tom angrily lashed out.

Brad stared blankly past his father as if he was intent on being coolly defiant, and ignored his every word.

"Whatever, old man," Brad mouthed.

Tom had lost his cool. He grabbed Brad by his left arm. "I want you to listen to me very carefully. I want your cantankerous ass to pack up your things and get the hell out of here this very instant. I'm not paying tuition and rent only to have you to flunk out of school, and move into a goddamn Neo-Nazi frat house," he said, his voice low and steeled, his jaws clinched. And just so you know, I'm cancelling your credit card."

Brad turned to a frat member. "I'll be at Lana's," he said, jerked his arm free from his father's grip, and stormed out of the frat house. Tom looked on in total disbelief. After a moment, he turned his attention to the frat members.

"Why are you all standing around looking like morons? I'll have each and every one of your little under-aged Hitler asses locked up and charged with the possession of illegal drugs and alcohol. Get rid of it now!" Tom threatened and stormed off.

Chapter 22

Friday, October 13th had finally arrived. A full moon glistened brightly in the night sky. Jason was at the apartment as he gathered records for the 70s themed party. Brad was across campus as he celebrated his birthday at the K T N frat house, and prepared for his initiation. Even though he had called and apologized to his parents, and promised that he would get his act together, he continued to party and associated himself with the frat. Brad had not slept or moved back into the apartment. He and Jason were on speaking terms, but there was clearly a great deal of tension in their relationship.

After Jason had gathered his records together, he sat down, wrote Brad a note, and wished him a *Happy Birthday*. Also, he had informed him about the 70s themed party being held in the student union, and that he would be spinning the music, just in case he were to show up at the apartment. Jason had quickly written the note, because he knew Romeo would've arrived any minute. As soon as he placed the note on Brad's pillow, he heard Romeo honk his horn outside the apartment. Jason exited the dorm apartment and jumped into the van with Romeo and a few of his friends for the short trip across campus. Upon their arrival in front of the student union, they'd begun unloading the equipment from the van. Jason soon realized that Romeo had forgotten the speakers.

"Romeo, man, where are the speakers?" Jason asked.

"I forgot to bring them. Fuck!" Romeo exclaimed.

"No shit! What time do you have?" Jason asked.

"Ten thirty-five," Romeo said.

"I have time. I have to make a quick run over to Lee's Music, just outside the campus. They rent out music equipment. I think they close at eleven," Jason said.

"Cool. You do that, and we'll start setting up for you," Romeo said and tossed the key to the van to Jason. Partygoers stood around in full retro style 70s clothes. Some wore bell-bottom pants, big collar shirts and blouses, platform shoes, and donned fake Afro wigs. Others wore big collar shirts and Saturday Night Fever Disco Leisure suits and Disco Diva Dresses, and the all-in-one Jump Suits.

"I'll be back," Jason said and rearranged the hair pick in the back of his fake Afro wig. He was completely hyped about the party, and determined not to let the equipment situation frustrate him, since he knew that it could easily be resolved with Mr. Lee's help. Jason jumped in the driver's seat of the van and sped off.

* * *

Back at the K T N frat house, all thirteen pledges were dressed in black jeans and sweatshirts with the big red letters K T N on the front. A deep techno track played while some dance on a make-shift dance floor. Others stood around and smoked pot or cigarettes, drank alcohol and distributed drug paraphernalia. Brad, who sat in a chair, was approached by Lana. She offered him powdered crystal meth. He refused. Lana straddled him, her eyes invited his, moved wildly as she ground her hips into him, her head arched back. She unbuttoned her blouse, her hands rubbed lightly over her breasts.

Lana reached down, with her right hand and grabbed Brad's crotch. Brad was drawn into the seduction. Desire twisted his face. He closed his eyes; his head was now arched back.

"Do it for me. Don't you want to make love to me?" Lana said and leaned in, "This will help you stay hard all night long. After all, a girl doesn't want to be disappointed on her first night," Lana whispered seductively into Brad's ear as she put the crystal meth up to his left nostril. Without hesitation, Brad snorted the crystal meth.

"*Whew!*" Brad exclaimed. He choked and coughed while being cheered on by everyone.

"Hey, Brad, we got a surprise for you," Ted said.

"What's that?" Brad asked as he sniffed and rubbed his nose.

"Well, why don't you just follow us downstairs to the basement and find out," Ted said.

"All right," Brad said as he still sniffed and rubbed his nose.

Lana had fastened the buttons on her blouse and removed herself from Brad's lap as everyone walked downstairs to the basement.

"You knew we were going to help you to celebrate your birthday, right? Ted asked.

"I had no clue," Brad said.

"Well, beyond this door is a birthday gift from us to you. This is the underground world in which we live. A world that's dark and unknown to most. Welcome to our world," Ted said and slowly opened the door to a crowded basement rave party.

Brad saw countless people who danced to deep dark minimal techno track in a large foggy and dimly lit room. Hot and sweaty ravers danced in provocative outfits, on a packed dance floor.

"Dirty house dancing," Brad whispered in total amazement. "Is this party really for me?" he asked.

"This is your party, man," a frat member said.

"But first, you and the rest of the pre-pledges will join the party after you all have crossed over," Ted said.

"When do we cross over?" Brad asked anxiously.

"You all will become honorary members once the thirteenth and final task has been completed. Let's go join the other pre-pledges and let the final task begin!" Ted said and proceeded upstairs.

"Lana, your dad's on the phone. He wanted to know how the party was going. We are like so totally busted," a kitten sweetheart whispered into Lana's ear and handed her a cordless phone.

"Daddy, what a surprise," Lana said nervously.

"I just called to see how well your party was going," Lana's father, Vince Burkeman said.

"The party's a huge success. Everyone's having a great time," Lana said.

"Good. I'm glad to hear it. Don't forget, you promised to come home and have dinner with the family next Sunday. Oh, and by the way, bring your new boyfriend? I would like to meet him," Vince said.

"If you're referring to Brad, he's not my new boyfriend. I'd just recently met him," Lana said in hushed tones, as she turned away from Brad.

"Well that's not what your little brother told me. He saw you two as you held hands before and after last week's church service. And now, you've thrown him a birthday party," Vince said.

"That little nerd needs to mind his business," Lana mouthed.

Vince was quick to backtrack. "I'm sorry, sweetheart. I didn't mean to ruffle your feathers. I just wanted to meet the young man. Just in case he was to become part of the Burkeman family. I needed to know what his views and beliefs were. I'm sure you know what I mean," he said.

"Look, Dad, I have to get back to the party. I don't wanna be rude and keep my guests waiting," Lana explained and shook her breast in Brad's face.

"Okay, angel, call me tomorrow, and let me know how the party turned out," Vince said.

"I will, Dad. Bye," Lana said and hung up the phone.

Ted was about to advise the pledges of their thirteenth and final task.

"May I have your attention, please?" Ted said as everyone had gathered around. "It's time for the thirteen pre-pledges to cross over into the K T N fraternity of brotherhood. In order to complete this year's induction ceremony, your final task will be to go out and shave the hair off a reggin's head. About an hour ago, I went to Rand's Mini-Mart, to buy beer and ice. While there, I had to take a leak. Inside the restroom was this big black buck standing over the sink combing his hair. When I went to wash my hands, I saw all these little disgusting Negroid hairs all over the sink. It made me sick to my stomach. And that's why you all will be responsible for shaving the hair off some big black buck's head and bringing it back to me in this sacred chalice. It will be used in a symbolic burning ritual. Here's an electric razor. You will have exactly one hour. So if there are no questions, get to it," he said, stepped up to Brad and handed him the razor and sacred chalice. "Don't let me down, again, Martin."

"I won't," Brad said and exited the frat house.

As the pledges scurried out of the frat house, both the official K T N members and kitten sweethearts cheered them on. Lana smiled smugly as she strutted up to Ted, and hugged him around the waist. He hugged her back and kissed her on the lips.

"Well done, my beguiling sweetheart," Ted said.

Once outside, all thirteen pledges had decided on which cars they were going to take.

"Brad, why don't we drive, since we have the two fastest cars," Scott suggested.

"Good idea," Brad said as five pre-pledges piled into his car, while the remaining six squeezed into Scott's red 1999 Pontiac Grand Prix GT Coupe.

Brad suggested that they'd split up and go in separate directions. He thought that this would help to increase their chances of completing the thirteenth and final task.

Scott and the pre-pledges all agreed.

"We only have one razor," Scott said.

"I have an electric razor in my car. Here, take this," Brad said and handed Scott the razor.

A few blocks just outside the campus, Brad drove up on a

potential victim as he loaded stereo speakers onto a van. He dimmed the lights and everyone exited the car. Brad, with the electric razor in one hand, bent over and scooped up dirt in the sacred chalice.

As the pledges stalked their unsuspecting victim, they crept alongside the left side of the van. Brad had thrown dirt into their victim's face while the others launched a surprise attack, followed up with a gauntlet of MMA–style blows.

In the course of the struggle, the black male, with his vision slightly impaired, had managed to temporarily break free from his attackers and begun swinging his fist violently, landing a powerful haymaker punch to Brad's jaw, and caused him to stumble to the ground. One of the pledges quickly picked up the razor and sacred chalice, and helped Brad to his feet. Brad, slightly dazed, stumbled back to his car, opened the trunk, and retrieved a baseball bat.

Brad walked briskly, his left fist clenched, toward the melee. The pledges spotted him coming with the baseball bat in tow. The pledges released their victim and scattered. Brad, grim as death, stood behind the exhausted black male.

"Kill the nigger!" Brad exclaimed in a loathsome voice.

The black male, exhausted and breathing hard, slowly turned around as Brad hauled back the bat and struck a powerful and stunning blow to the left side of his head that sent him crashing to the ground. A two-inch gash, at least, had begun to form a pool of blood.

The pre-pledges watched as the black male was sprawled out on the ground, convulsing violently. Moments later, the victim violent convulsion had slowed considerably before he finally stopped, and laid motionless in a puddle of blood.

"What are you waiting for? C'mon, Mark, shave the fucker's head so we can get the hell out of here," Brad ordered and shoved the razor and sacred chalice in his hands.

"I'm totally freaked out, man. Look at all this blood," Mark said in shock.

"Give me the razor. I'll shave the fucker's head," Dillon said and snatched the razor out of Mark's hands.

Dillon kneeled over the lifeless victim sprawled out on the ground and begun to shave his head and quickly realized that it was a fake Afro wig. He used two fingers to remove the blood-soaked fake Afro wig from the lifeless victim's head and flung it by his right foot.

"Jason," Brad whispered to himself as he looked on in disbelief as the baseball bat slid out his right hand, and fell to the ground near his feet.

"Here come somebody! C'mon, Brad, let's go!" Dillon said.

Mark scooped up the razor and sacred chalice.

"Leave it!" Dillon yelled as Mark dropped the razor and sacred chalice near the victim's feet and fled.

"Jesus! What've I done?" Brad whispered again to himself as he stared at his best friend's lifeless body. He took a few steps back, then turned and ran to his car and got in, started the engine, floored it, jerked the steering wheel, tires squealing, blew out of the area, took a left and sped off down the street, leaning hard on the curves.

* * *

The following morning, Lisa returned from her morning jog. As she entered the subdivision, she noticed a police car parked in front of their home with two policemen who stood at the front door. Lisa's expression turned to one of dread as she quickly made her way up the driveway. By the time she'd reached the house, her face read out-and-out fear. Mike had opened the door.

"What's going on?" Lisa asked as she tried to catch her breath.

"Mr. and Mrs. Taylor?" an officer said.

"Yes, we are Mr. and Mrs. Taylor," Mike answered. "Is there a problem?" he asked as Lisa stepped inside the house and stood behind him. The two officers removed their hats.

"I'm Officer Bob Hopkins, and this is my partner Officer Lance Carter. I'm afraid we have some bad news.

"I'm terribly sorry to have to be the one to tell you. It's about your son," Officer Lance Carter said with a grim face, a clear indication he doesn't know how to break the news.

"What bad news about our son?" Lisa asked and stepped in front of Mike.

"He was murdered," Officer Carter said and dropped his head. Officer Hopkins released a deep sigh.

Lisa shook her head, her face registered confusion. Suddenly, the reality of the news had set in. It proved to be way too much for her to bear.

"*Noooooo!*" Lisa screamed. She'd become unhinged, burst into tears, and collapsed into Mike's arms.

"What do you mean our son was murdered?" Mike yelled, with Lisa's face now buried in his chest.

"Sir, we are still investigating the incident. We have an eye-witness who'd seen six suspects who fled the scene. We'll need you both to come with us to identify the body," Officer Hopkins said.

"We'll be happy to drive you both to and from," Officer Carter added.

"That won't be necessary," Mike said, barely audible. "We'll follow you," he said solemnly.

"All right, we'll be waiting in the car. I'm terribly sorry," Officer Carter said apologetically as he and Officer Hopkins put on their hats and walked back toward the squad car.

Tom had just pulled into the driveway. He'd just gotten back in town from North Carolina. He and Rachel had rushed over to the Taylors' front door.

"Mike, I'd just gotten back in town. What happened?! Is everything all right?" Tom asked, genuinely concerned.

"Jason was murdered," Mike said slowly as he attempted to be

205

strong for Lisa, and fought back his tears.

"*What*?" Tom said, shocked by the news. "Mike, I'm so sorry," he said as Rachel put both hands to her mouth and slowly stepped over toward Lisa to console her.

"Lisa and I are on our way--" Mike said mid-sentence.

Tom cut him off. "We're best friends, Mike. We're going with you."

* * *

An hour or so later, the Taylors and the Martins were at the Aurora County Coroner's Office. A medical examiner, with piercing eyes who wore round horn-rim glasses, opened a storage rack, pulled out the tray, unzipped the body bag and revealed Jason's cold body with a blank toe tag ID. His name was Colin Dougherty.

"I'm terribly sorry for your loss. The cause of death was TBI or Traumatic Brain Injury. It resulted from a violent blow to the head along with his skull hitting the pavement with great force. If it's any comfort to you both, your son didn't suffer. He died almost instantly," the medical examiner informed.

"Oh, God! Look what they've done to my baby!" Lisa shrieked as tears streamed down her face.

The sound of Lisa's painful cry echoed throughout the morgue was unwelcomed confirmation, for Tom and Rachel who sat out in the waiting area that Mike and Lisa had positively identified Jason's body.

After the two grief-stricken families left the coroner's office, they headed directly to the Aurora Police Department. Spectators were clamoring. Sirens were wailing in the distance. Reporters, cameramen and crewmen swarmed Mike, Lisa, Tom and Rachel. Mike wrapped his arms around Lisa, shielded and protected her from the mob of television news reporters, as they pushed through the crowd. Tom had become furious by their blatant insensitivity. He stopped dead in his tracks to address their steaming litany of questions. Immediately, Tom was flanked by reporters, cameramen and crewmen. Cameras flashed from every angle. Microphones were shoved in his face.

"Can't you bloodhounds see that the family is in no state of mind to answer any questions?" Tom said angrily.

"Who are you to the victim's family?" a female reporter demanded.

"Thomas Ray Martin. I'm the family's next-door neighbor, best friend, and their attorney. I would just like to say a few words on behalf of my clients. The murderer or murderers responsible for this senseless act of violence will be caught. You know who you are, and sooner than later, you will be brought to trial. And within the scope of my legal powers, and the judicial system, I will take the all necessary steps, with due diligence, to prosecute those responsible to the fullest extent of the law. I will seek the death penalty," Tom said.

"Do you know who could've committed such a crime?" another reporter asked.

"No. I don't. The officials handling this case will have to answer any further questions. Then Tom voiced a dismissive, "Now, if you all will excuse me, I have to get to my clients," he said and pushed through the crowd of reporters and made his way up the steps and into the precinct.

Later that night, Brad was still hiding out at Lana's apartment. Lana, passed out cold on the sofa, was obviously strung out. Brad sat on the other end of the sofa and flipped through TV channels. He stopped, snorted meth, and then turned up a beer. Still in shock, Brad was unable to come to the realization that he had murdered his best friend. Neither of them had left the apartment since Brad arrived shaken and scared just after last midnight. With eleven o'clock drawing near, Brad had begun, once again, to flip through the channels to catch the latest newscast, and sure enough, the crime scene was in full display as the newscaster, with an umbrella in her left hand, presented the top story.

"Good Evening. I'm Angela Adams, here to bring you late-breaking details of tonight's top story that has already gained national attention. Around this time last night, an Aurora State University student, positively identified as 20-year-old Jason Lamar Taylor of Arlington Heights, an affluent suburb just outside of Chicago, was found bludgeoned to death in front of Lee's Music Store, near the corner of Galena and Randall. The saga of this high-profile murder case has quickly energized ASU students to rally, spurring thousands of demonstrators from around the metro Chicago area and other neighboring cities, believing race was a major factor in the victim's death by members of a white racist fraternity on the college campus, based upon an eye-witness who said one of the attackers assailed the victim with a racial epithet. Police would not comment at this time if this, in fact, was a hate crime.

As you can see behind me, evidence markers and crime scene tape still blocked off the entire corner as investigating police officers, detectives and crime scene technicians were back here again tonight, took more photographs, sifted for more potential evidence, a clear indication that this was still a very active crime scene. At this time, I can tell you that the police detective assigned to the case has confirmed that the victim was found in a supine position, and had apparently suffered blunt force trauma to the head, inflicted by a bloody baseball bat that was left at the scene of the crime. We were also told that the murder weapon has the initials JT on the bottom of it. Investigators were hopeful that the baseball bat, a fake blood-soaked Afro wig, an electric razor, and a black chalice found at the crime scene, all unceremoniously dumped at the deceased victim's feet, will be useful evidence in solving this case. Standing next to me is storeowner Mr. Kwan

Lee, who'd just finished doing business with the victim, was the only eye-witness, and has given us detailed accounts to this heinous and senseless crime," she reported and positioned the microphone in front of the storeowner.

"The young man came here to rent speakers. As he loaded them into van, I forgot speaker cord and went into the back of store to get. When I returned, I saw five white males beat my customer. Then, out of nowhere, one of them said "kill nigger" and hit my customer in head with baseball bat. And when they saw me, I locked the door, grabbed the phone and called police. They took off running, got in car and drove off like bat out of hell," Mr. Lee recounted.

As Brad watched Mr. Lee recount step-by-step, the gruesome crime, his hands clenched tightly around the remote control, causing his knuckles to turn a ghostly white.

"Do you think that you would be able to identify any or all of the suspects in a police lineup?" the reporter asked.

"Yes. Like I told the police, there were six white males wore sweatshirt with letters K T N on them."

"Thank you, Mr. Lee. Back to you, Angela," the reporter announced.

Before the reporter could turn it over to the anchorwoman back at the station, Brad had already turned off the television. He jumped to his feet and punched a hole in the wall of Lana's apartment. He opened and slammed the door shut. Lana was jolted awake.

* * *

Brad returned to the dorm apartment. He wanted to pack some clothes and get the hell out of Dodge before it was too late. He was sure that his parents and the Taylors had learned of his involvement in the now murder case, and would have tried to contact him. In fact, the phone had rung as he entered the apartment. Brad ignored the phone and plopped down on his bed. He lowered his head and begun to run his hands through his hair. He raised his head and looked toward Jason's side of the room. All his belongings were gone. The walls were bare. A neatly made bed. A grim reminder of what he had done. The fact that he'd murdered his best friend made him sick to his stomach. Brad jumped to his feet and rushed to the bathroom. He dropped his face in the basin where he coughed and vomited. Brad turned the faucet on and splashed a handful of water across his face. He raised his head and stared at himself in the mirror. Brad had begun to hallucinate from the usage of crystal meth, and seen himself as a former skinhead. He wore a T-shirt: a swastika on the front. On the back, the words: "DER FUHRER." Beneath them, in parenthesis, the words: "Supreme One." Brad laughed to himself as he sniffed and rubbed his nose. Once again, he lowered his face into the basin and splashed another handful of water on his face. The phone rang. Brad raised his head, and stared at his present self in the mirror. He exited the bathroom, left the faucet on, and slowly walked back into the bedroom. Brad stopped dead in his tracks. This time, as he walked toward his bed, he noticed a piece of paper that was placed on top of his pillow, and picked it up. It was the note Jason had left for him that read:

Brad, what's up?
It's after 10:00 p.m. I was hoping that you would've come back by apartment. I wanted to invite you to a 70s themed party that I'm going to be dj'ing at the Student Union. Hopefully, you'll get to check out my retro outfit that I'm wearing, complete with bell-bottoms pants, platform shoes, a fake Afro wig, and hair pick. Oh, and by the way, Happy Birthday! No matter what, we're still homies.
Peace out, Jason.

William Jaman Taylor

Brad dropped his head, crumpled the note, walked back into the bathroom, and turned off the faucet. He grabbed a red wash cloth, dabbed his face and head, exited the bathroom and begun to hallucinate again. Jason's belongings were in the bedroom. Jason was seated on his bed with his back to Brad.

"Jason," Brad whispered, shuddered with fear, and shook his head in disbelief. "This isn't real. You're dead," he said and dropped the wash cloth and crumpled note to the floor.

Brad lowered his head and rubbed his hands through his hair. After a moment, he looked up, hair extremely disheveled.

"Don't just sit there . . . say something," Brad growled. He looked like a crazed man. Still, there was no response or movement from Jason. An unnatural silence filled the air. "Look at me when I'm talking to you," he yelled.

Jason's head rotated 180-degrees. Blood slowly oozed out of the gaping head wound. Brad stumbled back onto his bed and hit his head against the wall just as, simultaneously, the apartment door was kicked in.

BOOM!

The door burst open with a pounding explosion.

Brad is bum-rushed by police officers with their guns drawn. Brad's eyes widen. Clearly, he's caught off guard, and scared out of his wits. It's a professional take-down. Police officers quickly yanked Brad up from off his bed, and slammed him up against the wall.

Lt. Bill Gibson, a fiftyish, highly decorated detective, stepped up to Brad.

"Bradly Thomas Martin, you're under arrest," he said and read Brad his Miranda rights, as one of the police officers hand-cuffed him.

Another police officer pushed Brad toward the busted door as he scuffled to look left of the bedroom that Jason had once occupied only to see all of his belongings gone, bare walls, and a neatly made bed as he's being lead out of the apartment.

Once outside of the apartment, students and onlookers watched as Brad was stuffed in the back seat of a police squad car and hauled off to jail.

Chapter 23

A somber hush had fallen over the Taylor's home. Days after Jason's murder were days clouded over with grief. Jon and Maddie had arrived the following morning only to find a hand-written note, by a despondent Lisa, taped to Jason's bedroom door. It simply read: *I want to be alone.*

Mike sat downstairs as he dealt with his own grief. Earlier, he tried to console Lisa, but it seemed that she would just cry uncontrollably, so he decided to respect her wish and let her grieve alone.

Maddie stood at the foot of the stairs and shook her head. She'd been grieving ever since she first heard that Jason would be attending Aurora University against her attempted warnings. Maddie had sensed danger was in store for her grandson, especially on the morning when she awoke to severe sharp pains, emanating from the left side of her head.

Jason's murder had been committed exactly thirteen weeks from the date of her nightmare. Maddie always had a superstitious belief and fear of the number thirteen.

Reflecting upon the chain of tragic events, in hindsight, Maddie had wondered if things would've been differently if she had commented on the Martins' home address, Brad's license plate number, Jason and Brad's apartment number, and Brad being the thirteenth pre-pledge member. Her grandson had been murdered on Friday, October 13th. Maddie knew that they would've dismissed her fears and superstitious beliefs as nonsense. Instead, she opted to keep quiet, felt that at no time would've been appropriate.

Lisa was secluded in Jason's bedroom as she looked up into the stormy heavens, but the rainfall that pelted the window and pounded the earth outside obscured her view.

213

She curled up on the bed, a wad of tissues in one hand, her face contorted in grief. Lisa wore the black dress that Maddie had purchased thirteen weeks ago. A red sweater rested over her shoulders.

The sky was dark. The wind has really picked up. A storm has moved in and rapidly intensified. A massive lightning bolt has streaked the sky followed with a loud thunder clap. A reflection of Jason's face popped up against the window.

The thunder outside rattled the windowpane. The snapping of twigs can be heard. Rain streaked down the windows of the room.

Lisa sat straight up on the bed, feet planted flat on the floor, shivered and pulled the sweater up on her shoulders. Her breaths formed tiny clouds in the cold air. An eerie stillness filled the room. She sensed something. An icy quiver ascended to the back of Lisa's neck, she was overcome by a sense of being watched. She rubbed her gooseflesh pimpled arms, turned and peered out the window.

Another lightning bolt streaked the sky. Lisa seen a quick glimpse of the subdivision's night skyline, and then her reflection in the rain streaked window.

Romeo had stopped by the night before, after he left the radio station where he hosted the six to ten spot three nights out of the week. He had told Mike that the only reason why he had gone to work at all was because he wanted to tell his listening audience how much Jason would be missed. Romeo dedicated his entire show to him and recorded it on a CD for Mike and Lisa.

Lisa reached over and pressed the 'play' button on a CD player that sat on top of the night stand, and allowed the room to be filled with Romeo's now solemn voice. She listened intently to the first song as Romeo dedicated a cover version entitled, *Goodbye, My Love*, to her and Mike. The hurt and pain in the singer's voice was so identifiable that Lisa found herself sobbing all over again.

William Jaman Taylor

As the rain falls
It washes our sins away
Burying our loved one
Sorry to meet this way

The love that I lost
Was the love of my life
Dear, dear God
Why the sacrifice
I know it's your will
To do what you do
But I can't take this feeling
That I'm going through

Please, please make it stop
And go away
I can't take this pain

Tell me why it hurts so bad
Tell me why it makes me mad
To think it had to happen to me
I guess it was meant to be

Tell me why it hurt so bad
Tell me why it makes me sad
To think it had to happen to me
Maybe it was meant to be
Goodbye, my love

Every day and every night
I'm hoping it'll be over soon
Knowing that only time
Can heal all wounds

I can't sleep at night
I can't get it off my mind
Along with this hurting feeling
That's buried deep inside
Please, please make it stop
It's killing me
I can't take it today

Tell me why it hurts so bad
Tell me why it makes me mad
To think it had to happen to me
I guess it was meant to be

Tell me why it hurt so bad
Tell me why it makes me sad
To think it had to happen to me
Maybe it was meant to be

Goodbye, my love

The song ended with the plink of a solo piano key as Mike, Jon and Maddie sat quietly with sullen faces on the sofa. A solemn silence overtook the Taylor's home. Seconds later, Lisa's grief was so profound that she released a heartrending scream that filled the entire house. The song had evoked the memory of the loss of her son.

Maddie was startled. She jumped up and scurried to the foot of the stairs, peered up at the top, with a hand to her mouth, eyes welled up. Jon arched his head back as he looked up at the ceiling and fought back tears. Mike dropped his head in near-total helplessness. He just wanted to be with his wife.

"She's in so much pain," Maddie said as she wiped away tears.

"I can't sit here another minute. I'm going for a walk."

"In the rain?" Mike asked dryly.

"I won't melt. I'm not a witch, you know," Maddie scoffed.

"Just let her be," Jon said as he picked up the remote control, and turned on the TV.

Mike sighed and nodded as Maddie grabbed her coat and umbrella, and exited the house.

Across the lawn, the phone rang inside the Martin's home.

"Hello," Tom answered.

"Thomas Ray Martin?" the caller said.

"Who's calling?" Tom asked.

"This is Lt. Barry Gibson over at the Aurora Police Department. I was hoping to reach you before the mid-day newscast."

What's this about?" Tom asked.

"Well, we have your son in custody. You might want to make another trip to the police department," Lt. Gibson said in a calm and direct tone.

"My son's in custody. What for?" Tom asked.

"Mr. Martin, your son and five other fraternity members were positively identified and charged with the murder of Jason Taylor last Friday night," Lt. Gibson said.

Tom dropped into the chair behind his desk. "*What!* Is this some kind of sick joke?" Tom asked angrily.

"I'm afraid not, Mr. Martin," Lt. Gibson said.

Tom's head was spinning. He and Rachel had tried to contact Brad ever since they'd heard the horrible news about Jason, but were unable to reach him. They figured that Brad had just gone off to grieve to himself, and would've shown up shortly before the memorial and funeral services. Tom was in complete shock.

"They were best friends," Tom said.

"During the interview process, your son had provided us with a very lengthy written confession that detailed exactly why he and five others had committed the crime. It turned out that your son was the one who struck the fatal blow that caused the victim his life," Lt. Gibson stated flatly. "And for the record, counselor, your son was not coerced in providing us with the written confession. He volunteered. Perhaps his conscious had gotten the best of him. The five other individuals implicated in the crime have been charged with complicity to murder. They were interviewed separately, and all have corroborated your son's entire confession.

Tom's shock turned to fury at the mention of a written confession. He rocketed from his leather office chair.

"What is my son's bail set for?!" Tom sneered.

"He's being held without bond," Lt. Gibson said.

"How am I going to tell my wife about this?" Tom thought out loud as he stared up at the ceiling.

"I think you should also consider how you are going to tell your next-door neighbors, best friends and clients. I expect to see you shortly," Lt. Gibson said and hung up. Tom stood frozen as he held the phone to this head.

"You don't have to worry about how you're going to tell me," Rachel said silently as she stepped into the home office, with the cordless phone clutched in her right hand. "I heard everything. We have to get him out of jail," she said.

"He's provided the police with a written confession. We're talking first-degree murder here. I'll see what I can do," Tom said as he dropped his head and placed his hands on his waist.

"See what you can do! You're his father and a fucking lawyer for Christ's sake, and all you can say is that you'll see what you can do," Rachel yelled and showed a side of her that Tom had never encountered.

"Regardless of who or what I am, first-degree murder is just that . . . first-degree murder! Not to mention there's a conflict of interest," Tom fired back, angered by everything and how quickly things were happening.

"A conflict of interest," Rachel repeated.

"That's right . . . a conflict of interest. I can try my best to circumvent the legal system, but there are federal and state laws and codes of ethics in place where a judge would make the decision to recuse me from the case or not. And if a judge was to rule in my favor, prosecutors for Mike and Lisa would formally file a recusal to have me removed from the case," Tom explained.

"Well I'm not going to sit here and twiddle my thumbs while my son is sitting in some jail cell like a common criminal," Rachel said.

"*Newsflash, Rachel!* Tom exclaimed. "This could be an open and shut case. The detective isn't looking for the proverbial needle in the haystack. Brad confessed to the murder. His participation alone has incriminated him. That made him a goddamn criminal," he yelled and smashed the cordless phone against bookshelves packed with law tomes and diplomas.

"Tom, we're talking about our son here. Whose side are you on?" Rachel asked as tears streamed down her cheeks.

"This is not about taking sides. Have you thought about how Mike and Lisa are going to feel when they find out that Jason was murdered by his best friend, our son, Brad? That has made Jason's tragic death all the more difficult to deal with."

"No. I haven't. That's not my problem or primary concern," Rachel gritted out through her teeth and wiped away tears. "My son, our son, Tom, is sitting in a filthy-rotten jail cell. That's my problem and primary concern now," she snarled, in utter coldness.

"How can you be so cold? Where's the woman I married, who-who was compassionate and overly friendly? I remembered how I teased you and said you had a trace of Williams Syndrome.

"That was before our misguided son needed us now more than ever. He's not from the wrong side of the tracks. We can help him, Tom," Rachel said.

"Help him? How? The therapy sessions obviously didn't work.

The trip to South Africa wasn't therapeutic. Our home was filled with authentic African-American art didn't serve as a daily reminder. An African-American family moved next-door to us sure as hell didn't help. Let's face it, Rachel, he's incorrigible. Beneath the surface, our son is a very sick-minded individual. He has a menacing persona," Tom said.

"Tom, don't you even care that we're about to lose our son, and--"

Tom angrily cut in. "And what, Rachel? Listen to what you've just said? Mike and Lisa have already lost their son. You can't compare a jail cell to a morgue. Jason is dead. Mike and Lisa will never see their son alive again!" he protested and snatched his keys off his office desk, grabbed his jacket off the back of the chair, exited the office, walked through the hallway and into the foyer, and headed toward the front door.

Rachel was close behind on his heels, her eyes had grown fierce. "Since you're not acting like a father and a lawyer toward your own son, why don't you just pretend that Brad is one of your fucking high profile cases and get him out of jail!" she screamed at the top of her lungs.

"Why don't you just pretend that our son killed his best friend? And while you're at it, any pity and sorrow that you can muster up, save it for Mike and Lisa. They are sure as hell going to need it," Tom said sarcastically, opened and slammed the door shut behind him, and left Rachel as she stood absently on the other end.

Once outside, Tom paused and allowed the drizzle to splatter down on his face. "What am I going to do?" he asked himself as he looked up into the steady drizzle.

"That's a good question, counselor. I heard everything," Maddie said as she walked toward him. Tom paused, his mouth opened a tiny bit involuntarily. He looked perplexed and wondered if, in fact, she had heard and known everything.

Standing face-to-face with Maddie, he read into her facial

expression that, in fact, she had indeed known everything.

"I saw you on the news yesterday. You spoke with great conviction about what was gonna happen to the murderers who killed my grandbaby. Counselor, now that you know that your very own son killed my grandbaby, are you still in favor of the death penalty?" Maddie asked as she shifted the umbrella from her right hand to the left, to get a good look at his face.

Tom had become despondent and fell against the side of the house, shook his head and slid down the side of the wall, huddled in a corner and shivered and wept. He'd become befuddled by the conflicting thoughts that raced through his head.

"I don't know what I feel or what to think. I'm so confused right now. So many things have raced through my mind all at once. I tried to make things right," Tom rambled and shook his head as he wrapped his arms around his shivering shoulders.

"What do you mean by make things right? Maddie asked.

Tom released a deep sigh and looked up at the drizzling sky.

"As a kid, I witnessed a black man being beaten and lynched by a racist white college fraternity. For years, I was haunted by ghostly visions and dreams of this black man. It was as if he'd been trying to tell me something. I was just a kid, for Christ's sake. There wasn't anything I could have done. That sense of helplessness is what led me to law school. I wanted to become a lawyer. I vowed to fight the prejudices and injustices of the world. I thought these nightmarish visions and dreams would go away." He broke down, sniveled and shook his head. "They didn't," Tom confessed and glanced over at her. "Maddie, you're wise women. What am I to do?" he asked.

"Believe me, counselor, there ain't nothing you can do. That decision has already been made," Maddie said and walked away and left Tom huddled in the corner as he wept and looked more perplexed.

Maddie made her way back across the lawn and entered the

house only to find Mike and Jon tuned into the mid-day newscast. The news anchorwoman had just dropped a bomb that sent Mike in a rage. He rocketed from off the sofa, swept past Maddie, rushed out the front door, and over to the Martins. Maddie whipped around and tried to stop him, but to no avail.

Mike's face turned to stone as he dashed across the lawn and headed straight for Tom.

Tom spotted Mike as he charged toward him like a raging bull. His eyes widen as he staggered to his feet. He slipped on the wet pavement, huddled in a corner, and cowered with both arms in a defensive position. Mike hovered over Tom, lifted him up by his jacket, and slammed his backside up against the side of the house.

"You knew about this K T N shit. You knew Brad was a danger to society. Didn't you?" Mike yelled as he run on pure adrenaline. He jerked Tom again by his jacket and demanded an answer. "Didn't you?! He yelled louder over the subdivision, his anger fueled by his own suspicion, and slammed Tom's backside up against the side of the house again.

Tom's expression registered sheer terror. "I warned Brad not to join. He went behind my back and got mixed up with the wrong crowd of people," he explained, in a tearful voice.

Before Mike could respond, a convoy of major local TV vans, channels 2, 5, 7, 9 and 32, had entered the subdivision, and pulled up in front of Mike and Tom's homes. In no time, cameramen and crewmen quickly exited their vehicles, got their satellite antennas up, each reporter with a microphone in one hand, an umbrella in the other as they trotted over the wet lawn to get to Mike and Tom.

"Mr. Martin, do you believe your son committed the murder of Jason Lamar Taylor? A reporter asked.

"How have your wives responded to this latest and astounding news?" a second reporter asked.

"Are the two families still friends? If not, do you think both families will ever reconcile? A third reporter asked.

"Mr. Martin, now that it has been confirmed that your very own son committed the murder, would you still be in favor of the death penalty?" A forth reporter asked.

"Do you believe the murder was racially motivated since news reports have confirmed the fraternity's name is indeed a double entendre? A final reporter asked.

"Why don't you bloodhounds just pack up and leave?! Mike yelled and turned to Tom. "Come inside," he said calmly.

Still, they were trailed and bombarded with a litany of questions by the reporters as Tom followed Mike back into his house. Once inside the foyer, they witnessed Lisa as she slowly made her way down the stairs. A deep pain was etched on her face--controlled, but evident. Her pained eyes were raw-heavy from crying but no tears.

"What's going on? What's with all the reporters?" Lisa asked in a melancholy voice.

Mike looked upstairs with glistening eyes. His face clearly indicated he doesn't know how to tell her the unfortunate truth.

"Sweetheart, so far, the police have arrested six students in connection with Jason's murder," Mike said as he turned and looked to Tom who dropped his head. He could not look Lisa in her grief-stricken eyes. Mike turned back to Lisa, released a deep sigh, and said, "One of them was Brad."

Lisa stood frozen on the stairs in disbelief. Tom stood motionless, his head still buried in his chest. After a moment, she turned to Tom; her eyes welled up as she slowly shook her head.

"No! Oh, God! No!" Lisa choked and shook her head as painful tears streaked her face. She had become unglued and screamed at the top of her lungs as she bolted downstairs, her footsteps thundering on the stairs. Lisa hurled herself at Tom and grabbed him by his soaking-wet jacket with her left hand as she pounded his chest with her right hand in total despair. "Tell me that Brad did not kill my baby. Tell me it's not true! Tell me it's not true! She cried out, her voice rose as she pounded her fist on his chest, before becoming weary, cried harder and collapsed on his right shoulder.

Mike gently removed Lisa's grip from Tom's jacket, hugged and consoled her.

Maddie stepped over and rubbed her grief-stricken daughter's back. Jon stepped behind Maddie and placed both hands on her shoulders. It pained Tom to see first-hand how the murder had gripped the family. He knew, at the moment, there wasn't anything he could've said or done to ease the family's pain. Tom had clammed up, dropped his head, and wept.

Lisa removed herself from Mike's comforting arms, and turned to faced Tom.

"I want to see him," Lisa gritted out through her teeth as Tom slowly raised his head, and looked at her. After a moment, he released a deep sigh and nodded.

Approximately twenty minutes later, Tom walked with Mike and Lisa toward their car in the driveway. They were headed to the Aurora Police Department. Jon and Maddie stayed behind just in case family members and friends were to call with questions and get information pertaining to the memorial service and funeral arrangements. Mike opened the left back door for Lisa. She stepped into the backseat of the car. As Mike was about to shut the door, Rachel had stepped out the front door and rushed across the lawn.

"Tom, where do you think you're going?" Rachel asked without acknowledging Mike and Lisa's presence.

"We're going to the jail," Tom answered.

"Why do you have to go?" Rachel asked, with a stoic look on her face.

"I'm going because I'm trying to make sense of it all," Tom said.

William Jaman Taylor

Lisa snapped, angered by Rachel's blatant rudeness. She disembarked from the backseat of the car to confront her.

"Look, Lisa, I'm sorry for what happened to Jason, and I can only imagine what you must be going through, but no matter what happens, he's not coming back. Brad is my son, and there is a chance of saving him," Rachel said, the cold tone implied.

"Saving him from what? Life in prison? The death penalty? Evidently you don't have a clue as to what I'm going through," Lisa said as she kicked off her shoes, picked them up, and thrust them into Rachel's arms. "Here, walk in my shoes, go stand in my living room and see how it feels to know your son won't ever walk through the door again. Walk in my shoes and go visit his body at the morgue, zipped up in a body bag. Wear my shoes to his funeral, and tell me how it feels to see your son's casket being lowered six feet into the ground. You wouldn't want to trade places with me. So don't you dare begin to think that you can imagine what I must be going through," she said, her lament too painful for mere words.

Lisa turned and galloped bare-footed back into the house. The crying had begun all over again. Lisa was too upset, and, understandably, had changed her mind about making the trip to the jail.

Rachel, who was also crying as well, turned and trotted in the opposite direction just across the lawn back toward her own house, with Lisa's shoes in tow.

Tom, with Mike in the car, backed out of the driveway, and headed to the Aurora Police Department. Approximately one hour later, they arrived at the jail.

Tom turned onto a side street, a block from the jail, pulled up curbside and parked the car.

Tom paused, took a deep breath as he looked at the steel door framing thick glass that is the entrance.

"Are you going to be all right?" Mike asked as he exited the car.

"I'll be fine," Tom nodded and exited the car.

Tom led the way to the entrance, opened the door, and stepped inside. Mike followed close behind.

The public lobby looked well-maintained and cleaned, showered in bright lights, one wall a thick bulletproof partition, behind which the sheriff's minions scurried about on their mission of confinement.

Lt. Gibson was waiting for him. He was surprised to have seen Mike with Tom, through the glass, and the jail guards buzzed them through a kind of airlock chamber, not much larger than a classic mall instant photo booth but with steel doors on each side. One is closed and locked before the other is opened.

Tom and Mike emerged on the other side.

There were three police officers who stood behind a desk. One officer took their information.

"Mr. Martin, Mr. Taylor, this is Officer Rosario. Follow me," Lt. Gibson said as he and the officer escorted them to Brad's jail cell.

Once the three were clearly out of sight, the other officers had begun to discuss Brad.

"Who's this Brad kid?" Officer Powell asked.

"The lawyer's son. You know . . . the basket case who sits there all day long mumbling "making things right," Officer Howard chuckled and shook his head.

"How does one who has everything going for him come to this?" Officer Powell said as he shook his head, and then released a deep sigh.

"It's always the rich kids who have everything going for them tend to fuck up in life," Officer Howard scoffed.

"That jail cell is now like his own purgatory," Officer Powell said.

Like dead men walking, Tom and Mike strolled down the corridor. Lt. Gibson and Officer Rosario led the way.

Moments later, they stood in front of the cement cell with steel bars about half the size of Jason and Brad's former college dorm bedroom. It had a concrete bed platform, stainless-steel sink and toilet fixtures in concrete stands, and an unbreakable window that showed nothing but a rectangle of the sky. An inmate can't even see the sun or moon. They found Brad, in an unresponsive state, as he sat on the bed in a corner, with the right side of his body pressed against the wall.

"I gotta make things right. I gotta make things right," Brad mumbled incoherently as he stared blankly off into space.

Once again, Tom felt completely helpless. He knew that he and his wife have already lost their son in more than one way as well.

Chapter 24

On a rainy Friday morning, the visitation was being held at Jamanson and Son Funeral Home, and unwelcome place where Mike and Lisa were both surrounded by a host of family members and friends as they bid farewell to their son. It seemed like hundreds of people had come up to them, young and old, talked to them, shook their hands, hugged them, and offered their condolences. Tom rode to the memorial service in the limo with Mike and Lisa, and her parents although he had intended on driving his own car to the memorial service and in the funeral procession. Even though Mike and Lisa had reassured him that in spite of everything that has taken place, he was like an honorary family member. Still, Tom felt the limos were for true family members. Not to mention a tug-of-war of guilt that raged within him. Tom felt very uncomfortable knowing that his wife had not planned on attending the memorial and funeral services, in addition to the fact that Brad had been charged with Jason's murder.

Inside the funeral home, Lisa stood at a podium on a platform in front of a large crowd of mourners. Just as she was about to deliver her son's eulogy, she spotted Rachel as she discreetly slipped into the back row and took a seat. Lisa took a deep breath and squeezed her eyes tightly shut, and willed herself not to cry. After a moment, she'd opened her eyes, and begun her heart-felt eulogy.

"Ever since Jason was born, I knew he was precious gift from God. He was my little angel for only a short time. I feel a great sense of impermanence. You're here today and gone tomorrow. Never in a million years would I have expected to bury my son. He was too young to die. And due to his untimely death, he's now God's angel. He was the happiest baby I had ever seen. He always smiled and laughed. Jason never gave his father and me any problems. He was a popular and well-liked student. Jason had always gotten good grades. He had many friends. He loved his music. Overall, he was a good kid," she said and incorporated a wistful smile into her utter sadness as she continued her eulogy. "Besides from being a little mischievous at times, like any child, I suppose, Jason had never wronged or disrespected anyone. He had no enemies. He made no enemies. Well, except for the few times he'd blast the music, and the neighbors had come over and complained. Like I said, Jason loved his music. In fact, he attended Aurora State University majoring in broadcasting, and dreamed of becoming a radio personality and talk show host. Once, he told me that he'd wanted to influence people's lives like Jack 'The Rapper' Gibson had done. That was his idol. But my son's dream has been taken away from him. My baby is gone." She choked up as she looked down from the podium, viewing her son's body. "He's ... gone," she said and wiped away tears.

Lisa raised her head, still wiping away tears and fighting back more as she looked toward the back row of the funeral home and spotted Rachel. "Goodbye, my son. Goodbye, Pookie," she said and dissolved into tears. Rachel, teary-eyed, put a hand to her mouth, stood, rushed pass two ushers, and quickly left the funeral home.

Mike rushed up to the podium to console his wife and escorted her back to her seat. Lisa stopped at the bottom of the steps. She walked over and stood in front of the expensive pearl white casket and bier. She leaned in; with a mother's loving look, as warm as her demeanor the day Jason was born. Lisa tenderly caressed her son's head. She leaned in closer and kissed his forehead. She resumed her stance, placed her right hand on her son's crossed hands, looked up at the ceiling, and mustered the strength to fight back the tears. After a few moments, Lisa released a deep sigh, removed her shaky hand from her son's and returned to her seat next to Mike, on her right, on her left were Maddie and Jon. On Mike's right was Tom. There, Lisa placed her head in her mother's bosom. She burst into a hard and uncontrollable cry. Mike looked on. He, too, finally broke down as tears slowly streamed down his face.

* * *

The following Monday morning, a sheriff's deputy, with his Marine-like haircut and muscular arms and his black leather gun belt, the handle of an automatic, perhaps a Glock--it looked like-ready to draw, around his waist, escorted Brad into the stuffy, highly guarded courtroom in handcuffs for his arraignment. He appeared to be troubled. Brad looked dazed, disheveled and tired, dark circles and bags underneath his eyes. The gallery was packed with a feeding frenzy of news reporters, crewmembers and courtroom spectators due to the nature of this highly publicized profile case.

Brad stopped and scanned the courtroom. He spotted Mike, Lisa and her parents, and then dropped his head to his manacled hands. The deputy jerked him forward as they walked pass the prosecuting attorney's table, a podium or lectern, and seated him with his defense attorney team.

Maddie sat quietly as she stared at the top heading of a document she gripped in her left hand that read 'The State of Illinois versus Bradly Thomas Martin'. She noticed the fact that Brad's first, middle, and last name all have six letters. With a pen in her right hand, Maddie wrote the numbers 666 under his first, middle and last name. "*Vous meurtrier,*" she muttered in French, anger had settled upon her face as she looked over at Brad and crumpled the document while Jon looked on, and discreetly nudged her.

Brad searched the rest of the courtroom for his parents, only to find his mother sitting directly behind him. He finally realized that his father wasn't in the courtroom.

Tom had pulled up outside of the courthouse ten minutes earlier. Unable to remove himself from his car, he sat with both hands firmly gripped to the steering wheel. Tom craned his neck and looked up at the three-story high building windows that reeked of history. The courthouse, surrounded by an impressive set of spike tipped black wrought-iron gates, displayed eclectic architectural styles: Traditional and Georgian.

Inside the courtroom, the bailiff approached the Judge's bench. "All rise," he said.

Brad, flanked by the sheriff's deputy and his attorneys, remained seated while everyone stood and acknowledged the Judge as she entered the courtroom. The deputy attempted to help Brad to his feet.

Judge Calhoun, a confident fair-skinned African-American woman, in her fifties, strong-willed, tough, but fair. She took her seat in a leather high-back chair behind the bench, flanked by the great seal of the jurisdiction and the flags of the appropriate federal and state governments.

"The Honorable Judge Ella L. Calhoun presiding in The State of Illinois versus Bradly Thomas Martin is now in session. You may be seated," the bailiff announced.

Suddenly, Brad broke free from the deputy's grip and made an awkward dash toward the front of the courtroom.

"I gotta make things right," Brad yelled as he dashed past the judge's bench. The sheriff deputy and bailiff lunged after him. The Judge quickly jumped to her feet. She looked confused and bewildered.

"*Brad, noooooo!*" Rachel yelled and jumped to her feet.

Judge Calhoun pounded her gavel as murmuring and chattering rippled through the courtroom. People stood, howled and gasped of horror and disbelief, as they looked on in shock.

"*Order!*" Judge Calhoun exclaimed and pounded her gavel.

Brad had managed to jump on top of a table that sat below one of the large courtroom windows, just as the sheriff deputy had drawn his gun, assumed the Weaver stance, and fired a single fatal shot. The fatal round entered him in the back, severing the aorta, perforating the left lung, piercing the ribs as it passed through the intercostal muscles or chest wall, instantly killing him. The muzzle blast, violent sound pressure levels of 140 ear-shattering decibels, sent Brad crashing through the plate-glass panes.

Just outside below, Tom had just stepped out of the car and heard the blast followed by the sound of shattering glass and looked up at the three-story building, simultaneously, as his son fell from the third floor courtroom window, with his hands still cuffed. Shards of glass rain down with him.

Tom watched in astounding horror as Brad's body connected with a spike tipped black wrought-iron gate that surrounded the courthouse below.

"*Noooooo!*" Tom echoed his wife as he dashed toward his son's impaled body on the spiked gate. Some horrified onlookers stood in shock, yelling and screaming. Others frantically looked on as they tightened around Brad's impaled body.

Seconds later, Rachel burst through the courtroom doors, holding onto the hand railing as she frantically galloped down the steps, skipped a step or two. Court spectators, city employees, cops, security officers, lawyers and reporters streamed out of the courthouse including Mike, Lisa, Jon, Maddie and Mr. Lee. Rachel rounded the courtroom building only to see Brad's body impaled on the spike tipped gate. Instantly, she'd become unhinged. Rachel released a blood-curdling and chilling scream.

Tom pushed through the crowd, grabbed Rachel, and tried to bury her face in his chest but to no avail. Rachel flailed her arms and kicked her legs violently to free herself from his grasp.

William Jaman Taylor

Somehow she had managed to turn in Tom's grasp and viewed Brad's impaled body. Rachel sobbed hysterically, with her arms extended as she reached for her son.

Chapter 25

Gray clouds covered the sky. A mix of rain and sleet fell. A host of family members and friends, all dressed in black, attended Brad's funeral. They stood and held black umbrellas around the gravesite. The Taylors and LaRues were present. They stood off to the side near a large oak tree. In the background, the press was visible, and was held back by private security guards.

Francis Knapp II, a priest of the Archdiocese of Aurora's St. John's Catholic Church, presided at the gravesite burial or rite of committal. "We've gathered together here today to commit Bradly Thomas Martin, to his final resting place. Along with his loving parents, we've also gathered to comfort each other in our grief and to honor the life of Bradly Thomas Martin. A life that was full of hope, happiness, and ups and downs . . . through good times as well as in bad. Bradly, as we honor your memory and the love you've left behind, we offer your spirit the following blessing: Until we meet again, may God comfort you in his eternal and loving arms. According to Genesis 3:19: for dust thou art, and unto dust shalt thou return. We commit his body to the ground; ashes to ashes, dust to dust."

A mix of rain and sleet continued and poured down on the assembled mourners as they watched Brad's casket being lowered into the ground. Rachel stood in front of the mourners, her head rested against Tom's shoulder. Tears had soaked through her veil. Tom stood, with an umbrella in his left hand, by her side and consoled her. Moments later, the service concluded. Mourners had offered their condolences and begun to solemnly file away.

William Jaman Taylor

Chapter 26

Inside a Cumberland County Courthouse, located in Fayetteville, North Carolina, the jurors had filed in from the jury room. The jury consisted of seven men and five women had convicted Andrew Brewer and Stanley King, and eleven others of capital murder and kidnapping and first-degree murder and kidnapping respectfully, with all twelve unanimously agreeing, after about thirteen hours of deliberations over three days after they'd carefully considered the case and heard closing arguments from prosecutors and defense attorneys.

The panel had taken less than one hour to determine the killing was especially cruel and inhumane.

The Honorable Judge Harold Stallworth presided over the case, which had begun Wednesday, December 13, 2000. Judge Stallworth was a gruff-spoken man in his sixties with a reputation for handing down strict sentences, usually the maximum the law would allow.

Harold Stallworth had been a judge for more than thirty years. His reputation was beyond reproach; he knew the law and executed it. He was a devoted Christian who made no apologies for his religious beliefs especially when it comes to cold-blooded murderers. He looked to the jury box. "Have you reached a verdict," he asked.

The male foreman stood. "Your Honor, we have reached a verdict," the foreman replied. "We, the jury, have found Andrew Brewer and Stanley King guilty of one count of capital murder and one count of kidnapping," he said.

The Honorable Judge Harold Stallworth handed down the sentencing for Andrew Brewer and Stanley King. "You've been convicted by a jury of one count of capital murder and one count

235

of kidnapping. You both have denied violating the victim's civil right, and having any knowledge or involvement of the brutal beating and murder. Unfortunately for you the jury did not believe you, and I must agree that I don't either.

My responsibility today is to impose a sentence that is sufficient and fit the crime. As far as I am concern, there are no mitigating circumstances that would warrant sparing your lives. Today's sophisticated forensic science proved that Brown, in fact, had been beaten, chained by his ankles to the back of a truck and dragged, stabbed, and ultimately hung to death. Miraculously, fingerprint evidence left on the knife and on a broken beer bottleneck had not degraded where super glue fuming was used to reveal and fix latent fingerprints on the two non-porous items, and placed you both at the crime scene. This circumstantial and physical evidence, beyond a reasonable doubt, corroborated both the compelling eyewitness and forensic expert testimonies. With that being said, I must hand down the following sentencing," he said.

Tom, seated in the courtroom, in an executive two-button wool patterned black suit, a white shirt and red silk tie, looked intently at the Judge. He'd assisted homicide detectives in the cold case that had stumped the department for over forty years, and served in the trial as a key witness in the case against the fraternity members for the 1959 murder of the black man, Jessie Lee Brown. The college yearbook group photograph in 1959/60 was used to positively identify all thirteen white men. Ultimately, Andrew Brewer and Stanley King were found guilty and formally charged with one count of capital murder and one count of kidnapping in connection with the death of Jessie Lee Brown. Both will face the death penalty by lethal injection. Eleven others have been found guilty of one count of first-degree murder and one count of kidnapping, each facing 20 to 60 years in prison without parole.

Tom also went as far as spearheading a campaign to have the nationwide K T N Fraternity Chapter shut down permanently due to the organization's underlying mission and involvement in one of the most grisly and shocking hate crime murders in North Carolina history.

After the sentencing was handed down, Andrew Brewer and Stanley King were led out of the courtroom in handcuffs. Tom stood with his briefcase and an overcoat in his left hand, and shook hands with the prosecutorial team as courtroom spectators stood and begun to engage in small talk.

A black man, dressed in a long-sleeve crisp-clean white shirt, blue jean overalls, and a pair of work boots, sat in the last row. He stood and held a dark-colored cap in front of him with both hands. Tom spotted the black man and instantly recognized him. His eyes had widened. Tom, with a free hand, had begun fumbling for something inside his suit jacket pocket. He extracted a harmonica. The black man, with a heavenly glow, smiled and nodded, put on his cap, and exits the courtroom. The vision of the black man had appeared before Tom for the very last time, only this time, no noose around the neck, his hands unbound, and no badly beaten bloody face and body. He excused himself, and rushed out of the courtroom.

Tom stood in the middle of the hallway. He looked around for the black man who was nowhere to be found. Tom dropped his head, and looked at the harmonica he held. A light bulb had come on, and he now realized what the black man wanted all these years.

Tom whispered, "Retribution. He wanted retribution," he said, pocketed the harmonica and walked down the hallway as people spilled out of the courtroom.

Chapter 27

On a brisk but sunny New Year's morning, Maddie was in Lisa and Mike's kitchen, humming a cheery tune as she prepared a holiday feast.

"Good morning, Mom. *Mmmm!* Something smells good. Do you need any help? Lisa asked.

"Child, I don't need any help," Maddie chuckled. "I've been cooking big family dinners for almost fifty years. Why are you up so early?" she asked.

"I've decided to go for a morning jog, to burn a few calories before I eat and put them right back on. Well, since you seem to have everything under control, I'll be on my way," Lisa said.

"Okay, baby. I'll make us some tea. And when you get back, we can sit down and talk, and have a slice of sweet potato pie before your father and Mike have gotten to it," Maddie said.

"I don't have anything to worry about. They're glued to the TV watching the sports highlights for the Wisconsin and Sanford College Rose Bowl game," Lisa said. She paused a moment. "On second thought, you guard those pies with your life until I get back."

"All right, child. Go on . . . get out of here," Maddie chuckled as she opened the oven door.

Once outside, Lisa surveyed the snow blanketed cul-de-sac. Garlands of tinsel and Christmas lights, from the recent holiday, rattled and rustled under the eaves of many neighboring homes. She stood in the shoveled driveway and stretched. Lisa, breath smoking in the brisk morning air, glanced over at the Martins' house. Weeks have passed. Lisa and Rachel haven't spoken to each other. She turned, dropped her head, and then released a deep sigh. Lisa gazed at her elongated shadow, which draped the driveway, and folded onto the concrete pavement. She raised her

William Jaman Taylor

head and jogged down the driveway, onto and out of the cul-de-sac, unaware that Rachel had been watching her through one of the mini-blind slats.

As Lisa made her way out of sight, Rachel walked away from the window and turned on the television. As she flipped through the television channels, she stopped at the *Oprah Winfrey Show* where a legendary female singer was being interviewed, and about to perform. Rachel took a moment to reflect how she and Lisa loved to watch the show together. She snapped out of it as the audience applauded, watched and listened intently as the iconic and fiery singer performed her latest hit single, *Where Did I Go Wrong*, which was featured on a soundtrack to a movie she recently had a cameo appearance in. The fiery singer transfixed the audience with her wrenching, emotion-filled performance. The lyrics struck an emotional chord within Rachel as she listened.

I remember the first time that I saw you
Your head coming first right out of my womb
Watching you grow and getting into things
Now you're all grown, I'm remembering
All the good time that we had together
How I never thought there'd be stormy weather
Every night I'm on my knees and pray
That tomorrow will be a brighter day

Tell me where did I go wrong
This time, tell me
I've always been there
To teach you right from wrong

Tell me where did I go wrong
This time, show me

I've always tried to be there
To show you love so strong

Tell me where did I go wrong
This time, all around
I realized what's been done
You won't be coming home

I've done all that I could
So what's else a mother to do
Provided you with everything
Including my love too
I never thought something like this
Would ever happen to me

I still believe and keep the faith
My faith in he
Believing everything will work itself out
Just be patient and you'll see

So why did it have to come to this
Lord, I just don't know
But one thing I do know
You'll truly be missed

Tell me where did I go wrong
This time, tell me
I've always been there
To teach you right from wrong

Tell me where did I go wrong
This time, show me

William Jaman Taylor

I've always tried to be there
To show you love so strong

Tell me where did I go wrong
This time, all around
I realized what's been done
You won't be coming home

Tell me where did I go wrong

The singer's song had captured and evoked the loving bond and heartbreak between a mother and her child wailed her versatile contralto over piano keys and melancholy orchestral arrangements.

Rachel wiped away the tears from her face, walked back over to the window, and peered out over across the separating lawns. After a moment of thought, she took a deep breath in. Rachel held it a moment and then exhaled slowly. She turned and trudged into the foyer, unhurriedly ascended the stairs to the master bedroom, stepped into the large walk-in closet, picked up Lisa's shoes that were neatly tucked in the empty space in the bottom right corner, looked at them and simply nodded.

Approximately thirty minutes later, Lisa returned from her morning jog and paused in front of her doorstep. She bent over and rested her hands on her knees. After a few seconds, Lisa resumed her stance and looked up directly into the heavens. The clouds parted and the sun had shone brightly. Blinded by the sun, Lisa used her right hand and shielded her eyes. She just stood there and gazed up at the sun's bright eye.

Rachel stepped outside, walked cautiously over to Lisa, and stood next to her. "The sun is rather bright this morning, huh?" she said.

"My mother once told me that if you look directly up at the sun, then close your eyes, you can see a vision of the person or thing that's dear to your heart," Lisa said as she continued gazing up at the sun.

"Does it work?" Rachel asked and squinted.

"There's only one way to find out," Lisa replied and closed her eyes.

"I don't know which hurts the worse . . . the blinding sun or these shoes I'm wearing," Rachel said.

Lisa opened her eyes and glanced down at Rachel's feet.

"It's true, I can see them practicing baseball," Rachel said with her eyes shut tight.

"I saw the exact same thing," Lisa said shockingly as she looked up and stared at Rachel. A single tear rolled down her cheek.

Rachel opened her eyes and turned to Lisa only to find her tearful eyes locked on her. Lisa, can you ever forgive me? I am so sorry for the way I've acted, and what I've put you and your family through. I've missed you and our friendship so much. I can't do it alone. I need you," she pleaded with tears rolling down her cheeks.

"Rachel, I never ended our friendship. I wished you would have been there. I needed you too, "Lisa said as tears streamed down her cheeks. She wiped away the tear and extended her opened arms to hug Rachel.

"Thank you," Rachel said and hugged Lisa as she sobbed uncontrollably on her shoulder.

Lisa shook her head in their embrace. "No. Thank you," she said as they continued their heart-felt and sincere embrace.

IN MEMORIAM

This book is dedicated to the victims and their families and loved

ones affected by a tragic accident, any lawless, senseless, isolated

and/or random act of violence.

May it be a source of inner strength and comforting to know that

we have a heavenly Father watching over us, and that, in our time

of need, he'll never leave us nor forsake us.

God Bless.

ABOUT THE AUTHOR

William Jaman Taylor makes his impressive fiction debut novel entitled, Nightmares in the Neighborhood, features "The Lawyer's Son," the basis for the suspense thriller. His goals are to continue to write novels and start a budding career at screenwriting. To date, he has adapted Nightmares in the Neighborhood to a screenplay, and penned his second fiction novel entitled, Reality Check (Historical Fiction).

Originally from Cincinnati, Ohio, a graduate of Robert A. Taft High School, and attended Wilberforce University, he now lives in Atlanta, Georgia. He is currently at work on his third novel and second screenplay.

PLEASE SHARE WITH US YOUR THOUGHTS. WE VALUE YOUR OPINION.

Was it a good book? _____

What did you like most about the book? _____

What did you like lease? _____

What is your overall opinion about the book? _____

Would you recommend this book? _____

How did you hear about us? _____

How would you rate this book? Please circle one of the following:

1 star   2 stars   3 stars   4 stars   5 stars

$5,000.00 CONTEST CASH AND//OR PRIZE GIVE-A-WAY! THERE ARE THIRTEEN CLUES THROUGHOUT THE BOOK THAT CONNECT THE DOTS TO THIS SUSPENSE THRILLER. CORRECTLY IDENTIFY ALL 13 CLUES AND WIN! DEADLINE: 9-30-2014.

1   7

2   8

3   9

4   10

5   11

6   12

                   13

PRINT ENTIRE PAGE AND MAIL TO:

GB WORLDWIDE ENT & BOOK PUBLISHING

C/O: CONTEST

PO BOX 7585

MARIETTA, GA 30065

NAME _____

PHONE (   ) _____ - _____ Email: _____

GROUNDBREAKING WORLDWIDE ENT.

GB BOOK PUBLISHING

PO BOX 7585

MARIETTA, GA 30065

Please <u>print</u> and completely fill out this mail-in order form.

Total number of books _____ X $9.99 + $4.99(S/H&P) per book = $ _____

[ ]Check box if book(s) are to be mailed to one mailing address.

[ ]Check box if book(s) are to be mailed to more than one address.

Name: _____

Street Address: _____ **Apt:** _____

City: _____ **State:** _____ **Zip:** _____

E-mail: _____

Name: _____

Street Address: _____ **Apt:** _____

City: _____ **State:** _____ **Zip:** _____

E-mail: _____

Name : _____

Street Address: _____ **Apt:** _____

City: _____ **State:** _____ **Zip:** _____

E-mail: _____

www.ingramcontent.com/pod-product-compliance
Lightning Source LLC
Chambersburg PA
CBHW070744180626
46818CB00007B/2980